Tomb of Souls

Tomb of Souls

Elice, the Great (Book Two)

Jennifer Roachford

Curly Tales Publishing

For those whose heart is as big as a mountain.

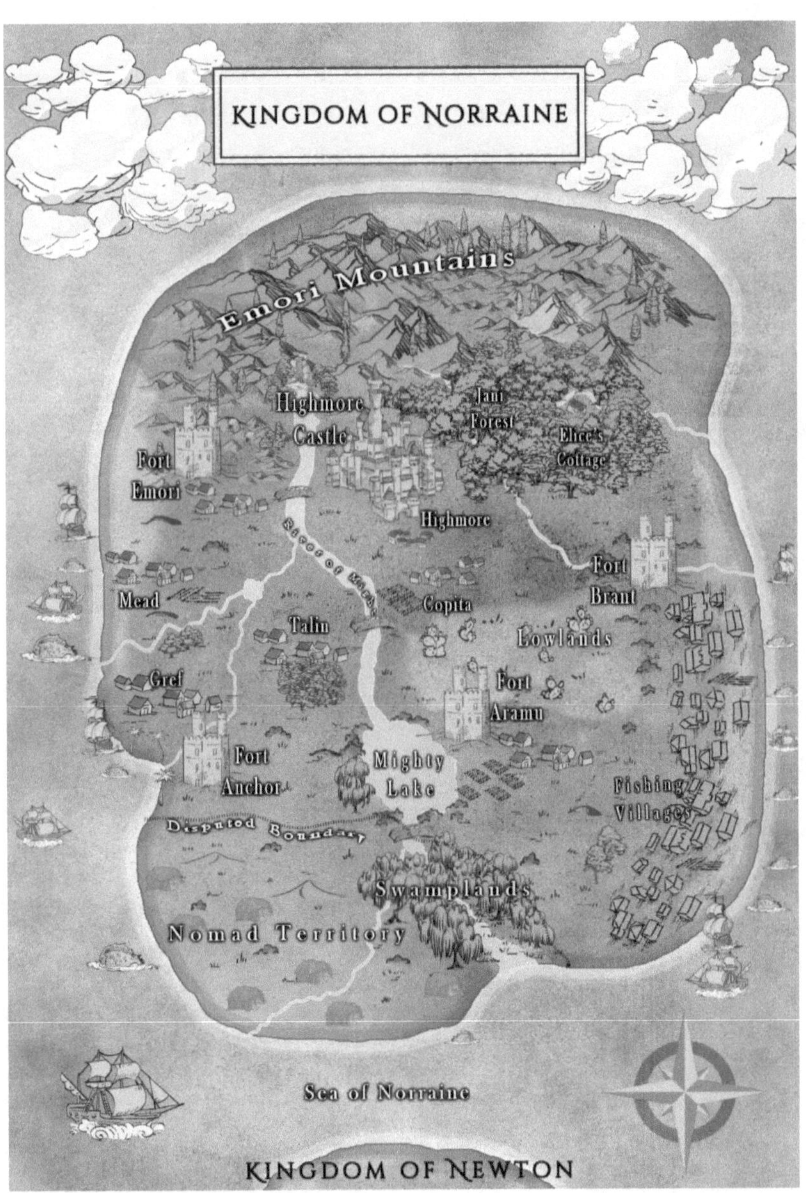

KINGDOM OF NORRAINE
Emori Mountains
Highmore Castle
Jant Forest
Elice's Cottage
Fort Emori
Highmore
River of Mead
Fort Brant
Mead
Copita
Lowlands
Talin
Gref
Fort Aramu
Fort Anchor
Mighty Lake
Fishing Villages
Disputed Boundary
Swamplands
Nomad Territory
Sea of Norraine
KINGDOM OF NEWTON

One

The sword came out of nowhere, slicing through the air beside her as she evaded his swing. Sweat ran down Elice's face, causing a chill to ghost her arms as the nippy fall air snaked across her body. She sucked in a deep breath just as another swing came flying by her head.

Angry, Elice blew a powerful gust of wind at him, forcing a few feet of separation so she could draw in a hurried breath. Her long, curly hair came loose from the silk white ribbon that held it in place behind her head. Now, her curls flew in all directions with the wind, and she quickly wiped a few stray strands away from her face with her free hand.

It was the middle of the afternoon, though a few rain clouds crept in from the west. She wore a thin beige sweater and matching trousers to keep her warm from the brisk wind that blew in with the approaching storm.

"Nice," James said, gasping as he changed his stance, crossing his right foot over his left. "But you're still not thinking ahead. Remember to use your sword as well."

He took a step to the left, and Elice adjusted her sword so she could match his steps like he taught her.

"I keep forgetting," she said as she glided her bare feet across the dirt floor of the open-air training arena. The wooden benches surrounding the sunken stage were empty, giving her privacy from curious eyes during her training sessions.

James shook his head as he adjusted the hem of the thin white shirt he wore. He usually removed his green uniform top during their practices, opting for his white undershirt over his dark pants. "The sword can help you in any situation, just like your magic can."

Elice took a step forward and waved her sword. James met her swing, using his momentum to push it away. Elice lost her balance and spun, readying her sword to attack, but James was too quick. He brought his sword up again, swiped it underneath the hilt of hers, and flipped it out of her hands.

It flew to the side, landing several feet away. With a flourish, he held his sword against her neck, gently and with calculating caution.

Defeated, Elice held up her hands. "What's that, twenty-five to zero now?"

With a smile, James lowered his sword and went to retrieve Elice's. He passed it back to her, bowing and looking sheepishly at the floor. "Don't worry. With more practice, you'll catch on."

"I think I prefer my magic, honestly," she said, digging the tip of her sword into the dirt. They had upgraded from wooden to blunted swords, but after two months of practice, she still felt like she didn't know how to move around with it.

"That's to be expected. We just need to find a way to get you to balance your magic with sword fighting."

Elice didn't know if there was a way for her to find a balance between the two, but her father wanted James to teach her how to use a sword. James, being the loyal servant he was, would try his best to follow the king's orders.

They walked to the sword rack on the edge of the circular arena and hung up their weapons. Elice climbed the steps to the first row and sat on the nearest bench to catch her breath. She almost swallowed the air, relishing the cool breeze that passed. James plopped down next to her and took a deep breath too.

She looked at him from the corner of her eye, noting how he didn't seem nearly as winded as she did. He sat with his hands in his lap, looking down at them as he cleared his throat.

"I was wondering," he began, then shifted in his seat and started again, still staring at his lap. "Have you heard of Talin's apple festival?"

Elice turned to look fully at his face, watching a bead of sweat glide down his cheek. "Yes, of course. It's a fall tradition, right?"

He met her eyes briefly before averting his gaze again. "I was wondering if, maybe, you'd like to see it this year. With me."

Her eyes grew wide, and she opened her mouth several times, but no words came out. Her lack of answer made James turn to her. "I just thought it would be nice for you to get out of Highmore and see a little of the kingdom. You know, before winter comes. I know the king said the family wouldn't be traveling to Fort Anchor this winter because of what happened with ... you know."

She nodded, knowing exactly what he was talking about, but not wanting to have a conversation about it again. She had spent countless hours with her father and General Thiery, going over every detail about the day she left the castle to find Lenore. The two men wanted as much information as possible from her to clear her name in Lenore's death, claiming it was self-defense. They also wanted to gather enough evidence against Lenore's fire mage accomplice, since he still sat in their dungeon awaiting his trial.

James raised a hand to scratch the top of his head. His hair was growing again, and Elice enjoyed looking at his curls, though she knew he would cut it soon to maintain his usual clean-cut design.

"And I think you'd like to meet Madam Verna," he continued. "She's sent me a few letters. And her niece, Cassidy, is still dying to meet you." The reminder of Talin's sight mage and her healer niece brought back another unwanted memory of Lenore.

Elice looked off into the sky. The clouds drew closer, and she could feel the rain in the air as it advanced. When she met his eyes again, she gave him another nod. "I would love to visit Talin."

A smile broke across his face, and he let go of the breath he had been holding. "I'll inform the estate right away. It's in a week, but they'll have time to get everything ready for your visit."

Elice scrunched her nose. "You're not going to make a big deal out of this, are you?"

James laughed and placed a hand on his heart. "Why would I do that to you, my princess?"

She gave his shoulder a light push before she stood. "I have to get going. I'll see you tonight at dinner."

James stood and kissed the back of her hand. "Until dinner, then."

Elice hurried to the castle, wanting to stay and enjoy the rain, but she had to check on her sister.

She stepped onto the terrace and wiped her feet on the thick woolly mat off to the side, then she ran through the double doors. She bypassed a security guard—it looked like Michael, who was assigned to watch her and follow her everywhere—and continued up the east-wing staircase that led to the bedrooms. Michael's footsteps came pounding behind her, and she rolled her eyes as he called her name.

"Princess," he called, "I've been waiting for you to finish your training session with Captain Taylor. The queen requests your presence."

Elice halted, her foot hanging in midair above one of the steps. Turning, she looked at her personal guard, his sheathed sword attached to his belt swinging as he ran to catch up with her. She walked back down the stairs. "Oh, well, why didn't you say so? Lead the way, Mr. Hall."

He blew out a breath and turned on his heel. Elice knew she drove him crazy, but she never asked to be hounded all day. It cut into her time wandering around whenever she wanted, and she always felt uncomfortable when he watched her all day. Especially when he was around James. James always acted so differently when Michael was near. He was more formal and didn't kiss the back of her hand like she had grown accustomed to, which was why she requested her training with James to be private. It was the only time she could get away from her guard, and she enjoyed her alone time with James.

In hindsight, she knew she should blame her father for forcing the poor man to guard her all day. Edgar was more paranoid now than ever after Lenore's death, not wanting to leave any members of the royal family alone without a guard or a soldier.

Michael led Elice to her mother's office on the ground floor. Her mother's guard, Mr. Banks, stood sentinel outside the door. Michael stepped to the other side of the doorway as Mr. Banks knocked, waited for the queen's reply, and opened the door for Elice to pass through.

Julice sat behind her desk, flipping through the pages of one of her books, her long curls flowing across the desk. A window at the back of the room allowed in a bit of light from the gloomy day outside, but several candles were lit and placed across the room and on her desk. She looked up as Elice entered and beckoned her closer. "I have a favor to ask," Julice said as Elice sat in the chair across from her.

Elice nodded. "Sure, Mother. What do you need?"

"I need you to sit in for your sister again today." Julice's face held firm, but Elice saw the tiniest of frowns.

Elice wanted to decline, but she knew how important it was to say yes. "The council hates me, though." She remembered the last time she sat in on a council meeting for Alice. Several council members stared at her as if she didn't belong, with narrowed eyes and tight smiles, and she nearly released her anxiety on them in a flurry of wind gusts and torrential rain.

Julice pulled at the long sleeves of her maroon gown, avoiding eye contact. "No, not in the council meeting. I'm talking about Alice's meeting with Miss Tabitha."

Elice blinked at her mother. "You're not serious."

Julice closed the book she was reading and pushed it away. "It's just for today. Your sister's not ... feeling well."

"But—"

Julice held up a hand. "I don't need to remind you what your sister is going through right now. And we need this dress fitted."

"But—"

"And you have almost the exact same measurements."

Elice opened her mouth to object again, but her mother narrowed her eyes. "All right," Elice said instead, making her mother smile. "But a wedding is the last thing on everyone's mind right now." She rushed the words before her mother could cut her off again.

Julice sighed and rubbed the space between her eyes. "I don't need this right now, Elice. Miss Tabitha graciously accepted the role of wedding planner, even though that is not her job, and she has been waiting for Alice for nearly two hours now. Your sister refuses to leave her room. I've yet to finalize the guest list because we are still a few months away, but the caterers will need a head count soon. The flower arrangements are all wrong. Your father barely has time to sit down for a proper dinner for longer than thirty minutes before he shuts himself in the council room all night. And I think I found another gray hair." Julice looked down at the thick curls that rested against her shoulder before huffing and tossing them behind her back, not wanting to look at them anymore.

Elice chewed on her bottom lip. "This might be a bad time to ask if I can go to Talin with James for the apple festival."

Julice pursed her lips before she got up and walked toward the door. She pulled on the gold doorknob and motioned for Elice to leave through the opening. Elice's shoulders sank low as she walked toward the door. Before she walked out, her mother touched her shoulder. "You can go," she said, a tiny smile peeking through her grim expression. "But you should take your sister with you. It might do her some good to get out of the castle."

Elice smiled and gave her mother a hug, lightly resting her cheek against the soft velvet of her dress. Julice squeezed Elice back and kissed the top of her head.

Elice turned to leave, but her mother gripped her shoulder again. "And you will meet with Miss Tabitha. For your sister. And your mother."

"Yes, Your Highness," Elice said, giving her mother a dramatic bow, her hands clasped one over the other across her chest. She laughed as Julice pushed her out the door.

Shaking her head at herself, Elice walked past Michael, who fell in line behind her, and continued on her path to Alice's suite.

Elice nodded at Mr. Corte, her sister's guard, who knocked on Alice's shiny white door. She ran a finger across the embellished flowers etched along the border, tracing the intricate petals while she waited for her sister's reply.

She waited a few more seconds before giving up. Turning the knob, she nudged the door open and peeked her head in.

"Your Highness," Mr. Corte whispered, eyeing her as she placed a finger to her lips in a plea for him to be quiet.

With her head through the crack, she looked for her sister in the front sitting room, but it was too dark to see anything.

Looking behind, she saw Michael posting himself against a wall just a few feet away. He usually allowed some space while in the east-wing suites in case someone was changing or otherwise indisposed in their rooms. Mr. Corte shook his head and copied Michael's stance, his gaze directed away from Alice's room.

Elice fully entered the suite and walked through the dark with her hands in front, feeling for the door that led to Alice's bedchamber.

When she reached the door, she fumbled around for the knob. When her hands found the solid gold handle, she turned it and pushed the door open. "Alice," she called, hoping her sister would forgive her intrusion.

A single candle lit the room, perched in front of Alice where she sat at her vanity. The faint glow barely illuminated her sister's face, casting an eerie shadow that made Elice's skin prickle.

After a second of silence, Elice crossed the room to stand in front of her, almost bumping into the edge of the vanity. "Hey, Alice," she said a little louder. Alice continued to stare off to the side, her eyes glazed over like she was stuck in a trance.

Elice bit her lip and bent closer, afraid to startle her sister but wanting to make sure Alice heard her. She looked at the top of the dressing table and saw one of Alice's notepads open, a few charcoal pencils resting off to the side. She reached for the book, and when her fingers brushed against the page, Alice grabbed her wrist, squeezing tight.

"Ow," Elice exclaimed, trying to pull her hand away. "Alice, wake up. You're stuck again." When Alice's hold on her wrist didn't let up, Elice raised her voice. "Come on, Alice. It's me. It's Elice."

Alice's eyes fluttered. She looked at her hand gripping Elice's and yanked it away like she had burned it on an open fire. "Elice! By the Fates, I'm so sorry."

Elice rubbed her wrist. "It's all right. I just came to check on you." She looked down at the notebook. "Have you been drawing again?"

Alice closed the book and pushed it away. "No, I haven't. It's nothing."

Elice frowned, taking in her sister's messy hair piled loosely on top of her head and the heavy bags under her eyes that appeared darker under the low light of the room. It had been weeks since her sister last painted or created some kind of art. It worried Elice that her sister had stopped drawing and painting, but the worst part was the nightmares had not gotten better. In fact, Elice thought they had gotten worse.

Her sister sat in trances several times a day, only breaking out of them when someone shook her or called her name loudly. Sometimes, her sister's screams woke Elice in the middle of the night, so she would crawl into Alice's bed to hold her while she sobbed.

The family's doctor thought it was trauma, related to what she went through that day at the old cottage. Sure, Elice knew it must have been frightening having a murderous old woman hold a knife to the side of your neck, but she wondered if there was a more sinister reason. Her thoughts flew back to Lenore's last words: 'Our fates have already been decided.'

Shaking her head, she reached down and brushed Alice's hair

away from her face. "Did you know Miss Tabitha was waiting for you?"

Alice stood and walked to the foot of her bed, somehow finding it in the dark. She sat on the edge and stared at a spot on the floor. "I know. I just don't feel like trying on wedding dresses right now."

"I think the dressmaker needs those measurements, like last week."

Alice sat quietly, wringing her fingers. Elice followed her sister and sat next to her, placing a gentle hand on her shoulder. Alice flinched slightly, and Elice pulled her hand away.

"Don't worry about it." Elice pushed herself up and gave her an encouraging smile. "Mother said we have almost the same measurements, so I'll fill in for you again today."

Avoiding eye contact, Alice nodded. "Do you think you could fill in for me at the council meeting today as well?"

Elice held back the groan that threatened to escape. Instead, she muttered, "Of course." She turned to leave before she remembered the other thing she wanted to talk to her sister about. "Before I forget, I spoke with James, and he invited me to go with him to Talin in a couple weeks. You should come with us. It'd be nice to see some of the kingdom with you. That is, if you're feeling up for it."

Alice sat still for a moment, and Elice wondered if her sister even heard what she said. Then, like a spark of flame, Alice's eyes lit up and a genuine smile graced her tired face. "Yeah, I think that'd be nice. To get away for a little while. I'd like that."

Elice exhaled a sigh of relief. "I'd like that, too."

"But we'd have to invite Andre. I know father wouldn't allow us girls to travel with another man without my betrothed."

Elice couldn't hold back the groan this time. "I'm not sure James—or Andre—would like that much."

Alice shook her head. "No, but if father says it, they will have no other choice."

Elice pursed her lips. "I wish I had that kind of power."

"Yeah, me too." Alice looked toward her desk, eyeing the mysterious notebook on the corner.

Elice eyed the notebook too. "Don't forget to take your medicine," she muttered, her gaze lingering on the book before she left.

Two

Tabitha huffed, her hands on her hips as she stared daggers across the room toward Elice. "Would you hold still?"

"I would, if only I could breathe," Elice said in between gasping breaths. It seemed Alice was actually thinner along the waist than she was, and the white gown squeezed the air out of Elice's lungs. "Is this actually a good idea? What if I pop the seams of her dress?"

Miss Gwen lifted her head over Elice's shoulders. She had a pin in her mouth as she tucked in pieces of fabric along the back of the dress. The seamstress pulled the pin from her mouth and mumbled an angry response. "I'm not waiting another day, Your Highness. It will take me several weeks to hem the rest of the skirt. Not to mention taking in the back and adding the jewels to the bodice. And the wedding is only a few months out now. You're the next best thing we got to the real model."

Elice held her breath, sucking in as much as she could. Air

brushed against her face, reminding her to exhale, so she slowly expelled some from her lungs before pulling it back in.

Tabitha did a full circle around the raised wooden platform Elice stood on as Miss Gwen worked on the dress. Every so often, she would adjust Elice's shoulders to help her stand straight, humming in approval as the seamstress added another pin to the layers of taffeta fabric along the bodice. "Don't worry, Princess Elice. When it's your turn to get married, the measurements will be fitted exactly to your body."

At those words, Elice sucked in a large breath, causing her to choke. She coughed several times, a weak noise from the back of her throat as she tried to stifle it, but the motion caused the seamstress to accidentally stick a pin right into her back. Elice yelped in pain and hopped off the platform.

"Princess, my apologies," the seamstress exclaimed, her eyes wide in shock.

Elice rubbed the middle of her back where the pin stuck her. "I'm so sorry, Miss Gwen."

Tabitha walked over and waved her hands. "Are you trying to destroy the dress?" Elice opened her mouth, but Tabitha cut her off. "Don't answer that. Please, let's just get you out of this gown before you ruin it."

With Tabitha's and Miss Gwen's help, they managed to get Elice out of the wedding dress before she wrecked the seamstress's hard work.

Now wearing a long-sleeved green dress, Elice took a moment to catch her breath by sitting on a chair. She had been running around all morning, and next she had to sit in for her sister at the council meeting. The only other meeting she attended was when her sister first fell sick. It was right after Lenore's death, when Alice had her first bout of nightmares.

Alice had been awake all night, screaming at the top of her lungs. Elice could still hear the words she cried out.

"He's coming," Alice had yelled, tears streaming down her face. "We can't stop it. He's coming!"

"Princess," Tabitha said, gently touching Elice's shoulder. Elice blinked up at the woman. "You looked lost for a minute. Is everything all right?"

"Yes, I'm fine," Elice answered. She stood, mentally preparing herself for the meeting.

Tabitha cocked her hip to the side, one perfectly sculpted eyebrow raised in silent question. Today, Tabitha wore a purple cropped shirt with tight-fitted black trousers that cinched at the ankles. A matching purple and black striped headscarf wrapped around her curly hair. Elice took a moment to admire Tabitha's daring outfit before she stood from her chair.

"I don't want to be late for the council meeting," Elice said before Tabitha could question her further. Miss Gwen nodded and gave a curtsy, and Tabitha followed Elice out of the seamstress's office.

"Tell me," Tabitha whispered as they left the room, "how is she, really?"

Elice glanced over her shoulder where Michael leaned against a nearby wall. She gave a subtle shake of her head and lowered her voice. "We don't know what to do. She's not getting any better."

Tabitha gave Elice's shoulder a squeeze. "Is there anything I can do?"

Footsteps reverberated down the hallway, and both women paused as a servant entered the hall. Elice looked at Tabitha and forced a smile. "You could tell me where you got those pants."

Tabitha winked. "I'll send you a pair." With that, Tabitha sashayed away, heading toward the corridor where her office was located. Elice was grateful to still have Tabitha around to teach her more princess etiquette, and even more thankful to have someone to talk to.

With a sigh, Elice walked toward the assembly room.

As soon as she entered the space, a hush fell across the room as the council members stared. She stood with the door open, looking around for a familiar face. A man with a thick, bushy mustache nodded at her before resuming his conversation with a woman wearing thin glasses. They stood behind their seats along the wide oval table.

Elice's eyes continued to roam the group. Not everyone had arrived yet, which meant she wasn't late, as per her usual. Her shoulders rose with a deep inhalation as she walked to her seat on the left of her father's chair. His seat sat at one head of the table and had a bright-red velvet upholstery on the back and cushion, while the others had a light-gray cloth covering. Alice's folder rested on the table, and, to busy herself, Elice opened it and perused the contents. A few of the documents were simple ordinances or regulations recently put in place, so she spent a moment scanning them.

Movement across from her caught her attention, and she looked up to see the face of one of the young lords. She remembered him from her birthday ball and from their brief interaction during her first council meeting. He wore a light-gray vest over a blue shirt, and a silver watch glistened from its spot on his wrist.

He gave her a smile as he took his seat. "Good afternoon, Princess Elice."

"Good afternoon, Lord Torenti." Elice nodded at him and returned his smile. A few other members gave them their attention, turning fully in their chairs to stare at Elice and Lord Torenti's exchange. Elice felt their inquiring gazes on the side of her face at their obvious eavesdropping, hoping to hear her explain why Alice wasn't present for the meeting.

"There's a terrible storm outside, have you seen?" Lord Torenti leaned back in his chair and rested his folded hands on his lower stomach.

Elice shook her head, thankful he didn't ask where Alice was or why Elice was filling in for her. "I only saw the clouds rolling in this morning. I'll be sure to look the next time I pass by a window."

He laughed, and a few older members returned to their conversations. "You mean a water mage like you won't go outside to enjoy it?"

A heat rushed to her cheeks as all conversation stopped once again. She could feel everyone's gaze on her, waiting for her to confirm her mage status. It had been three months since her father made the proclamation that ended the ban on the use of magic. Still, the tension in the air was as thick as a dense forest. She knew there were several people in her father's court who disapproved of his declaration. Many were even quite vocal about it.

Lord Torenti sat up in his chair. "What I mean is, I'm sure

you'd love to take a walk outside instead of just look at it from the window."

Someone coughed, yanking Elice out of her worry. She gave him a vigorous nod, drawing herself up in her chair as well. "You're right. I'd much prefer a walk in the rain. I'm also an air and earth mage, so a storm is perfect for someone like me."

Lord Torenti smiled and opened his mouth, but was cut off when the double doors opened. The remaining council members, who were all members of the King's Army, walked in, and Elice saw James among the group. As usual, he wore his green military uniform, looking like he had changed into a fresh outfit after their spar. He grinned when he saw her.

"My princess, what a pleasant surprise," James said, causing all heads to turn toward him.

Elice tucked a long strand of hair behind her ear. "I'm just filling in for Princess Alice today."

James found his seat next to Elice's, and they shared a smile as he sat. "It's nice to see you again, my princess."

She had to look away from his eyes, otherwise another blush would have warmed her face.

The doors opened again, and her father stood in the doorway. The gold crown above King Edgar's head reflected the light from the candelabras hanging from the ceiling. His long, flowing blue cape draped over his pearly-white shirt and fitted gray pants.

Everyone stood from their seats and hung their heads. Elice followed their movements, pushing herself up from her chair and bowing her head. His footsteps echoed in the small room as he made his way over to his velvet chair. As soon as he sat, the council members took their seats, ready to begin the meeting.

The king caught Elice's eye and leaned toward her. "Everything all right?"

Elice leaned in to whisper. "If I have to stay for the entire meeting, it won't be."

Edgar grunted in reply and sat tall in his chair, placing both palms on the desk. "May the Fates bless our meeting," he told the chamber.

"And may the Fates bless our king," the council members said in unison.

"First order, General Thiery," Edgar said, motioning to his general on the opposite side of the table. General Thiery opened his folder and passed a document down the line until it reached the king.

"Your Majesty," General Thiery began, "a new report from Fort Aramu."

Edgar scanned the sheet of paper, his eyes roaming over the words. After reading, he passed it along to the person on his right. "These are excellent numbers. Recruitment has gone up this month."

"Thanks to your latest proclamation, more citizens are signing up for the cause," the general said with an approving nod. He had a thick brown beard, which was quite uncommon for soldiers, but Elice guessed being a high-ranking officer allowed him some privileges.

"Thanks to the fear, you mean," one man grumbled. He was an elderly man with deep wrinkles and a stern-set mouth.

Elice noticed her father clench his fists on top of the table. Across the room, heads looked back and forth between the king and the grumbling old man. A couple angry stares were directed her way.

"Is there something you wish to share with the council, Lord Cove?" her father asked through clenched teeth.

Lord Cove shrugged a shoulder. "We all know the real reason people are signing up for the army. They fear a war is dawning, and they want to be prepared."

"There is no proof a war is coming," said the woman with glasses, one of the few ladies on the council.

"Besides," James added, "there haven't been any attacks to cause worry."

General Thiery coughed and passed another sheet across the table. "There's just been a report of an attack, Your Majesty."

Edgar snatched the paper, and he swept over the document with wide eyes. "This was last night."

He passed the paper to Elice, and James looked over her shoulder as she read it. "It happened in a small fishing village," she said, meeting James's eyes.

James looked at the general. "There's no mention of a possible suspect or motive. We have no way of knowing it was a mage attack."

"That's because the people are too afraid to share the full details of the incident," said the general.

"Send a special investigation team," Edgar said, his eyes set on his general. "I want to find out who did this and why."

General Thiery nodded and took down a few notes. Elice returned to the document as the general called another item to be discussed.

The document reported several damaged huts, all burned to a crisp with nothing but charred wood as evidence. There were no deaths or injuries reported, but the victims and witnesses all refused to speak to the patrollers on the scene. The reporting officer stated he sensed foul play but was unable to find a culprit or a motive. He ended his report by saying the villagers all seemed too scared to speak to him, and he wondered why they wouldn't come forward.

Elice looked up at the end of someone's speech. Applause rang across the room, and she leaned closer to James. "What did I miss?"

James leaned in to whisper in her ear. "Captain Yusef is getting married next spring. He and his bride-to-be have finally settled on a date."

She nodded and pulled away. "Oh. How nice."

He smiled and returned to sit properly in his seat. She didn't miss the way her heart had skipped a quick beat or the way his eyes seemed to light up.

She cleared her throat and attempted to focus on the rest of the meeting, though she could feel James's eyes on her the entire time.

Three

As she wandered through the upper level of the library, the smell of old paper filled her nose, refreshing her mind after the long meeting. After Captain Yusef's wedding announcement, the council quickly took a turn for the worse. At one point, a council member accused her father of being too soft on mages, which caused James and a few others to accuse them of disloyalty to the king, until Edgar finally stood from his chair and asked if anyone wanted to question his decision making.

The room grew quiet at that, and one by one, each member shook their head and pledged their loyalty to him. Even Elice spoke up and said that she would follow the king's rules. This earned her a smile, which seemed to lighten her father's load enough to make it to the end of the meeting.

To forget the jumbled mess that was the council, she went straight to the library. Only one thing remained on her mind now that she was out of that council room: Alice.

Over the last few weeks, she would spend her free time trying to find as many books on magic as she could. She figured with a library as large as this one, there was sure to be a substantial amount of research material.

What she had come to find, though, was a measly total of four books, and only one had any worthwhile information.

She held on to the tiny ray of hope that the last few shelves in this section would have a book that might help her find out what was wrong with her sister.

A built-in staircase led to the higher shelves, and Elice climbed up to begin her search. One by one, she scanned the book titles, pulling a few from their spot to peruse the contents before deciding whether it would help her. After several hours, she had looked through each book in this last section of the castle's library.

It's no use, she thought as she plopped down in her little nook on the first floor. Not a single book in this extensive space had any information about magic, other than it being banned and was not allowed. She realized she would need to upgrade the library's catalog very soon.

The clock on the wall beside her indicated it was almost six in the evening. With a sigh, she stood and headed to her suite to dress for dinner.

As soon as she entered, her maid, Serena, looked up from the wooden table she was polishing in the sitting room.

"Good evening, Princess Elice," Serena exclaimed. She gave Elice a quick curtsy. "I've laid out your dinner gown and set out your favorite slippers."

"Thank you, Serena," Elice said in reply. She slipped into her bedroom to change, sliding on the scallop-necked maroon gown Serena had picked out. The sleeves went midway down her forearm and the bodice was cinched tight to her chest, flowing away at her hips and bunching on the floor. Once fully dressed, she opened her door for Serena to enter.

The two girls had fallen into a comfortable routine. Elice learned that Serena actually enjoyed her job, so she let her maid help every once in a while. Serena would set out her training clothes in the morning and her dinner dress in the evening, then help her tame the wildly long curls that gradually became frizzy throughout the day.

Elice sat on the tiny stool in front of her vanity while Serena worked a light cream through her hair, spiraling a few strands around one of her fingers to get them to coil.

"Did you have an enjoyable day, Your Highness?" Serena asked.

Elice frowned, her first thought going to her sister. "It was fine. I had to sit in on a couple of my sister's meetings, which I didn't enjoy."

Serena held back a laugh, but Elice could see her smile in the mirror's reflection. "I heard you helped with the wedding dress fitting."

Now Elice rolled her eyes, not sure if it was Miss Gwen or Miss Tabitha who was the biggest gossip in this castle. She wondered when people were ever going to get sick of talking about her. Didn't Alice say everyone would grow tired of her and would soon leave her alone? She didn't want all this attention on her all the time.

Sensing her discomfort, Serena placed a hand on her shoulder. "Don't worry. We all think it's a nice thing you're doing for Princess Alice."

"Who's we?" Elice eyed her.

"The staff. We all know how much she is suffering. For you to step up the way you are…"

Elice shifted in her chair, avoiding Serena's stare in the mirror. "I'm not really doing anything. And half the time I have no idea what's going on in the meetings. I shouldn't even be there."

Serena wrapped another strand of hair around her finger. "Well, I think you've been a big help for the crown princess. One day, when she's better, she'll have nothing but praise to give you for always being there for her."

Elice sat quietly until Serena finished working. After the final twist, Serena dabbed a bit of blush to Elice's cheeks and smeared a dark pink lipstick on her lips. Satisfied with her work, Serena excused herself and left Elice alone.

She sat there for several minutes, going over Serena's words. The staff thought she was a good sister. All Elice could do was doubt whether she deserved their kind words. Ever since they returned from Elice's old cottage, a tiny part of her mind blamed herself for letting Alice and Andre join her in finding Lenore. They had come to her asking to help, but she knew she should have tried harder to get them to stay at the castle. That was why she left them in the middle of the forest after Alice injured her ankle. Deep down, she knew one of them would get hurt, and she still hadn't forgiven herself. They could have died, and it would have been her fault.

A shiver ran down her spine, causing the hairs on her arms to lift as bumps covered her skin. She remembered the stony stare Lenore gave her as she held a knife to Alice's throat.

Then she thought about the scruffy-looking prisoner—whose name they learned was Freddy Owens—in the dungeons. He was a fire mage, and her father suspected he was a low-level Fire Lord—the king scoffed at that, calling it a false title—sent to help Lenore. So far, the man had been less than forthcoming. He refused to talk, even under interrogation.

James hinted he had even been tortured for information, yet the fire mage still held tight, a dark smile playing on his lips as he waited for each interrogation session to end. Elice thought James was exaggerating, but she still shuddered when she remembered the wicked grin he gave her that fateful morning.

The morning she killed Lenore.

She shut her eyes and tugged at the crystal charm that hung around her neck, resting beneath the neckline of her dress. That was the only thing she owned that belonged to Lenore—the woman who raised her, who had lied to her every day.

Elice pushed off the vanity and stood. She needed to get down to the sitting room before everyone wondered where she was. *Besides, James and Andre will only make the wait awkward,* she thought as she walked down the east-wing staircase.

Everyone had already arrived by the time she walked through the sitting room doors.

"Ah, finally," King Edgar said with a huff, standing from the purple sofa and extending his hand for Queen Julice to grab. "Now we can eat." He tugged his wife's hand, and they rushed to the dinner table.

"Thank you for waiting for me," she sputtered as her parents left, Miss Tabitha's etiquette lessons kicking in automatically. She caught the quirk of Alice's lips, but it was gone just as quickly as it came.

James walked up to meet her where she stood by the open doorway. He wore a fitted navy suit that complimented his brown skin and shiny dark brown shoes. He crooked his elbow, and she slipped her arm inside, allowing him to guide her to her chair. It was a gesture she now considered normal, yet she could still feel her cheeks blush every time she gripped his muscular arm.

"Good evening, my princess," he said, quietly enough for only her ears to hear.

"Hi, James." She cleared her throat, mentally kicking herself because her voice always dried up like this in his presence whenever he cleaned up so nicely. *If only he could wear his generic soldier uniform all the time*, she thought as they walked behind Alice and Andre into the formal dining room.

James led her to her seat and pulled it out for her. She gathered her billowing skirt before sitting down as James pushed the chair in. He took his seat to her left, and everyone else sat in their normal seats. Her mother and father took opposite ends of the rectangular table, Alice sat across from her, and Andre sat across from James.

Usually, the two men avoided eye contact, only speaking directly to each other when necessary. Ever since Andre admitted his feelings for Elice and James found out, the uncomfortable tension in the room hung over everyone like heavy clouds that threatened rainfall.

Andre never brought it up again, not since the birthday ball when Elice was forced to use her magic to prevent their altercation from turning physical. He knew it was his fault her magic was exposed to the party guests, and the king was then forced to remove the magic ban and formally announce Elice's powers to the kingdom when they weren't yet ready to handle the fallout from the council.

However, Elice was a little glad it had happened. Now she was free to practice magic whenever and wherever she wanted. Every mage could. It was only a shame they had to worry about the Fire Lords coming out of hiding again, risking everything her father had done to protect the kingdom from those who wished to destroy it.

She looked at James as the servants brought out the first course. James never rehashed anything about that night, and he never pushed Elice for anything other than her training. He was the perfect gentleman, always on his best behavior, even when he and Andre went toe-to-toe during an argument.

He caught her eye as he lifted his spoon to his mouth, quietly sipping the warm vegetable broth with a faint smile. "Why are you looking at me like that?" he whispered after he swallowed.

Elice shook her head, realizing how intently she was staring. "I just noticed you have a scar on your jaw." Now her cheeks burned as bright as a fire.

James brought a hand to his cheek, then his eyes glanced across the way at Andre. "That's an old memory."

"Very old," Andre cut in, wiping his mouth with his napkin.

"So you're not going to tell me about it?" Elice said, annoyed with their behavior already.

"Perhaps another time," James answered.

Elice faced forward, looking at Alice for help, but her sister raised one of her shoulders and continued eating her soup.

"Speaking of memories," Julice said after an uncomfortable silence. She looked at James. "Elice tells me you've invited her to Talin's apple festival."

"Yes, Your Majesty." James nodded his head and looked across the table at Edgar. "With your permission, of course."

Elice noticed a glint in her father's eyes—something like a warm affection that quickly became guarded as he turned on the worried father expression. "That's next weekend, is it not?"

"Correct. The first weekend of fall."

"And there will be travelers from all across the kingdom, no doubt." Edgar raised an eyebrow, and Elice wondered if he would refuse to let her go because he was so overly cautious these days.

James sat straighter in his chair. "It's an important festival for Talin, so I'm sure many citizens will show their support. But security is always strict, and I have made special arrangements because of recent events."

Edgar gave a slow nod as he brought his hand to his chin, rubbing his coarse beard as if in thought. "Have you enough room for personal guards?"

"I can arrange for accommodations with my staff. There are plenty of rooms and always enough food."

A smile spread across her father's face, and little wrinkles appeared beside his eyes. "It's settled then. I'm sure the four of you will have a fun time."

Elice spit out her drink, the water spraying across the table and almost hitting Alice's plate. Her sister barely reacted, with only the slightest quirk of her eyebrows. Elice didn't think her father would automatically assume all four of them would attend the festival.

Andre coughed, almost choking on his own drink. "Excuse me, King Edgar, but did you mean Alice and me as well?"

Edgar placed his glass of wine on the table and picked up his spoon to continue eating. "Of course. You don't expect me to send Princess Elice on her own, do you?" He eyed James, and Elice was reminded of the time they were caught alone together in the shed only a few months ago. Granted, she was only practicing her magic, but since magic was banned at the time, she and James were on the receiving end of the king's glare.

"No, Your Majesty," Andre said, his tone unusually low and quiet. He returned to his food and avoided making eye contact with anyone else.

James's jaw tightened, and Elice knew this change in plan was not what he expected. She would have to speak with him tomorrow and apologize for not warning him sooner. She sent a quick prayer to the Fates that the two boys would behave themselves once they arrived in Talin.

Four

When the weekend of her trip arrived, Elice hardly slept the night before and awoke before Serena came to help her prepare for the half-day journey to Talin.

She jumped out of bed and threw open the curtains, taking in the rolling clouds as they continued to pour fall's first rains across the castle grounds. To anyone else, they would be wary to travel on such a stormy day. Elice breathed a deep sigh and gathered the clothes Serena had laid out last night.

Tabitha had sent her a pair of those pants Elice questioned her about, along with a matching shirt. The black shirt hung loosely off her shoulders but had a tight waist that tucked into the top of the high-waisted black pants. The bottoms wrapped tight around her ankles, and she wore low-cut boots with a small heel.

In front of the mirror, she took in her casual outfit and felt completely comfortable in it. Her hair flowed longer than ever, well past her hips and curling towards the tops of her legs.

A soft knock drew her attention. It had to be Serena, so she yelled for her maid to enter.

Serena poked her head inside, curtsying before making her way inside. "Wow, Your Highness. That's quite the outfit."

Elice sat in front of her vanity. "Miss Tabitha says these pants are popular right now. And they are much more comfortable than heavy ball gowns, especially for a long carriage ride."

Serena grabbed a few strands of hair from Elice's face and pulled them behind her head. "Well, I'm sure Lord Talin won't be able to take his eyes off you either way."

"Please, I don't want to talk about that." Elice held back the heat from her face as much as she could. Serena smirked but didn't say anything else.

When Serena finished styling Elice's hair into one long braid, a few loose strands curling around her face, she grabbed the necklace from the vanity and hung it around her head. "There," Serena said with a tight smile, "you're all set." The young maid's eyes watered, and Elice turned in her seat.

"Serena, what's wrong?" Elice asked, worry in her voice.

"I don't know why I'm getting so emotional. Maybe I'll just miss seeing you for the next few days. And when you and Lord Talin marry—"

"Oh, I *really* don't want to talk about that," Elice interrupted. "Besides, I'll only be gone for the weekend."

"I know. I'm just being silly." Serena sniffled and wiped away the stray tear that had fallen.

"And…" Elice began slowly, "*if* I ever married, I would want you to come with me. That is, if you'd want to."

Serena's eyes lit up. "Your Highness, that would be wonderful."

Elice held her hand and squeezed. Then she gave it a pat and dropped her smile. "But I'm not talking about that."

Michael waited for them outside the door and followed close behind. The grand doors that led to the veranda outside the front of the castle stood open, and Elice felt the chilly air sweep across her face. Several guards and servants stood by the door, waiting to see her and her party off. Serena walked her to the opening and whispered goodbye. Elice gave a shy wave before she turned and hurried outside.

Her mother was just outside the door, and she eyed Elice upon arrival. "Why are we always waiting for you?"

"Because you are so kind," Elice said in reply before her mother pulled her in for a hug.

"Be safe out there. And stick together." Julice ran her hands down the braid on Elice's back.

Elice nodded and pulled away. She couldn't open her mouth to say anything in reply, a sudden tightness in her throat causing her to choke up. This was the first time since returning to the castle that she would be leaving her parents overnight, and this trip was for four full days. A heavy stone settled in her stomach, and she remembered all that transpired the last time she took off.

This is different, she told herself. I'm going on a vacation. I'll be with my sister. I'll have two highly trained soldiers and several guards around me. Nothing bad can happen.

Together, she and Julice stepped onto the front steps. James was the first to see her, and he paused, holding a luggage case in both hands. His eyes trailed down Elice's body, taking in her new attire with wide eyes and his mouth slightly ajar.

Andre almost bumped into James as he came up right behind him with two cases of his own. He narrowed his eyes at James's back, then he followed James's gaze and his own mouth fell open.

Julice pulled Elice down the steps, and Elice eyed the two men with a curious smile on her face as she approached.

"Good morning, gentlemen," Elice said. James and Andre snapped their mouths shut, shaking themselves from the trance they seemed to be in. Andre cleared his throat, bowed, and then stepped away with his cases.

James set the luggages down and bent low in a bow before he grasped Elice's hand to place a tender kiss upon it. "Good morning, my princess," he said, his voice strained and raspy. He then turned to the queen to bow to her.

"I think you all are ready now," King Edgar said, walking up to the carriage with Alice's arm wrapped around his. Elice didn't notice where they came from, having been too enthralled with the attention she received from James.

Alice gave a single nod before she pulled herself from her father's grasp. "We should be heading out now."

James picked up his cases. "Right. We need to leave now if we want to arrive in Talin before it gets dark."

Elice felt a familiar weight in her stomach, pulling her down to the stone walkway and cementing her to the spot she stood in. She looked toward her mother, her eyes pleading and her bottom lip quivering. She opened her mouth to say something, yet no words came out.

Julice held both of Elice's hands. "You're going to have so much fun, my dear. There's no need to worry."

"But how do you know?" Elice whispered, her voice nothing more than a hollow sound escaping from her parted lips. She didn't know why she felt so scared, when just a few days ago she couldn't wait to leave the castle and spend time with James at his estate.

Her mother reached out and ran her fingers along Elice's cheek. "Because I just know."

Elice leaned into her mother's touch, grateful their relationship had grown so close over the last few weeks. The queen leaned closer and placed her lips on Elice's forehead. The soft kiss gave Elice the last bit of confidence she needed.

With a nod, she stepped away and turned toward her father. He raised his arms for a hug, and Elice all but collapsed in them.

"Just make sure you don't have too much fun," he grumbled above her head. She felt the breath from his chuckle blow across the top of her hair, and she smiled along with him as she pulled away.

"I'll see you soon," she said. Alice came to her side, and the two girls shared a look before they waved goodbye to their parents.

The two girls walked to the carriage door, and Michael stepped forward to pull it open for them. Alice climbed in first, and Elice waited for her to sit down before she followed.

The interior of the carriage was decorated in the castle's signature gray and white color scheme, with a velvety gray fabric on the walls and white trim along the windows. Above her head, the white roof curved down on both sides, ending on the top of bright red upholstery that made up the back of the benches on both sides of the carriage. Thick padding cushioned her seat, and she sank into the tiny red pillows behind her back. The plush red curtains on her left and right were drawn open, letting in what little natural light shined in from outside even though it was a cloudy day.

Elice drew in a deep breath and closed her eyes. She reminded herself once again that she had nothing to worry about on this trip, and the bad case of nerves she felt was simply the thrill of the new experience that awaited her.

The carriage shook as Andre hopped inside, wearing his usual exuberant smile. "Nice trousers," he said, a chuckle following his words.

Elice rolled her eyes. "Don't be mad that I look better in pants than you do."

His grin only grew as James entered. "If I looked as good as you do in those pants, I definitely wouldn't wear anything else."

James's eyebrows grew taut, and Alice choked on the sharp intake of breath she took. To avoid any more awkwardness, Elice ignored his comment and turned her attention to James. "Are we ready to go?"

He slowly lowered himself into the seat next to Elice, eyeing her with a guarded expression that she couldn't read. "Yes, all set." He knocked his knuckles against the window, and Michael closed the door. She heard shuffling outside, and after a few seconds, several horses neighed, and the carriage jerked forward.

Elice faced the back window, looking at her parents and the staff as they all waved. She pressed her palm to the glass as they continued past the high metal gates and into the town of Highmore. It was an odd sight as the castle became blocked from her view, replaced by the shops in the small village that surrounded her family's castle.

Only a few merchants bustled about this early, setting up their shops and opening their doors to the public. She had never seen this side of the village before, especially this early in the morning. The sun rose behind the clouds that hung high in the brightening sky. The fog was just clearing, yet it lingered in corners and above rooftops as the sun's rays peaked through.

A sigh escaped her mouth. The beautiful view before her helped calm her nerves. Finally content, she turned around in her seat, finding James looking at her again.

"What?" she asked, wondering why he had a smile on his face.

James gave a quick shrug, then relaxed in his seat. He rolled his shoulders and rested one arm behind her on the bench. "You seemed stressed earlier, but now you seem at peace."

She didn't know how he could read her moods so easily, but it tugged at something inside her. The heavy rock that had settled in her stomach earlier seemed lighter in that moment.

Andre yawned and stretched out, his feet reaching over the narrow aisle to bump into James's legs. Elice wondered if it was intentional, since a smirk played on his lips. "Well," he drawled, "I'm going to take a nap. Let me know when we take our first break."

They would stop halfway into their ten-hour trip through the countryside to rest and feed their horses. Elice knew she would need a break to stretch her legs and possibly to take a break from the tension that always hovered around the two men and their ridiculous feud. She still thought about Andre's needless anger at James and wondered if Andre was simply jealous of James's skills as a soldier and his popularity with everyone around the castle.

Alice used a pillow as a neck rest, laying her head against the side of the carriage for support. "I think I'll take a nap too." She yawned, her eyes slipping closed as she settled into her position.

Elice pursed her lips. The last thing on her mind was a nap, especially when there was a whole countryside to explore from the window at her side. She looked at James, who sat with his gaze out the window to his right. "Will you stay awake with me, James?"

He gave her a smile and a nod. "Of course. I miss traveling to my childhood home. I don't think I could sleep even if I wanted to."

She grinned, taking his free hand as he leaned closer. With his other arm still resting behind her, she nestled inside his arms, and a warm comfort spread through her body at their intimate proximity.

He looked down at her, his thick lashes moving as he blinked several times. His lips parted slightly, drawing in a deep breath. It was in that moment she wondered what it would feel like to press her lips to his, to feel their fullness against her own.

Her throat tightened, and she swallowed against the dryness that suddenly overpowered her. "Do we have water?" she asked, her voice sounding raspier than ever.

James removed his arm from the back of the bench, and just like that, the warmth was gone. The moment was over, and she cursed her awkwardness for the first time in her life. Why did she always find a way to ruin these moments?

He reached under the bench and pulled out a large basket. Inside were several water canteens, fruit, pastries, and her favorite ham and cheese sandwiches. With the food and water in sight, she dove inside the basket for her beloved sandwiches, knowing James must have had them packed for her. He knew how much she loved those simple little lunch staples, since she brought them to their lunch picnics almost every day.

James laughed as she bit into the square morsel, her eyes closing as she savored the thin slices of meat and cheese. He had recently introduced her to flavored condiments, and this sandwich had a savory basil dressing between the loafs of bread that made her moan in delight. "By the Fates," she said in between bites. "What is this sauce?"

He finished chewing his own bite before he answered. "It's my chef's old recipe. She finally sent it to me, so I gave it to your kitchen staff just for this trip."

"Mm, I hope you'll share it with me. It's like a little piece of the spirit world."

They shared a laugh, tucking into their food as a quiet conversation flowed.

After several minutes and a few more sandwiches, James leaned toward her window and pointed something out to her. "See those hills over there? I tried to climb them once, but before I made it to the top, this jerk right here threw a rock at the side of my head and made me fall over. I rolled all the way down the hill and got several scrapes and scars to show for it."

Elice's mouth fell open just as Andre bent over in laughter. He gripped his stomach, clearly not asleep, and Elice wondered if he'd even fallen asleep to begin with.

"Oh my Fates," Andre said, sucking in several breaths. "You remember that?"

James narrowed his eyes, but a smile played on his lips. "How could I forget? I was racing you to the top and beating you by several yards. The only way you could beat me was to cheat."

"That was classic." Andre wiped the tears from his eyes, still chuckling as the memory continued to hit him. "Oh Fates, our moms were furious."

Alice shuffled beside him, turning over to face them with the pillow miraculously still tucked behind her neck. "I remember that, too. There was so much blood gushing out of your head, I almost fainted."

James shook his head, his hand running along the base of his hairline behind his ear.

Elice leaned over and saw a faint line. "There's still a scar! Dre, you're the worst!" She grabbed the pillow behind her back and chucked it at Andre. He merely caught it with one hand, still laughing uncontrollably.

"It's all right," James said, leaning back with his arms folded behind his head. "I was already used to Dre's jealousy by then."

It was Andre's turn to scowl as both Alice and Elice chuckled. "Whatever," he muttered, tossing the pillow back at Elice. He settled into his previous position, with his legs outstretched and in James's foot space, and closed his eyes again.

With a smile, Elice repositioned the pillow behind her lumbar and leaned back as well, finally ready to relax as the carriage rolled along.

Five

She had never ridden in a carriage for so long before. Those brief trips to the Highmore Square and back were a breeze compared to this half-day ride through the Norraine countryside. Soon after the carriage settled on the smooth dirt path, her nervousness had all but disappeared in exchange for boredom and numb legs.

Elice looked around at her napping companions with a hint of envy. They had likely traveled this path so many times before that another trip through these lands was nothing new to them. All the excitement was gone. They seemed so relaxed and comfortable with such a long trip.

Leaning toward the window, she inched open the thick red curtain. Tall green stalks of corn grew as tall as their carriage. The crops passed by in a blur as the carriage plowed down the path, and Elice had to pull the curtain back even more so she could get a better look.

A few farmers and their staff were in the middle of the massive corn field, harvesting the fall crop before the winter cold set in. The leafy green casing was all she could see for several miles as she continued to stare out the window.

After she grew tired of staring at the same setting, she closed the curtain with a huff and sat back against her seat. She folded her arms across her chest and huffed again.

Her travel companions continued to sleep, which irked her to no end. Instead of dwelling on it, she decided to turn her focus to something that could distract her from her current listlessness.

Elice closed her eyes and drew in a deep breath. All the years of being forced by Lenore to meditate came back to her memory, reminding her she had a place to go to whenever she needed. In her mind, she pictured a serene space, just like her old guardian had taught her. Before, she had a difficult time envisioning such a place, since she lacked any real knowledge of locations other than her meager, broken-down cottage. Now she had several places to draw inspiration from.

Her mind immediately went to the royal library, where she spent several hours every day wandering the shelves, searching through the countless books for new information or new stories. She saw the bench in her little nook with the cushions that were already indented because of her constant presence upon it. The smell of the books and wooden shelves filled her memory. She felt the warmth from the sun's rays as they crept in through the open window, with a gentle breeze blowing in to greet her, and she almost felt as if she were really there in her library.

A contented sigh escaped her mouth, drawing her to the present. She felt a tug on her mind as she tried to pull out of her meditation. It was a heated touch, almost like someone had tapped her brain with a hot metal poker. A searing pain shot through her head, spreading down her spine and making the hairs on her arm stand on end.

Her eyes shot open as she yelped, and she jumped in her seat, hitting her head against the window she had unknowingly drifted toward.

"Elice," came James's concerned voice beside her. "Are you all right?"

She rubbed the side of her head. For a brief moment, she could still feel the burning pain inside her head, like the poker was still connected to her brain. Just as quickly as the pain came, it disappeared.

Frowning, she touched the other side of her head where she bumped it on the window. "Yes, I'm fine," she muttered, her eyes finally meeting James's. "I just had a ... bad dream."

Elice swallowed the lump in her throat. Alice shifted in her seat, and when they locked eyes, a fog settled on them.

"Stop that," Andre said, scooting toward the opposite wall. "You're going to drench us all."

Looking up, Elice saw a rain cloud forming above them. She closed her eyes again to push away the dark thoughts that entered her mind before she lost control of the heavy cloud she had created.

When she opened her eyes, the cloud was gone, but the look in everyone's eyes was still there. James reached over and grasped her hand.

"Do you want to talk about it?" he asked, giving her hand a little squeeze.

She squeezed it back and nodded. "I was meditating, which I haven't done in so long. I've never actually done it so well before. I could literally feel the space I saw in my mind, like I was really there. But then I felt something. Almost like a presence. It was..."

Shaking her head, she drew in a breath to give herself the courage to continue. "It was hot. Burning hot. I tried to leave, but it was trying to get me to stay. If I hadn't felt the pain from the imaginary burn, I might have stayed there."

"Where's 'there', exactly?" Andre asked, still eyeing her from the farthest corner of the cabin.

"It's not really a physical space. Lenore called it 'the plane.'"

"Wait." Andre lifted a hand to stop her from saying more. "Lenore taught you how to go to this place?"

"Of course. Who else would've taught me anything about magic?"

"And you trusted her enough to continue going to this plane?" Andre quirked an eyebrow, clearly not happy.

Elice crossed her arms. "It's not that I trusted her. There are books about meditation and envisioning, even for non-mages who simply want to quiet the thoughts in their head."

"Well, maybe you should ask someone else for advice on how to access this place. Lenore's teachings are suspect, to say the least."

James crossed his arms. "Why are you attacking her right now?"

Andre turned to face him. "I'm not. I'm just stating the obvious. What if the way Lenore taught her is some evil Fire Lord way to enter? What if there's a better, safer way that doesn't involve her brain getting burned to a crisp?"

James opened his mouth to retort, but Elice yanked on his hand before he could continue the fight. He looked at her and his eyes softened, already forgetting the argument.

"I won't do that again until I know for sure it's safe," she promised, and she meant it. The feeling of that intense heat scared her, and she wasn't looking forward to that again.

James nodded, looking down at their connected hands as he threaded their fingers together. "I think that's probably a good idea."

Andre scoffed and threw his hands in the air. "I literally just said that."

Alice leaned forward and patted his leg. "Yes, but you're not as cute as Elice. At least, not to James."

⁓

Since Elice had jolted everyone from their nap, they couldn't go back to sleep. Even though the circumstance behind it was horrible, she was happy they were now awake and talking with her. James pulled open the curtain on his side and began pointing out things to her as they passed. The corn fields were now long behind them, but several more farms surrounded them on either side. Around the midway point in their journey, they made a stop beside a clearing to stretch and rest their horses. Once everyone rested enough and the horses were ready to travel again, they boarded the carriage and set off.

"The Drew family farms this land," James explained, pointing to a neat plot of land they passed. "They grow wheat and several vegetables. Marcus is around our age. His father wasn't called in to the war, so the whole family lives on the estate."

Elice thought back to her birthday ball just a few months ago. "I think I remember meeting Mr. And Mrs. Drew. I thought it was odd they were farmers with land but had no title."

"That's because we're still in Copita," James answered. He glanced toward Andre, who merely shrugged his shoulders. "Several families manage farmlands throughout the kingdom, and they lease the land from our lords."

"I know that. It just seems like such a big piece of land that can be seized by a greedy lord at any time." Elice looked around the cabin, noticing the raised eyebrows. "Not that I think you two are greedy. But there are definitely some suspicious lords currently occupying council seats that I don't completely trust, to be honest."

James held back a laugh. "You have no idea. But the majority of us actually care about the citizens. Isn't that right, *Dre*?"

Andre pursed his lips. "Call me that one more time—"

"Oh, look," James said, ignoring the warning tone in Andre's voice. He pointed toward the window beside Elice, and she turned and leaned toward it. The tall brown stalks of wheat gave way to a clearing, and beyond that, Elice could see the beginnings of a bridge.

She pressed her face closer to the glass. "Is that the River of Might?" Her voice rose as excitement flooded her. If she could open the window and crawl to the top of the carriage to get a better look, she would have. As the carriage driver slowed down on their approach, she had half the mind to actually do it.

"Yes it is," James answered. He laughed as he leaned in to stare out the window above Elice's head.

The grass along the dirt path was a dark green even through the changing season but became much shorter as it grew closer to the banks of the river. Elice could see the blue water shimmering with the fading sunlight, casting it in a bright blue as clear as the sky on a warm summer day.

The wooden bridge leading from Copita into Talin was straight ahead. It was an impressive size; there was room for two carriages to pass safely alongside each other with room to spare. As they rode across it, Elice could only see the bridge on her side of the carriage. Every several feet were tall wooden posts secured to metal plates at the joists. On top of the posts were unlit lanterns.

A small wooden boat in the distance caught her attention. A man sat in the middle, his hat askew as he waved up at them. Elice waved back, smiling at the sight.

The man lowered his hand and picked up his row again to continue down the river. Where he was headed, Elice could only guess. The river led to the Mighty Lake, and past that were the mucky Swamplands in the Nomad's territory. From what Elice knew, no one willingly crossed into Nomad territory, let alone the Swamplands. More than likely, he would dock his boat near Fort Aramu on the eastern side of the lake.

They rode the bridge at a slow pace for several hundred feet. This was not the widest point of the river, yet the trip across seemed to last several long minutes. As they approached the opposite shore, Elice saw a few houses along the river and a grove of trees in the distance.

"Welcome to Talin," James whispered beside her. She didn't realize he was still close behind her, and she turned in surprise to see his smiling face close to hers.

The carriage bumped across the end of the bridge and settled on the smooth ground. Elice returned her gaze to look at the new scenery, taking in the multitude of trees that were already various shades of yellow and orange.

As they passed the first few houses, she heard a few excited shouts as villagers exited their houses to catch a glimpse of the passing royal carriage. Alice's back shot up straight as she cupped her hand and waved to the people outside, all of them smiling and waving as their crown princess acknowledged them. Elice noticed even Andre, who had been slouched in his seat, sat up and set his face to stone. She knew this was all an act the two of them had rehearsed all their lives. The future queen, with her consort, needed to be the stoic leaders of this kingdom, which meant they couldn't slouch or lower their gaze.

Elice sneaked a peek at James, who wore a huge grin on his face. He seemed so happy to be back in his hometown, among the people he strove to protect as their landlord. His smile brightened up his face as he waved at his townspeople. She could feel her own smile grow as she admired the look of adoration on his face. James genuinely loved the people, and it was nice to see how happy it made him feel to be home.

More people rushed onto the path, and soon, the carriage had to slow down even more so they didn't accidentally run over anyone. The sun was setting to the west, and lanterns were being lit in the streets. As soon as they passed this village, there were fewer lanterns, and Elice lost sight of her surroundings outside the window.

She closed the curtain and leaned back into her seat, finally relaxing for the first time in hours. "How much longer until we get to the estate?" she asked before a yawn reminded her of how tired she was.

James stretched and rolled his neck. "About another hour. My family home is in the center of the province. Maybe you can try to get some sleep." He rested his head back against the bench, as if he were going to try to sleep as well.

"Good idea," Alice said, a yawn escaping. She curled one ankle under the other and turned on her side, hugging a pillow and closing her eyes.

Since Andre had already relaxed into a comfortable position, Elice hunkered down in her seat, wanting to close her eyes, yet she was reminded of the last time she shut them. As if on cue, the stinging inside her skull threatened to return, though it went away again as soon as she felt it. She couldn't shake the unease or the deep pit in her stomach as the group quieted down, the only sound coming from the rolling of the wheels beneath her.

Six

The carriage came to a stop, and Elice, who hadn't been able to rest for the last hour, almost burst out of her seat. The others also felt the sudden halt and woke with a start.

"Are we finally here?" Elice asked, bouncing in her seat. She pulled the curtain open but could only see the silhouette of thick trees.

"We must be," James said. He looked out his window, and Elice leaned over his shoulder. They were stopped in front of a mansion, lit by several lanterns along the front pathway. She only had a moment to look before the carriage door opened.

Michael stood beside it and ushered the way for James to step out. James immediately turned and extended his hand to help Elice climb out the carriage. Her legs were numb as she stretched them, but her discomfort was only momentary as she took in the place around her.

The Talin estate was different from the others she had visited—considering she'd only been to Copita and Highmore Castle, her list was relatively small. Those mansions showed off their regality, with their shiny stone exteriors and elegant topiaries strategically placed along every corner. In contrast, James's family home didn't look like a mansion at all.

Lanterns hung around all the windows along the exterior walls of both levels. Dark blue window shutters adorned the sides of the beautifully arched windows. The house had a natural wood tone, a soft, warm brown that reminded her of the oak tree in her sister's secret garden that she spent many afternoons with James in, hiding beneath the shade of its branches. Several evergreen bushes grew to an impressive thickness all around the perimeter.

"Welcome to my home," James said, and then he guided her toward the steps in front of the main door, which was painted in the same blue as the shutters. Right beside the door stood a woman, who barely seemed able to control her excitement.

She rushed forward and pulled James into a hug. Elice tilted her head to the side, taking in the sight of a servant showing so much enthusiasm. All the other servants she had ever met barely maintained eye contact with the nobility, let alone hugged them.

"My lord, welcome back," the woman said as she gave one last squeeze.

James returned the hug. "It's good to be back, Miss Wanda."

As soon as Miss Wanda let go, she spun on her heels and pulled Elice into a hug. Then, as if she caught herself, she pulled back just as quickly and lowered her gaze. "My Fates. I apologize, Your Highness. I'm just so excited to finally meet you. We've all prepared for your arrival. It's all we've been talking about. Please forgive me."

Elice took in the woman before her. She was around middle age and of average height, with a curvy figure and long braids twisted into a bun behind her head. She wore a wrap around the top of her head to keep the shorter braids out of her face, and a dark blue apron wrapped around the waist of her brown tunic. Her expression was so friendly Elice could only smile.

"It's all right, Miss Wanda," Elice said. "I've recently learned that I actually enjoy hugs." After living most of her life never having been hugged by Lenore, her first few embraces had taught her it was one of the best feelings in the world.

Miss Wanda bit her lip and gave a fast curtsy. That was all the encouragement the maid needed because she hugged Elice again before rushing to Alice and Andre. "It's been years since I've laid eyes on you two. Now look at you! Dear Andre, you're just as tall as the front door. You used to be a short little thing. And my word, Princess Alice, you're just as beautiful as I remember."

"Hi, Miss Wanda," Alice said, holding the woman's hands in hers with a soft expression on her face. There was a shimmer in her eyes, and Elice knew she was on the verge of tears.

Andre scratched the back of his head. "It's good to see you too, Miss Wanda." His voice cracked on the last few words—even after everything that had happened between him and James, he still must have felt some sort of way about being back in Talin after all these years.

Miss Wanda must have noticed, too, because she waved a hand at him. "Oh, let's get you kids inside the house. We have plenty of time for catching up. Dinner will be ready shortly, so you can freshen up in your rooms." She led the way into the house, opening the door for them and standing off to the side.

James held Elice's hand as they walked. He stopped just a few paces inside, letting her take it all in. "It's not as fancy as the castle," he said, almost to himself. She could feel his gaze on her as she looked around the main entry.

He was right—it was nothing like the castle. The castle was all bright white walls and deep red carpets, while the Talin manor had a subtle mix of browns, greens, and blues. The interior walls were painted a soft beige, and there were wooden beams along the ceiling that reminded her of a luxury version of her old cabin. Houseplants could be found in every corner, and a few vases with vibrant flowers adorned the wooden side tables along the foyer. Along the entry were beautiful paintings of the River of Might, the long, winding river painted across several canvases to create one giant portrait.

This house didn't just speak to her innate powers; it welcomed her in with open arms.

Andre appeared beside her. "Well, at least it's a step up from your cottage, right, Elice?"

Elice rolled her eyes. Instead of answering him, she turned to James. "It's perfect. Like it was made just for me."

James grinned, then tugged her through the hallway and into the main sitting room, where about a dozen of the staff members lined up. The staff all waved as the four of them fully entered the house.

Miss Wanda stood in front of the line. "Your rooms are all

prepared." She pointed at a couple of servants, and they rushed over toward Alice and Andre. After bowing, the two servants led them toward a staircase in the back of the main room. "Lauren," Miss Wanda continued, "please lead the future lady of the house to her room."

Elice froze in her place. Her eyes shot to James, who quickly looked at the floor.

"Right this way, Your Highness," Lauren said as she approached. Elice barely registered that she was following the maid up the stairs and into a hallway.

"I'm sorry," Elice began, "but what does 'lady of the house' mean?"

The maid, who was just a bit taller than Elice and wore her thick hair in a puffy bun on top of her head, looked over her shoulder as she spoke. "It just means you'll be in charge of the estate."

"But isn't that James's—I mean, Lord Talin's job?" They had been walking toward one end of the hallway and had passed several doors on the way before stopping in front of a door at the corner.

"Well, as his future betrothed, it will also fall to you." Lauren raised an eyebrow and cocked her head to the side.

"Oh, right, because ... we're supposed to be ... engaged."

Lauren blinked. "Right."

"Yes." Elice stood in front of the door, shifting her feet back and forth. Lauren stared for another impossibly long second before she pushed it open. Elice stumbled in, wanting the distraction but also craving some alone time to process the conversation.

Unfortunately, Lauren followed her inside and shut the door behind them. Elice was used to her own handmaid, Serena, constantly wanting to help her get dressed for dinner, so she accepted Lauren's help without complaining.

The suite was almost as large as Elice's bedroom back at the castle. It had a sitting room on the right side with two cushioned chairs and a low table, and it led to a small patio that overlooked the back of the house. On her left was a wardrobe and a vanity, and directly in front of her was an enormous bed. In the back of the room was a door that Lauren said led to a bathroom.

Elice excused herself to wash up while Lauren waited for one of the other servants to bring up her luggage. In the bathroom, Elice took her time, enjoying the few moments of quiet. Her mind was exhausted, and she couldn't help but think about the long day she'd had. All she wanted was to forget about dinner, crawl under the warm blankets, and fall right to sleep.

However, she couldn't do that. Not when all the servants downstairs expected to see her. They all assumed she was going to marry James and become the lady of Talin. And why shouldn't they think that? Tabitha had already explained whoever Elice chose as her date to her birthday ball would be her betrothed. It was only through the deal with her father that she got to postpone an official engagement if she behaved—and she did well, on most days.

She got Edgar to agree to put off the engagement until after Alice's wedding, which would take place just after their eighteenth birthday. Once that wedding took place, though, all talks of her and James's wedding was fair game to her parents.

Her stomach twisted at the thought, but her heartbeat quickened, and her palms began to sweat. *Would it really be so bad to marry James?* she wondered, looking at her reflection in the mirror.

Her hand wandered to Lenore's necklace, and she ran a finger across the crystal surface.

A knock at the door brought her back to reality. "Yes?" she said, her voice croaking.

"Your Highness," Lauren's voice came from the other side of the bathroom door. "Your luggage has arrived. I'll begin setting out your clothes."

"I'll be out shortly," Elice said, raising her voice over the sound of the running water from the sink. She finished washing up and adjusted the long braid down her back, using water to tame the flyaway strands by her face.

When she emerged, Lauren was organizing her things around the room, carrying a few clothes and shoes in her arms as she set about putting them in their proper place. "I don't know how you like your things arranged, but Lord Talin told me you like your independence and that your lady's maid only sets your things out for you to dress yourself. Until I learn your routine, please allow me some time to adjust."

Elice smiled and waved her hand. "He's absolutely right. I do like to do things on my own. But I'm grateful for your help. Please, you don't have to be so formal around me."

"As you wish, Your Highness." Lauren grinned, nodding as she placed the shoes inside the wardrobe and then grabbed hangers for the clothes.

Turning to the bed, Elice found an elegant purple gown with lace trim on the bottom of the long sleeves. When she slipped it on, it hugged her chest but flowed away from her waist until it fell just above her ankles. She grabbed her pair of black closed-toed slippers with straps that wove a couple inches above her ankle. Elice smiled, thinking how proud Tabitha would be of how far her sense of style had come.

"All right, I'm ready," Elice said to Lauren. The maid stopped emptying the luggage case to give her attention to Elice.

"That's a beautiful dress, Your Highness." Lauren walked behind Elice and set the long braid down the middle of her back. "There, now you look perfect."

"Would you mind if I walked down to the dining room by myself? I could use a little more alone time before dinner."

Lauren's eyebrows scrunched, but she nodded. "As you wish, Your Highness. The dining room is on the opposite end of the house, on the other end of the foyer you entered." She bowed, placed her hand over her heart, then excused herself from the room.

With a vague idea of how to get back to the house's main entry, Elice left the suite and wandered down the hallway the same way she came. Instead of turning toward the stairs, she kept walking down the hall, hoping for more time to clear her mind as she wandered the house. It seemed to be another wing of suites, but once she passed a few closed doors, the hallway opened up. A thick mahogany rail lined one side of the path, with ornate balusters connecting it to the floor.

She stepped up to the rail and looked down to take in the view. Below was an open sitting room with brown sofas and a wooden table in the center. The heat from a roaring fire crept up to her. A long, winding staircase a few feet away from where she stood led down to the private sitting area.

Just as she turned to leave, she spotted James leaning against the wall in the corner of the massive room. She hesitated, unsure if she should even be in this area of the house, when Miss Wanda entered from a nearby door.

"Dinner is ready, my lord." She lifted her hand to her chest in respect. "Princess Elice has yet to arrive in the sitting room, though."

Elice heard James sigh as he looked around the room. "Let's give her a few more minutes. She likes to run a little late."

"Princess Alice and Lord Copita are already enjoying drinks in the parlor. Won't you join them?"

There was a long moment before he answered, and Elice wondered if he was thinking about saying no. "I'll be there in a moment."

Miss Wanda nodded, then left through the same door she entered. Elice stood still for an extra second before she quietly turned on her heel to leave as well.

"You know, you're not supposed to be here," James called out, causing Elice to stop in her tracks.

She turned and leaned against the rail, catching James's smirk as he looked up at her. "Well," she said, "I didn't see a 'Do Not Enter' sign, so it might as well have been an invitation."

He chuckled, pushing off the wall and motioning for her to walk down the stairs. "I should've known you never follow the rules."

Elice laughed as she made her way below, her dress swaying as she walked. "What rules?"

"This is my private study. No one is allowed in here."

"Is Miss Wanda the exception?" Elice finally made it to the

bottom and came to a stop right before him. She noticed his hands jerk as if he wanted to reach out and touch her, but then changed his mind. A part of her wanted him to grab her hand like he always did, but his mind seemed preoccupied with something, almost like he was more hesitant than usual.

"I suppose you are too." He blinked slowly, his thick eyelashes fluttering. Elice didn't even realize people could blink slowly, but James seemed to do it all the time. Especially when they were this close, only inches apart.

Was he leaning closer, or was she? Her mouth went dry, and she swallowed, bringing her eyes down to his full lips.

When she looked up again, his deep brown eyes were on hers, holding her gaze with a fire that caused one to light inside her. She didn't know what that feeling was, but she pulled away from him and took a step back before she could find out.

"I heard dinner's ready," she managed to say, her mouth drier than ever.

James raised a fist to his mouth and cleared his throat. "Yes, let's eat." His voice sounded rough and raspy, so he cleared it again before he walked toward the door Miss Wanda had used.

He held it open for her, and as she walked past him, she tried to catch his eye, but he set his gaze just above her head.

She stopped in the next room, which was an open hallway with ornamental trees in large pots. Family paintings hung on the walls, and several candles burned from bronze sconces. Walking up to the closest frame, she took in the painting of a family of five; a mother, father, and three sons.

"Those are my grandparents, my father, and my uncles," James said, coming up behind her.

Looking over her shoulder, she noticed his eyes on the painting rather than on her. She turned toward him, but James was already walking toward another room. Following close behind, she could hear Andre's voice booming down the hall.

"There you two are," Andre said, eyeing them as they came into view.

James slowed so they could walk in together, and once they entered, he turned toward the back of the room and headed for another door. "I'll let Miss Wanda know we're ready," he called as an afterthought, shouting over his shoulder rather than turning around. Then he disappeared into the other room.

Elice, feeling awkward and not wanting to stand in front of the room, wandered toward one of the blue vases in the corner, admiring the swirly decoration along the surface.

"Where were you two?" Andre asked, a questioning tone in his voice.

Alice elbowed him absentmindedly, her eyes far away. Elice wondered if she was stuck in one of her nightmares, yet she somehow knew how to get Andre to keep quiet. Andre rubbed at his side as James returned.

"Dinner's ready," he announced. He stood to the side to allow everyone to enter the dining room.

Elice followed her sister to the table. It was quaint, with only four chairs even though it was large enough for six. There were minimal decorations in the dining room—only the gorgeous mahogany table with matching chairs, a buffet table along one wall, and several paintings hung throughout the space. The table settings were modest, crisp white plates with shiny silver utensils. White napkins with green stitching were folded in a triangular shape and rested on the table directly in front of each chair.

Her companions had already chosen their seats by the time she finished admiring the room. The only space available was the one directly across from James at one head of the table. As she approached, a servant pulled her chair out, and she was reminded of one of the first times she attempted to sit while someone pulled out her chair. She chuckled as she remembered nearly falling to the ground. Now that she had more practice, she was able to sit without falling over.

It seemed Andre had the same memory because he laughed along with her. "I know you're thinking about the first time you embarrassed yourself in front of your parents."

She held back a roll of her eyes as someone poured her a glass of water. After she thanked them, she unfolded the napkin and placed it gently on her lap. "And how would you know that?"

"Because I was thinking about it too," he answered, bringing his glass of wine to his lips with a smirk. "And I saw your face. You were definitely thinking about it."

"I really was." Her face broke out in a grin as he laughed again.

James passed a glance at each of them. "What's so funny? I must have missed the joke."

"That's because it's an inside joke," Andre replied. He continued to sip his wine as the servants set a plate of food in front of everyone.

Elice caught James's eyes from across the table. "No, it's not. I almost fell to the floor the first time I had dinner in the castle. You know how clumsy I am."

James held his lips in a tight line, but nodded as they all began eating. Elice didn't realize how hungry she was until she picked up her fork, looking down at her plate of vegetables. The only sound at the dinner table was the clinking of forks and the occasional slurping of drinks.

As she took her first bite, she wondered how this dinner could get any more awkward.

Seven

After a filling dinner of local roasted ham, creamy mashed potatoes, and stewed vegetables, Elice almost didn't have room for dessert. At least, not until the servants brought out slices of freshly baked apple pie. As soon as they placed a piece in front of her and she saw the cool whipped cream on top start to melt, she knew she had to make room in her stomach for the entire plate.

Once the plates were empty and cleared away, the party of four drifted away from the dining room and toward the stairs. The only thing on Elice's mind was a proper night's rest. Everyone else seemed to have the same idea, because they bid one another good night before walking to their respective rooms.

James was the only one who seemed to hesitate with his good-byes to Elice, but he shook his head once she yawned. He kissed her hand, and she only had enough energy to blush mildly this time. As she opened the door to her suite, she wondered if she'd ever get used to those little kisses from James, as innocent as they were.

When her head hit the pillow, she immediately fell asleep. The next thing she knew, the sound of curtains being drawn woke her from one of the deepest sleeps she'd ever had. A groan escaped her mouth before she could stop it, and she heard Lauren chuckle from the other side of the room.

"Please excuse my noise, Your Highness," Lauren said as she continued moving about, picking up Elice's shoes from the middle of the room. "We like to get an early start in this house, especially when Lord Talin is in residence. Even more so when he has guests. Actually, we're really only doing this for you. His lordship never cares for such formalities."

Elice sat up in bed and stretched. "Well, treat me the same way, please. I care even less than he does about these kinds of things. And please, I'll clean up my mess. I was just so exhausted from the trip I didn't have the energy to put my clothes away."

Lauren stopped moving, her body caught in the middle of bending down to pick up Elice's dress from the floor. "I don't know, my lady. I know Lord Talin said not to smother you, but..."

Sensing her discomfort, Elice decided to just go with whatever the household normally does. "You know what? Never mind me. I'm just acting weird."

Lauren lowered herself to the floor, her eyes on the dress. She scooped it up before Elice could change her mind, and with one corner of her mouth quirked into a smile, she continued with her duties. Elice forced herself out of bed, groaning again as her muscles protested the movement.

When she emerged from the bathroom, freshly bathed and at

least a bit more prepared to start the day, Lauren had already set out an outfit and left the room. Elice tilted her head, admiring the maid's ability to give her just the right amount of space and independence she needed to feel as if she had a semblance of control in her life.

The dining table had already been set when she walked in. She had heard her sister and Andre as she walked down the stairs, so she followed their voices into the dining room to find them already snacking on breakfast.

"Oh, you're finally awake," Andre said, his voice full of humor.

"Good morning," Alice greeted as Elice sat down. "I hope you don't mind we started without you. James was adamant we get an early start today. He wants to go into town to make sure the villagers have everything they need before the festival starts."

"Where is James?" Elice asked. She dug into her own plate of eggs as she listened to her sister.

"He's running around somewhere. He only popped in to tell us to get started without him."

Elice swallowed her mouthful. "So he hasn't eaten yet?"

Alice shook her head before she took another bite of food. Elice stood from the table, intent on bringing a plate of food with her as she searched for James since she knew he would need to eat before they rode into town. Just as she stood, James entered the room.

"So sorry, everyone," he said, slightly out of breath. "I've had some last-minute things to take care of. But that's done now, so we can head out to the village as soon as possible."

"I'm not done with my food," Andre said, lifting the fork to his mouth to prove his point.

"And Elice only just got here," Alice chimed in.

"I was just on my way to find you, actually," Elice said, returning to her seat. "You should eat before we go."

James looked around the table. "I suppose I could sit and eat a little something."

He sat in his seat, and a servant quickly placed a plate in front of him. When everyone had enough to get them through the morning, they headed toward the front door where James said the carriage waited for them.

With the castle guards flanking the carriage on all sides, the group packed into their coach and settled in for the quick trip to the town square.

The excitement of visiting a new town made Elice bounce in her seat again. "I can't wait to see what it looks like," she said as the horses started moving.

James reached across her and opened the curtains so she could look outside as they passed. "I love the square. Everyone is so friendly, and the local food is always amazing."

Elice looked out the window. There were so many trees, all turning various shades of yellow. As they drew nearer to the center of town, the trees thinned enough to allow wooden houses to crop up in between. They had angled roofs with red shingles, almost all of them matching and forming a cohesive design. The dirt road became a smooth cement as they entered the square and finally came to a stop.

Before the door opened, she could hear the roaring shouts the villagers made. The guards were there in an instant, forming a protective circle around the wagon as the citizens rushed to the carriage door.

James looked back at her with a smile. "They never greet me like this. They must be doing it for you."

"Why would they be that excited to see me?" Elice could feel her face warm at the absurd notion—surely the citizens were excited to see their crown princess, not Elice.

He shrugged, his eyes betraying the movement since they glistened with an all-knowing glimmer. James stepped out, followed by Andre. Elice waited for Alice to exit first so she could draw enough courage to leave the carriage.

As soon as she set foot on the ground, the crowd roared with calls of her name. She caught the faces of the citizens before her, most of whom smiled and waved their hands at her. Elice waved back as the guards pushed the crowd further away.

James held out his hand for her, and she slipped her fingers into his palm. They all walked in the middle of the circle of guards, making their way to a produce stand. The man and woman behind it placed their hands over their hearts and bowed as Elice and her group approached.

"Your Highnesses, Princess Alice and Princess Elice," said the man, and the woman beside him greeted them as well. They turned to Andre and James and gave them the sign of respect. "My lords. Thank you for visiting with us. The other farmers and I have almost everything ready for the festival. There are a few things we'd like to go over with you, Lord Talin, if that's all right."

"Of course, Mister Blake," James said, patting the man on the back. "That's why we're here."

Andre grumbled something under his breath, but Alice hooked

an elbow through his arm before he said anything else.

For the next hour, they met with several farmers to ensure they had everything they needed for the festival. All the stands were stocked with freshly picked apples, a wide variety that included some Elice had never even heard of. There were other types of produce stands as well—corn, squash, plums, and peaches—but apples were the main attraction.

As they surveyed the square, they saw other vendors already setting up their shops. There were stands selling various cured meats for the upcoming winter months, hot drinks, warm clothing, and even sleds.

Elice walked up to one of the sleds and admired the sharp blades along its bottom. She never had the chance to go sledding before, since Lenore always kept her locked up tight in the cottage during the winter. She remembered how she snuck out once when she was around eight years old, just before a bad snowstorm. The wind had picked up, blowing gusts of snow all around her and freezing her to the bone since she didn't have the right clothes or shoes. Even now, she still remembered Lenore's sharp yell as she chased after her and the fiery look on her face when they sat in front of the fire to warm up.

"It's a nice model," James said, creeping up beside her and pulling her from her memory.

She shook her head and tucked a strand of loose curls behind her ear. "Oh, is it? I wouldn't know."

James stared at her for a moment before he turned to the vendor and pointed at the sled. "How much for this one?"

The man's eyes widened. He dropped whatever papers he held

in his hand and rushed to their side. "For you, my lord and lady, it's free."

"No, I can't take it for free," Elice said, waving her hands.

James caught her by the waist before she could walk away. He leaned in close to whisper in her ear. "It's considered rude to turn down a gift. The people of Talin would consider it an honor to be able to give you something."

Elice looked up at him and bit her lip. "But it looks so expensive."

"That's exactly why it's special. He probably worked really hard on it, and you've taken a liking to it."

The man stepped around the table, but Michael stepped in at the same moment before he got too close to Elice. "Please," the man said, looking back and forth between Michael and Elice. "It would mean the world to me to tell my grandchildren I gave the princess and future lady of Talin one of my best sleds. They could tell all their friends this winter that Princess Elice is riding on one of grandpa's sleds right now."

Elice took a few steps closer until she could hold the man's hands in hers. She looked at them, the wrinkles soft but the pads of his fingertips rough from his years of woodwork. When she looked at his face, his pale gray eyes reflected the surroundings back to her. A chain pulled on her heart as if something were trying to sink it to the floor. In all her years looking into Lenore's cold, dark eyes, she had never felt the warmth she felt when looking into this man's eyes.

She swallowed the rock that seemed to have formed in her throat. "I think I'm the one that's honored to have such a fine sled.

It's the best gift anyone has ever given me."

The creases in his face grew as he grinned. Then he let go of her hands and clapped his together once. "By the Fates, this is a blessed day!" He turned to the sled and lifted it off the table. James and Michael ran to his side, grabbing the heavy sled from his arms before he could take a step with it.

"I'll have this sent to the manor," Michael said. He waved one of the other guards over and passed it to him, giving him instructions to have it packed for the return journey to the castle.

Elice turned to the man again. "Thank you so much. Please tell me your name, sir."

The man bowed. "I'm Henry. Henry Thurnmore."

"Well, Mister Thurnmore, I won't forget your kindness today." She reached for his hands again and held them for a moment.

His eyes filled with tears as he squeezed back. "And I'll never forget either. My grandkids will never believe me."

They shared a laugh, and James shook Henry's hand before they turned to leave.

"I can't believe I have a sled," Elice said, her voice light as she felt a gentle breeze blow through her flowing hair.

James clasped hands with her and they walked down a lane full of shops. "I take it you've never been sledding?"

Elice shook her head, swinging their hands back and forth. "I've only ever been in the snow once before, and it wasn't pleasant."

"Maybe we can take a trip to the mountains this winter. Fort Emori has some of the best hills for sledding." He glanced at her, catching her eyes briefly before turning his head to the other side of the street.

Elice smirked and stepped a little closer to him, causing him to turn to her once more. "I'd like that," she whispered.

Whatever James was about to say was interrupted when Alice and Andre came up beside them.

"You two always seem to go off on your own," Alice said, a small smile on her lips.

James scratched behind his head before he drew their attention to one of the nearby shops. "Actually, I'm glad you two are here now. This is Madam Verna's shop."

Elice turned to the store directly behind her. A sign with a shiny round object and the seer's name was nailed across the top of the building, and a small sign below said, "Medicines and herbs". Her heart raced as she realized it was finally time to meet the woman James had told her so much about over the last few months.

Now that the magic ban was lifted, she was finally going to meet another mage without having to hide who she was.

Eight

James led the way into Madam Verna's shop. As soon as Elice passed through the door, she felt the pull of magic in the air. The healing herbs from the shelves called to her, and she was reminded of the time she walked into Madam Olivia's shop with Andre all those months ago. Not for the first time she wished she were a healer, able to use her powers to help someone instead of merely being able to conjure three elements to her will.

As if knowing her thoughts, a gust of wind brushed past her, shoving against her skin in a show of insult. Sighing, she raised her hand and ran it through the wind at her side, begging for forgiveness. It slowed its angry assault until it was no longer rushing through the open doorway.

Andre was the last one in, so he closed the door and stepped up beside Elice. "Brings back memories, doesn't it?"

Elice nodded absentmindedly, turning to the back of the shop where a lone teenager, maybe a couple years younger than Elice, stood behind a desk. She had her braids tied back behind her head and a long, braided scarf wrapped loosely around her forehead. The girl didn't even notice their arrival, since she seemed so enthralled with the book she was reading.

James continued walking until he stood in front of her. "Does your aunt know you're ignoring the customers?"

The young girl's eyes snapped up and a grin spread across her face. "Lord Talin!" As quickly as she said his name, she shot out from her chair and peered over his shoulder. A squeal rang from her mouth, which she immediately covered. After another shriek, she lowered her hands. "I can't believe it. Princess Elice. In my shop!"

A hand came out of nowhere, gripping the girl's shoulder to keep her from running up to Elice. "It's not your shop yet, little one."

A woman stepped forward from her place behind the girl, and Elice didn't notice where she came from. Her dark black hair hung loose behind her body, running to the middle of her back. It was wild and free, almost as curly as Elice's. Her brown skin was almost identical in complexion to the young girl's, and she wore a green and purple frock that flowed down to the floor.

"Madam Verna," James said, lowering his head toward her. "It's so nice to see you again."

"Likewise, my lord," Madam Verna said, looking at him for a moment before her eyes met Elice's.

Elice stood frozen to her spot on the other side of the store. Alice and Andre stood beside her, but she felt a light push against her back. She looked at Alice, who gave another push and a gentle nod in the seer's direction.

That was all the encouragement she needed. With a deep breath, she walked forward until she stood before the other mage. The woman nodded, then placed her hands over her heart. "Ah, yes. It's nice to finally meet you, little one." She then turned to Alice and Andre and gave them the same sign of respect.

Elice didn't know whether to bow or shake the woman's hand, so she placed a hand on her chest. Her words came out breathy as she spoke. "By the Fates. I've never met another seer before."

The woman pursed her lips. "And the one seer you knew happened to be the worst."

Elice took a step back. She opened her mouth to rebut the woman's harsh words toward her old guardian, but no words would come out. *Have I finally run out of words to defend that old woman?* she wondered.

Madam Verna sighed and shook her head. "I apologize for my harsh words. Please don't mistake me for someone who speaks badly about others for fun. Madam Lenore was someone I came across quite often, and we never ... saw eye-to-eye. If you understand my meaning."

Nodding, Elice recovered from her previous recoil. "Yes, I understand. Believe me, I know what she was like."

"So she came to Talin often?" James asked, standing off to Elice's side with his arms folded across his chest. "How come I never knew?"

"I'm sorry, my lord," Madam Verna said. "Madam Lenore liked her privacy, especially her secrets." She walked up to Elice and gripped her hands, holding them between their bodies as she searched Elice's eyes.

"What secrets?" Elice asked in a quiet voice.

Madam Verna blinked, pulling herself from what looked like a vision. "Why don't you all come with me? Cassidy, please watch the counter." The woman turned toward her niece and pointed at the front desk she was originally sitting behind.

Cassidy frowned and crossed her arms. "But Auntie Verna—" she protested, but her aunt raised a hand to stop her.

"Do as I say. This is important."

The young girl pouted but nodded her head before she turned on her heels to return to her designated spot. She continued to stare at them as Madam Verna guided them behind the counter to the back of the shop.

"Again, I apologize for all the secrecy, Your Highnesses, my lords." Madam Verna led them down an aisle of bookshelves, the contents of which were an eclectic mix of books, medicines, and other knickknacks Elice couldn't name.

They came to the end of the row, where a round table and five chairs sat along the back wall. A rainbow-colored cloth took up the center of the table, and on top was a brightly glowing crystal ball.

Unable to take her eyes off it, Elice felt the command of its magic as she walked over. With a trembling hand, she reached out to touch it, but something stopped her from making contact. She looked down at her hand, where someone else lightly gripped her wrist.

"Please don't disturb the energy of the crystal, Your Highness." Madam Verna had her lips in a tight line, yet her eyes were soft as she stared at Elice.

"What is it?" Elice's voice came out barely above a whisper. The rest of the group hovered close to her, their eyes scanning their surroundings, trying to make sense of the energy that flooded the room. She wasn't sure if they could feel the magic in the air, but they definitely sensed something.

"It's a crystal ball." The woman motioned toward the empty chairs before she wandered to the one closest to the orb. She smoothed her skirt as she sat down, then scooted her chair closer.

The rest of them followed suit, sliding their chairs across the splintered wood floor. Elice sat beside Madam Verna, and Alice took the spot next to Elice. Andre and James pulled in their chairs on the opposite side of the table.

"What does it do?" Alice asked, her eyes narrowed in on the glowing ball. Now that Elice was closer, she could see a bright light swirling around inside. The movement reminded her of a slow-moving stream swirling around in a complete circle rather than down a hill.

Madam Verna lifted her hands and kept them hovered above the ball. It responded immediately, the light dulling until it became a dark gray. "It helps me center my visions. I can focus on either the past or the future, depending on the nature of one's energy. That's why I didn't want you touching it, Your Highness. It would change the outcome of the vision."

"But how does it work?" Andre leaned forward with his elbows on the table.

"How does any magic work?" Madam Verna answered with a shrug. "It's a gift bestowed upon us by the Fates, completely in tune with our spirit. Some of us just need a little more help figuring ours out." She passed a glance at both Elice and Alice, giving them a knowing stare that made Elice shiver.

"You knew we were coming," Elice said, already knowing the answer.

"Of course. Lord Talin wrote to me a few days ago to let me know." The woman winked, smiling as she moved her hands in a circle above the large crystal. "And I had a vision."

A cloudy figure emerged from inside the ball, shifting from side to side like a distorted shadow. Madam Verna focused her gaze on it, following its movements as it continued to sway. "I know why you're here, Princess Elice and Princess Alice. Your pasts are troubled, and your futures are cloudy. If you'll allow me, I will do a reading on the both of you. But I warn you: you might not like what you are about to see."

Elice looked at her sister, her hands trembling as she reached for her twin's hand. Alice's eyes were wide, her bottom lip quivering as she opened her mouth. No words came out, so she gave an imperceptible nod. Elice took a deep breath, then returned her gaze to the seer.

"Please, Madam Verna. Show us what we need to see." Elice set her jaw, her eyes locked on the woman before her.

Madam Verna hesitated, looking back and forth between the two girls. Then she nodded toward the boys. "Do you want them to stay?" she asked the twins.

Alice nodded. "Yes. They're very much a part of our lives."

Andre and James glanced at each other, and Elice wondered what they would do or say to each other. Andre sat high in his chair, lifting his head in challenge. James merely stared at him, his gaze never wavering. Then Andre gave a single nod, and the weight in the air lifted with it. Everyone let out the breath they held before turning their attention to Madam Verna.

She closed her eyes and held out her hands across the table toward the princesses. Elice reached a hesitant hand out, afraid to touch the seer. Was she ready to see what the Fates wanted her to see at this moment? She risked a peek at Alice and found her also slowly reaching her hand toward the woman.

Elice squeezed her sister's hand, which was still in hers, and they both took the last inch together to connect with Madam Verna.

Nine

The room spun. It became dark and cloudy, like a thunderstorm waiting to happen. Elice felt as if she had become trapped in one of her tornadoes as she swirled around in a seemingly endless wind tunnel.

Just as she thought her stomach might just empty its contents, the room became still. Her eyes had closed at some point, so she forced them open to take in her surroundings.

She looked around the room she now stood in. A pristine wooden staircase was in front of her, exactly like the one in the castle's sitting room. The same paintings of Norraine's various landscapes graced the walls, and the same mauve drapes hung from the massive windows. Instead of the purple couches, a dark brown sofa with a matching chaise took up the center of the space. A woman, her belly heavily pregnant, rested on the chaise, her legs stretched atop a pillow and her bare feet exposed.

Elice's breath hitched. She stared at her mother, seventeen years younger and resembling Elice almost identically. Her eyes roamed Queen Julice's body, taking in the same thick head of curls Elice had and her plump belly where she and her sister must have been at that moment. She shook her head at the thought—how was she able to see this?

A loud thumping resounded throughout the room, the unmistakable thud of a walking cane. Elice's blood ran cold. She recognized that sound, and she knew whose cane approached.

Apparently, the young Queen Julice knew who was walking down the hallway as well. With a groan, the queen pushed herself to a sitting position and let her feet fall to the floor. She slid them into the shoes that were beside the foot of the chaise and crossed one ankle behind the other. Her hands came to rest below her belly, and she fixed her expression on the door, waiting for Lenore to enter.

Behind her mother, another door swung open, and in ran a breathless man. He was the picture of youth, with shiny black hair cut short and a clean-shaven face. Her father ran into the room, startling Julice in her seat.

"Is she here?" King Edgar asked, his breathing coming out ragged, as if he had run all the way there from the opposite side of the castle.

Queen Julice shook her head. "Not yet. Give her a minute. She's not used to walking with a cane yet."

"Serves her right." Edgar huffed his usual laugh, and Elice almost laughed with him. She covered her mouth before she alerted them to her presence, but then she realized they probably couldn't see her. She had been standing in the middle of the room the entire time and they still hadn't looked her way.

Finally, after a couple more thuds, the double doors to the sitting room opened, revealing an aged and withered Lenore. She wore her normal grimace, the corners of her mouth turned down in a perpetual pout. That was the way Elice remembered her.

Elice involuntarily took a step back, away from the woman who had raised her. How was this even possible? She wondered why she needed to see the face of this woman again, the face that sometimes haunted her dreams.

The face of the woman she killed.

"To what do we owe the ... *pleasure*, Lenore?" Edgar asked, smirking as he placed a gentle hand on his wife's shoulder.

Lenore's frown deepened at the insult to her name with the term 'madam.' "I'm sure you know, *Edgar*." She used her cane to take a few more steps into the room.

"I'm honestly at a loss. I gave you everything you asked for. You have immunity. I don't even know where you live, nor do I care. So please, tell me what you want so you can be on your way."

The old woman came to a stop near the couple and leaned on her walking stick. "I've come for a reading, as is tradition. Or did you stop caring about that as well?"

Queen Julice gripped the king's hand on her shoulder.

"Why would we want you to give our child a reading?" Edgar stepped forward, bringing himself closer to Lenore.

"If you don't want to know your child's future, that's fine by me." Lenore turned on the spot, a slow circle made easier with the aid of her cane.

Elice saw the desperate look her mother gave her father. He closed his eyes, his hands balling into fists. "Fine. Just make it quick."

From her viewpoint, Elice could see the look on Lenore's face. The sinister look made her sick to her stomach. The bile that had threatened to escape earlier returned as Lenore smiled, her back still turned to the soon-to-be parents.

In all the time Elice had known her, she had never once seen Lenore smile like that. As Lenore turned, so too did Elice.

She was spinning again, the scene before her shifting into a new room, this one a bedroom.

Her parents' bedroom. And her mother was giving birth. Lenore burst into the room just before Alice was born, dismissing the doctor and staying until her mother had Elice.

As soon as she wrapped the newborn Elice in a soft white blanket, Lenore turned to leave. Elice watched with her mouth wide open as her parents cried out.

"At least let me hold her," her mother shouted, tears streaming down her face.

"It's for the best," Lenore said, her voice dull and void of any emotion.

"Lenore," the king yelled, his voice booming in the large room. "You will honor our agreement."

Lenore turned toward the door, ignoring the king's words.

When the scene changed again, tears cascaded from Elice's eyes. She didn't know why she had to endure these events. She couldn't understand why the Fates were forcing her to relive her horrible past, especially moments she couldn't even remember.

Once the new room stopped moving, she sank to the floor, her hands covering her face as sobs racked her body.

She felt weak, but her ears picked up the shrill shriek of a young girl. She lifted her head from her hands and looked around, taking in her old living room in the cottage she used to share with Lenore. It looked the same as she remembered, with the tattered couch and the old wooden furniture.

A young girl ran past her where she sat crumpled on the floor. Elice watched as the four-year-old version of herself landed on the floor at her usual spot in front of the couch. With a smile on her face, the tiny Elice opened her palm and formed a large water droplet. It grew before her young eyes, and Elice remembered how excited she was to have formed her first ball of water.

Elice rubbed at her wet eyes as she chuckled at the memory before her. She used to become so thrilled whenever she learned something new. Now she could shoot a stream straight through the air and mix it with earth and air magic, but it was nice to be reminded of a time when little victories brought a grin to her face.

The smile fell as she heard Lenore's walking cane. Young Elice tried to wipe her hand on her dress, but Lenore had already entered the room.

"What did I tell you about practicing spells you're not supposed to," Lenore said. She hobbled closer to the four-year-old and looked down at her with a sharp glare. The same glare Elice knew all too well.

"I'm sorry, momma," young Elice said, her voice small and fragile.

Lenore pursed her lips. "I told you. I'm not your mother. Your mother is dead. Your father is dead. There's no one in this world who will care for you. That's why you need to control your powers. You're the only one who can take of you. The sooner you learn that, the sooner you can leave this place."

Young Elice looked at her lap. Elice could see the tears in her young eyes and felt fresh tears form in her own. "Yes, ma'am," little Elice whispered. Then she closed her eyes, practicing her meditative stance so she could calm her breathing. As soon as Lenore left, though, little Elice opened her eyes and blew out a breath.

Elice laughed as she watched herself draw on more water behind Lenore's back. She had never cared about what Lenore taught her, at least not until the woman was dead.

Now she wondered just how important those meditations and controlled breathings were and if she should have paid more attention. After her last encounter in the meditative space, she knew she would have to spend some time researching it.

Elice crossed her legs in front of her body, facing her young self—still trying to grow her water ball, Elice noted with a shake of her head. Closing her eyes, she willed her mind to slow down. She thought about the things Lenore had told her to focus on. A wall came to mind, but she pushed it away, walking through the dark space of her mind until she came to a bright corner.

The light grew brighter until she had to squint. Then she realized none of it was real, because she was in her thoughts inside of a vision. None of it made any sense, but she kept her eyes open through the brightness anyway.

She continued walking until the light dimmed just enough to make out a figure. The figure looked exactly the same as the figure in the crystal ball—all shadows with little-to-no solid form.

As soon as Elice approached the figure, the light faded to normal, and the form solidified.

Elice stared at the woman before her. She wore long braids down her back that were tied together with a string at the nape of her neck. Her tan tunic reached to the floor, covering her feet. A long chain wrapped around her neck, and at the end was a clear crystal.

"I see you've finally made it," the woman said. There was humor in her voice and one corner of her mouth turned up.

Elice eyed the woman before her, the woman who seemed so familiar, and the even more familiar necklace that dangled across her chest. She looked down at her own neck, and she knew it was the same one. "What are you doing here?" she asked, slowly putting the pieces together.

The woman shook her head. "That's the wrong question. I always knew you were difficult. It's like you never listen to me."

Elice's eyes widened. "L-Lenore?"

"As if you didn't know, child. Please, try to keep up." The woman, whom Elice realized was a young Lenore, turned on her heels and walked away, waving her hand and beckoning for Elice to follow.

After catching her breath, Elice hurried after. She walked by Lenore's side, looking at her old guardian, who was definitely not her old guardian. This woman seemed more poised, youthful, and wasn't overtly glaring at her.

Something inside Elice felt warm when she walked beside her, but she pushed it away. This couldn't be the same woman she knew, could it?

"If you're really Lenore, how come you look so…"

The woman chuckled, giving her a sideways glance. "Young? If you'd have meditated like I taught you, then you would already know that answer."

"You never taught me how to do this."

Lenore came to a stop and turned to face her. The scene around them morphed, and a couple of chairs appeared behind each of them. "You mean I never taught you how to clear your mind, put up barriers, and create a safe space?"

Elice frowned. That's exactly what Lenore had told her to do, but for some reason, she never quite got it until now.

After Elice's silence, Lenore sighed and fell into her chair. "That's why he was able to find you here."

"What are you talking about?" Elice sat on the edge of the seat.

"When you went into the meditative space in the carriage on your way to Talin. You failed to put up your protective barrier, so he was able to get in your head."

"How do you know about that? And who got in my head?"

Lenore sighed again and ran her fingers through the bottom of her braids. "We don't have enough time. You need to do something when you get back to Madam Verna's shop."

"How do you—"

"Stop asking silly questions, girl!" Lenore raised her voice, and in that moment, Elice could see her old guardian. The woman breathed deep before she spoke again. "I'm sorry. Old habits. Just listen, please. When you get back, you need to give your sister the protection charm. It's protected you so far, but she's the one who needs it now."

Elice opened her mouth but snapped it shut. She tried again but couldn't find the right words. Seeing the annoyed look on Lenore's face, she hurried to get the words out. "So ... it really works?"

Lenore sucked her teeth, clearly trying not to lose her cool again. "Her visions are getting worse. If you want your sister to finally feel at peace and sleep through the night for once, you will give her the necklace. She must wear it every day, all day."

Elice's eyes narrowed. "How can I trust you? How do I know this isn't a trick? Since you apparently know everything, you should know what happened between us. What you did. What I did."

The woman's gaze lowered, her bottom lip trembling. "It's all according to Fates' design."

Elice stood from her chair. "Stop with your lies! I saw you. I saw what you did to my parents, to me. I can't trust you. I could never trust you."

"Elice," Lenore said, her voice quiet. The woman opened her mouth to continue, but the space around her began turning over.

Elice gasped. "You've ... never called me that before," she said, but it was too late. She joined the spinning, her body twirling around itself until it all came to a stop.

Ten

Elice sucked in a breath and noticed she was breathing real air. She opened her eyes, finding herself back in Madam Verna's shop, surrounded by her sister and her friends.

Elice met Madam Verna's knowing eyes, and in a matter of seconds, Elice was ripping off the necklace and handing it to Alice.

Alice snatched it from her grasp and threw it over her head.

Elice stared at her, gulping more air into her lungs to steady her beating heart as she carefully observed her sister.

Her twin closed her eyes and sighed. When Alice opened them, she looked at Elice, and her eyes seemed clearer as a grin appeared on her face. Elice tilted her head as she surveyed Alice's quickly changing demeanor.

"What's going on?" came Andre's voice, but Elice chose to ignore him. Right now, she was fascinated by the way her sister seemed to ... glow.

"Alice," Elice said slowly, afraid to jar her sister. "Are you all right?"

"I..." Alice began, then she laughed. "I've never felt better."

Elice turned to Madam Verna, who sat back against her chair. The woman's eyes drooped closed and her arms hung limply on the armrests. "I'm fine," the woman answered before Elice could ask. "That just took a lot of power out of me. I'll be fine in a few minutes."

James stood from the table. "I'll find you some water."

"Can someone please tell me what happened?" Andre said. "One second you were all holding hands, then the next you were throwing your silly charm at your sister's face."

"We were gone for longer than one second," Elice said, frowning at Andre.

He shook his head. "It was one second, literally. You can ask James. And what do you mean by 'gone'?"

"I'd love some pie right now," Alice chirped from her seat. She had slouched all the way back, her body angled lazily in the seat. "We should stop by a baker's cart next."

Andre looked at Madam Verna, a fire in his eyes. "What did you do to her?"

"It wasn't her," Elice interrupted before Madam Verna had a chance to explain. "It's the protection charm."

Alice pushed out of her chair. "Turns out that's all I ever needed. Funny how things work out, isn't it? Let's go before all the best pie slices sell out." Alice turned to leave, but then she spun around and bent down to hug the exhausted seer. "Thank you so much for all your help. I'll be sure to send payment for your services." And with that, she walked down the aisle toward the front of the shop.

Elice's mouth hung open as she watched her sister go. When she turned around, Andre's jaw was slack as well.

"What did I miss?" James asked a moment later, walking to the table with a glass of water for Madam Verna. He looked over his shoulder at the departing Alice, his brows furrowed, before he sat beside Elice.

"I'll try to figure out what's wrong with her." Andre stood and excused himself.

Elice shook her head, looking at Madam Verna. "I don't get it. I know what I saw, but I'm not sure I completely understand any of it."

Madam Verna placed her glass on the table. "You went to the mind realm, didn't you? There was a moment when you disappeared from my sight, but I could feel your presence. There was someone else with you too."

Elice looked at her hands as she played with her fingers. "I saw Lenore. Well, she was waiting for me, I suppose. She's the one who told me to give Alice the necklace. It's a protection charm."

The seer nodded. "Yes, crystals have immense magical properties. If infused properly, one could be used to harness unique qualities. My crystal ball, for example, allows me to focus on specific points in time. It seems that necklace of yours was imbued with healing magic."

"It was Lenore's, actually. She was wearing it in the—you called it the mind realm?"

"Yes. One of several otherworldly spaces that we can access, with the right training. It takes great practice and mental strength to be able to access the mind realm. You said Madam Lenore's spirit was waiting for you there?"

"That's what she said, but she looked and acted completely different from the Lenore I used to know."

Madam Verna took another gulp of her water. "The mind realm has a way of altering perspective if you're not careful. It can also show one's true self. Perhaps this version of Madam Lenore was the real one."

Elice pursed her lips, mulling over what that could have possibly meant.

James placed a hand on Elice's shoulder. "What happened? Did Madam Lenore say something about what you did to her?"

She shook her head, avoiding eye contact. "She seemed ... ashamed. Almost regretful. It was like she wanted to help me." Tears rimmed her eyes, and she thought back to the visions of the past she just witnessed. "But maybe I was reading her wrong. I also saw pieces of the past, times when I was in my mother's belly or just born, when I couldn't have possibly remembered anything. How could I see parts of my past that I can't remember?"

Finished with her water, Madam Verna sat up straighter in her chair. "It's entirely possible to access dormant memories, or those from a time most people can't remember. Just think of the old readings we seers used to perform on fetuses in a mother's womb. Those events are crucial periods in our lives, so they will leave an imprint that can be used when doing future readings of someone's past. If that makes sense."

Elice wanted to say it didn't make sense, but she experienced it firsthand "Lenore said something else about Alice. She said she has visions. Is Alice a seer too?"

The woman paused, pursing her lips. "From what I gathered, Alice has a rare form of visions that only happen in her dreams. Some call it dream sight. Others call it cursed sight, but that name belongs to another form that doesn't originate in our kingdom. It's actually more common in Newton, where your mother's people are from."

"Is Alice cursed, then?" James asked, shifting in his seat. His eyes were wide once again.

"It's not a real curse in that someone is punishing her for something. It's just a name, my lord. At any rate, Alice doesn't have cursed sight, and her visions are more or less harmless. Well, until recently." Madam Verna gave Elice a look, suggesting she knew all she needed to know about what had been going on with Alice over the last few weeks.

"But the necklace will take it away, right?" Elice chewed on her lip. She needed to know her sister would be all right now.

The sound Madam Verna made didn't give Elice much hope. "I'm not quite sure, Your Highness. There isn't much literature on dream sight, or on healing crystals. I'll look through my bookshelves before you return to Highmore to see what I can find for you. In the meantime, it seems to be having some sort of effect on her. Don't let her take it off, and be sure to monitor her."

"Would there be any negative side effects?" James asked.

"I don't think so. Again, I'll see what I can find and send it to the estate as soon as possible." Madam Verna pushed herself to stand, obviously much clearer-headed than she was right after the visions.

Elice and James stood and thanked her for her help. As the

woman showed them out, they stopped by the front counter to say goodbye to Cassidy, who eagerly waved at them.

Stepping out into the late afternoon sun, Elice squinted as she scanned the crowd. There were now a large number of people wandering from stand to stand, buying and selling different wares or goods as they chatted with their neighbors.

As soon as they exited the shop, her guard, Michael, and one of his partners appeared by her side.

James raised his hand to point toward one of the stands near the central fountain. "There they are."

Her sister and Andre were sitting on a bench next to the fountain, flanked on either side by two more guards.

"Oh good. Let's go." Elice began to walk, but James held her hand.

"First, I want to make sure you're all right." He gave her a once-over, focusing on her face as he stared into her eyes.

Elice blew out a breath. "I think I'm all right. This was all just too weird. I can't believe I saw her."

James held both of her hands and gave them a reassuring squeeze. "What was it like? Did she really seem remorseful?"

"It felt like it. But it could have been another one of her tricks. I know I shouldn't trust her."

"Then why did you give your sister the charm?"

Elice looked over to where her sister sat, eating what looked like a slice of pie with a pile of whipped cream on top. Even from this distance, she could see the smile Alice wore as she listened to Andre talk. Then Alice burst out laughing, covering her mouth with one hand and trying not to spit out the bite of pie she was chewing.

Andre gripped his belly as he joined her laughter, and Elice smiled as she realized the two of them actually looked like a couple for once.

She met James's gaze again, the chocolate brown eyes of his that she could easily get lost in. "I would do anything to make sure my sister gets better. Even if it means I have to trust the word of the most untrustworthy person in all of Norraine."

James reached out and tucked a stray curl behind her ear. "Even if it means you don't have the protection of the charm anymore?"

Something heavy fell in her chest. Now that she didn't have the necklace, would that mean she could get hurt? She remembered Lenore's words in the mind realm.

It's protected you so far, but she's the one who really needs it.

What did it protect her from? She had only begun wearing it when she took it from Andre and left her cottage to find Lenore, back when she thought her old guardian was lost. If she didn't need it all those years leading up to it, what had changed now to make her need it?

She scratched at the spot near her ear where James had touched, her mind going over everything that had happened in the last few months. The only thing she could think of that changed was Lenore's death by Elice's hands.

Her hands shook as she looked down at them, remembering Lenore's blood caked on her brown skin. With a shake of her head, she cleared her mind of the bloodstains and focused on James.

But she couldn't ignore the dark feeling of dread from the pit of her stomach.

Eleven

Before Elice could open her mouth to tell James she would be fine, a shrill voice called her name. She looked toward the sound and saw Alice skipping—by the Fates, her sister was *skipping*—toward her. Andre bounded after her, balancing two plates with melted cream and bits of pie in his hands.

"Sister," Alice yelled, excitement ringing through the air, causing the citizens to look their way with amused smiles on their faces. "You must try the pie. No one bakes it better than Norma Wood. And she's almost out, so let's hurry."

Elice blinked. Her sister had never been this loud before, and Elice was not at all prepared for it. As soon as Alice reached her spot, she grabbed Elice's hand and pulled her through the crowd toward Norma's booth.

"Two more slices please, Miss Norma." Alice held up two fingers at the elderly woman, who smiled graciously as she scooped out two big piles of pie, then loaded them with fresh whipped cream.

Miss Norma reached across her booth to hand the girls the plates. "You made it back just in time, Your Highness. The cream's all out and we're down to our last few slices."

Elice thanked her and turned in time to see James and Andre appear behind them, scooting past the guards.

"Alice," Andre said, his voice clipped. "You can't just take off like that. Please wait for one of the guards if you're not going to wait for me or James."

Alice waved him off as she passed the plate in her hand to James. "James will forgive me. After all, I got this slice for him."

Elice watched as James eyed the pie, a smile spreading across his face.

James took the plate and thanked Alice, then reached in his pocket for a few coins to pay the baker for the pie. "I suppose nothing bad can happen when we're all close by. But, as much as it pains me to say it, Andre's right. You shouldn't wander off, especially in such a big crowd."

Alice nodded hastily, then turned on the spot and started perusing the booths. Elice couldn't understand her sister's sudden change in personality, but she would definitely have a long talk with her once they returned to the manor.

Elice looked down at her plate and forked a portion of the pie into her mouth. At least Alice was right in that regard—the pie was *delicious*.

They spent the next hour following Alice around as she bought a few more items from the sellers. Once the sun hung just above the tops of the houses and the chilly evening air whipped against their faces, the townspeople began clearing up their booths.

James talked to a few of the townspeople as they passed, asking if they needed any help with cleanup or checking how their day went. He seemed to know exactly what to say to each person he saw, charming them with his warm smile and perfectly worded jokes. Everyone seemed to love him, and they joked back or thanked him for his kindness.

Elice kept her eyes locked on him and his genuine love for the residents of Talin, and everyone else, for that matter. His generosity and warmth never seemed forced or fake in any way.

A young child dropped her wooden toy doll right by James's foot, and he bent down to pick it up for her. James wiped a little of the dirt off, passed it back, and ruffled her hair before the girl thanked him and ran off.

As James stood, he caught Elice's eye, and he gave her one of his signature smiles. She didn't know what to do with that look right now, so she averted her stare to watch her guards as they helped facilitate cleanup.

Andre walked toward her, wiping his hands on his slacks that were now a bit dusty from moving tables across the ground. He raised an eyebrow as he came to stand right by her side. "Weird day, huh?"

Elice quirked one of her own eyebrows and nodded. "And that's saying something."

"So, we're going to have a big team meeting when we get back, right?"

She nodded again. "Definitely." Just as she spoke, Alice appeared at her side, draping an arm across her shoulder and resting her head on Andre's arm.

"I'm pooped," Alice said, then covered her mouth as if she had said a bad word against the Fates. "Wow, Miss Tabitha would have made me read lines from the etiquette book if she had heard me."

Elice looked over Alice's head and gave Andre a look, one that he reciprocated.

James finally approached, his slacks in the same state as Andre's. "I think the townspeople can handle the rest of the cleanup, so we are free to go."

"Finally," Alice said, already heading toward the carriage. "I am in need of a long, hot bath."

Elice yawned, feeling the weight of the day's events. "And a nap."

They all piled into the carriage, the guards flanking them on their horses as they took off toward the Talin estate.

No one said a word as the carriage bounced along the dirt road, and Elice spent the entire time looking out the window at the passing landscape. When they arrived on the smooth pavement in front of the mansion, they quietly poured out of the carriage and walked inside.

The maids and butlers greeted them, ushering them all inside and up to their rooms. Lauren guided her to the bedroom and went straight to the bathroom to draw warm water in the large soaker tub. "I take it today was tiring?"

"Oh, you have no idea." Elice slipped out of her dress, then pulled on one of her thick cotton robes. Another comfortable pair of pants from Tabitha and a soft, silky shirt awaited her on the vanity stool. "All we did was walk around, chitchat, and try glorious food. You'd think we'd run all the way to Highmore and back, but it's much more tiring putting on a regal face than I ever thought."

She had shaken so many more hands today than she was used to, considering the only other big event she had attended was her birthday ball. She couldn't imagine doing something like this very often.

"Don't you worry, my lady. I'm sure next year will be much more enjoyable now that you have one festival under your belt. Soon, you'll be used to it. And I'm sure the people loved seeing you there today."

Elice thought back to the old man who had gifted her the sled. He was thrilled to have met her and even more honored to give her something. But he seemed especially excited to be able to return home to tell his grandkids about the story of meeting Princess Elice at the apple festival. Then she remembered meeting Cassidy, and how ecstatic she was to have Elice in her shop.

A smile appeared on her face as she thought about the people—her people. She would never get used to having so much positive attention aimed at her. And now that they all thought she would one day become their lady on top of being their princess...

Lauren headed toward the door. "I'll let you get some rest. I'll return when dinner is ready."

Elice hummed her response as the door shut, and she slipped off the robe and stepped into the tub, her eyes sliding closed as soon as her body relaxed against the warm ceramic. As soon as she closed her eyes, a sharp pain stabbed at the side of her head, and she lurched forward. Water sloshed over the edge of the tub, sending splashes across the tiled floor.

"Weird," she mumbled, rubbing at the offending spot near her temple. The pain reminded her of the scorching heat she felt in the carriage. "Maybe I'm just tired." She realized she didn't have much water or food today, besides the little sips and snacks she had at the festival.

She rested against the tub again, letting the water soak up all the apprehension from her shoulders, until Lauren peeked her head through the door.

"I'm sorry to disturb you, my lady," she whispered. "Dinner is ready, and everyone is gathering in the sitting room."

Elice stretched before she sat up, then rubbed the tiredness from her eyes. After the long day of traveling, plus spending all day outside, her body was exhausted. She hoped to feel better tomorrow after she got another night's rest, since they didn't have any events to attend.

After she dried off and changed into her lounging outfit, Lauren fixed her curls, setting them in her usual style down her back. When Elice finally made her way into the sitting room, everyone was laughing and enjoying a warm mug of some steaming drink.

"And that's why I'll never take Dre shopping with me ever again," Alice said, still laughing and wiping stray tears from under her eyes.

Andre took a sip of his drink, still chuckling. "How was I supposed to know you're not supposed to touch the glass? There wasn't a sign that said, 'Breaks on impact.'"

"You idiot," James said under his breath. "You're not supposed to hit a glass casing."

"Well, now I know," Andre mumbled, taking another gulp.

Elice cleared her throat, and all eyes turned to where she stood at the opening of the door frame. "Sorry I'm late, as usual."

James stood from his seat, taking in her attire. The last time she wore pants, he had the same heated expression on his face, and she kind of liked it.

"We were just having some warm cider. Let me get you a cup," James said, hurrying over to the buffet cart.

She followed him, taking the hot mug from his grasp.

"Let's all head into the dining room." He motioned for Elice to lead the way, and everyone started toward the table after her.

Having a hot meal warmed her belly, and the cider was so perfectly spiced that she almost forgot about her anxieties. Everyone listened to Alice as she shared story after story, the boys adding in their own jokes and laughing along. Elice sat back against the chair as she listened to her sister prattle on. She laughed to herself, knowing Alice would need lots of water or healing tea for her throat since she probably had never talked so much in her life.

"Isn't that right, Elice?" her sister said, bringing her attention back to the group. "Miss Tabitha is a horrible influence on you. I mean, she's got you wearing those pants."

"I like those pants," James said from across the table.

Elice swallowed the last of her cider. "Don't judge them, Alice. They're much more comfortable than a heavy ball gown."

"I'll take your word for it." Alice pushed her plate away, tossing her napkin on top before a servant took it away from the table. "I have an idea! Let's have a bonfire. Like we used to." Andre and James exchanged looks, and Alice scoffed before they could say anything. "You guys are a real pain, you know that?"

"I've never had a bonfire before," Elice said, drawing their attention.

"That settles it," Alice exclaimed. She turned toward James with a raised eyebrow, one that said she knew he would never turn something down if Elice was on board. That knowledge was both sweet and scary.

James shook his head, but the way he smiled as he turned to a servant made something twist in Elice's stomach. "Jacob, can you please ask Miss Wanda to prepare the fire pit?"

"Right away, my lord," Jacob said, bowing before he left the room.

One by one, they pushed their plates away and stood from the table, filing out of the dining room and back into the sitting room, where they all collapsed on the couch as they waited for the fire pit to be ready.

Alice actually sat in quiet until Miss Wanda emerged from the hallway, announcing the pit was roaring and ready to go.

A bubble of excitement grew in Elice's stomach. She didn't know what they would do at the bonfire, but she had seen the soldiers down by the barracks all huddled together by the fire, sharing stories and drinking as they ended a long day. From her outsider's perspective, it seemed to help them unwind and grow closer together. She even witnessed some arguments that helped people sort out their differences. The thought of gathering with her three companions in such a close way made her feel like part of a group—like she belonged somewhere, instead of just floating along reading or serving as an unwanted replacement for her sister.

James led them through the house, and Alice looped an arm

through Elice's as Andre brought up the rear. When they stepped out of the back doors and onto the patio, Elice could see the circle of fire a few yards away.

She realized she never got to see the yard properly, and since it was dark out, she still didn't have a great view. The light from the lanterns and the fire illuminated the center of the garden, where a fountain bubbled in the middle of a square patio. A few benches lined the opposite sides, and directly behind the fountain was the fire pit with a few wooden chairs snuggled close together. Pillows and throw blankets had been placed in a wicker basket beside the circle of chairs. Off in the distance, Elice could barely make out the trees that James had said was his family's orchard.

With an arm outstretched, he motioned for the girls to head to the fire pit first. They walked to the chairs, sitting next to each other. Alice reached over and grabbed a couple of pillows and blankets, passing one of each to Elice.

With a pillow behind her back and a plush blanket wrapped around her, Elice relaxed in her seat, embracing the warmth from the fire as a cool breeze blew around them.

The guys found their own chairs, Andre settling beside Alice and James pulling his chair next to Elice. For a long while, they sat in silence, enjoying the quiet after their long day. After a beat, James patted his legs, then stood, walking over to a basket of ice to rummage through it.

When he returned, he had a couple of sticks and a package of cold, raw meats. He stuck a cubed piece on one end of a stick before he passed it over to Elice. She looked down at it, wondering what in the Fates' name she was supposed to do with it. Surely people didn't eat raw meat on a stick at bonfires.

James chuckled as he loaded another stick in the same way. "Don't worry. We're not going to eat it like this. We're going to cook it in the fire."

Her mouth formed a perfect circle as understanding dawned on her. She watched as James scooted his chair a little closer to the pit of fire and hovered his stick above the flames. Not wanting to miss out on the new experience, she pulled her chair closer to his and copied his movements, rotating her stick every few seconds as she held it next to his.

Shuffling to her left let her know that Andre and Alice were doing the same thing, and soon all four of them had their sticks of meat cooking over the fire.

A giggle came from Alice's mouth. "Do you guys remember the snowstorm?"

Andre groaned while James sighed and shook his head.

Elice caught her sister's smirk. "Okay, now I have to know what this story is about."

Alice turned in her chair, tucking her legs beneath her as she all but forgot about her meat. "One year, all three of our families vacationed here in Talin because we had to escape the worst snow-storm in Norraine's history. I think we were only eight or nine. Everything north of Copita was covered in ice, the crops planted in the fall for next spring were destroyed, and people couldn't travel because the dirt paths were so slick. Anyway, Lady Talin, James's mother, invited Andre's family and our family to stay for a few weeks to wait out the storm and the eventual snowmelt. What we didn't expect was the storm to reach all the way down here."

Elice leaned in toward her sister as she spoke, absorbing her words. Her sister had suddenly become such a great storyteller, and she didn't want to miss a single word.

Alice set her stick on the ledge of the fire pit and continued. "We were outside playing—James, Andre, and I. There's a pond in the back, in the middle of the grove, so we went out there with our little coats on, thinking we would just put our feet in the water. The sky had been gray for days, so when the snow started to fall, we were excited the weather had finally changed. All of a sudden, huge blankets of snow fell on us, and we were almost frozen with our feet still in the water. I still don't know how the water froze around us so fast, but the whole pond turned to ice in the blink of an eye. We scrambled to get out as fast as we could, but by the time we made it back to the courtyard, we were shivering something fierce. Our mothers were so angry. And we had the worst cold of our lives."

"I think it lasted two weeks," Andre said, looking down at his stick. "But the real punishment lasted almost a month. Our mothers took away the toys we brought with us, wouldn't let us play outside, and I think I had to read every book in James's library at least twice."

Elice squinted her eyes. That last part didn't sound like a punishment to her. If anything, she wished she would have grown up with James's library, so at least she would have had a bigger collection of books than the one she had.

"You guys were stuck here a whole month longer than planned," James added.

Alice hummed, picking up her stick and returning it to the fire. "Other than that instance, all our memories of this place—and that pond—are great."

Andre chuckled. "Yeah, I suppose we've made great memories here."

"I wish I had the same memories as you guys," Elice whispered, loud enough for everyone to hear.

James reached over and placed a hand on her knee. "We'll make new ones."

"Exactly," Alice exclaimed.

Elice looked down at James's hand still on her knee and she shivered. She knew the reason was not because of the cold chill in the air.

Twelve

Drip. Drip. Drip.

Elice looked around for the source of that annoying sound. It seemed to come from everywhere, even below her feet. She squinted her eyes against the darkness, unable to see anything.

Slowly, she placed one foot in front of the other, taking her first cautious step. When she placed her foot down, it splashed in water, a light layer underneath her soft, silky slipper. The water soaked the bottom of her feet, and she realized they had been wet the entire time. But she didn't know how long she had been here, or even where *here* was.

She took another step, and the water squished again. After several more paces, she saw a bit of light in front of her.

Finally, she thought as she picked up the pace, sending water everywhere as she hurried toward the light. It grew brighter until she could finally make out her surroundings. The walls on either side of her were closer than she originally thought, made of wide stones that glistened as water slid down every crevice. She passed a few doors as she scrambled down the path, and that was when she realized she was walking down some sort of tunnel, declining lower and lower into the earth.

It seemed as if she had been running for almost ten minutes when she decided to take a break. She sucked in a few breaths, thankful James's training had conditioned her for this jog. Placing a hand against the stone wall to catch her breath, she felt the cold from the wall seep into her arm. An icy chill ran up to her shoulder, making bumps grow on her skin.

She snatched her hand away from the wall, but the chill continued down her chest and across to her other arm. With both hands, she frantically rubbed her arms and stomach, afraid the cold would freeze her over if she didn't warm herself up.

"Help!" she yelled into the dark expanse of stone, but her voice echoed off the walls until it faded to nothing. "Somebody, please help!"

She sucked in a deep breath as the cold enveloped her entire body. Closing her eyes, she wondered how she got stuck in this predicament, how she let herself get trapped in this Fates' forsaken place.

Then a quiet laugh resounded in her head, making her eyes snap open. Another type of chill ran down her arms, and then came the pain. She recognized this feeling, this sharp burning in her brain.

Elice gripped the sides of her head, and she sank to her knees, her pants soaking in the water as she fell.

"Make it stop," she cried, rocking back and forth in the dark water. The laughter grew louder, and the burning grew more intense as she curled into a ball. "Please, make it stop."

"Elice," a voice said, and she felt her shoulders shake.

"Just make it stop!"

"Elice!" The voice was louder now, drowning out the laughter.

She opened her eyes, then closed them again as the bright light almost blinded her.

"By the Fates, Elice, please look at me." It was Alice, and Elice's shoulders shook again as her sister tried to jar her awake.

This time, Elice peeked through her eyelashes, making sure her eyes had the chance to adjust to the lit lantern in the room. When she saw the outline of her twin's face, she opened her eyes fully, focusing on Alice's eyes.

"Are you all right?" another voice asked. This time it was James, and she turned toward the sound, finding him, Andre, and Lauren standing at the foot of her bed.

Elice opened her mouth, then closed it. No, she was not all right, but she couldn't get the words out. She shook her head, then turned toward her sister. Alice pulled her close, wrapping her arms around her shoulders.

"Could you all give us some privacy, please?" Alice called out to the others. Elice heard a few mumbled words as they shuffled out of the room, but she didn't look up from the comfort of her sister's arms. Alice kissed the top of her head and smoothed down her curls. "It was just a bad dream. Go back to sleep."

She knew that was not a possibility. Even now, every time she blinked, she could see the dark tunnel, feel the cold spreading across her body, the blazing fire in her brain, and the water soaking her skin.

Elice shook her head, and Alice shifted their bodies until they were both lying on the bed. Alice held her that way until Elice's eyes drifted close. She heard the same dripping noise as before. The darkness had appeared again, consuming every inch of the space she was in. The water, the chill seeping out of the walls—it was the same as her last dream.

What is this? she asked herself. Then she started running again, hopefully in what she thought was the opposite direction from the last time. When she stopped for a breath, she refused to touch the walls, but the voice found her nonetheless. The high-pitched laughter rang in her ears until she forced her eyes to open.

Elice was back in her room in Talin, looking directly into her sister's eyes. Alice wore a frown, the skin around her eyes crinkled as she looked at Elice.

"What's happening to me?" Elice choked out, a single tear sliding out of her eye.

Alice swallowed. "It's the dream sight. It's what's been plaguing me for years, becoming more aggressive after Lenore's... After *you know what* happened."

Elice shook her head, not understanding. "But I don't have visions. You're the seer. How am I having these dreams?"

Alice's shoulder shrugged, then she shifted from her side to her back, staring up at the ceiling. "We're twins, right? And now I'm wearing this protection charm. Maybe..."

After Alice's hesitation, Elice leaned on her elbow to get a better look at her. "Maybe what?"

Alice glanced at her, then looked away. "Maybe he's moved on to you."

"What do you mean?" Elice was afraid of the answer, and she wondered why she asked in the first place. She didn't want her sister to explain. She didn't want to know.

"He's probably been after you since the beginning, anyway, and was just using me to get to you, but I've always had weird dreams. And during the carriage ride here, when you entered the plane, or the mind realm, that's when I realized he might go after you next."

"Who, Alice? Who are you talking about?" Elice sat up, her frustration growing.

"Him. The one I've been talking about during my fits. Orser. He's trying to come back. He *will* come back." Elice scooted away from her sister as Alice sat up, her eyes intent on Elice's. "Now you see what I've been talking about. But I can't let you go through what I've been through." Alice reached for the necklace and began to pull it over her head.

Elice realized what she was doing and grabbed her hands. "No, Alice. You need it more than I do. Even weird, mind-realm Lenore knew that. You have to keep the necklace."

Tears formed in Alice's eyes, and her bottom lip quivered when she spoke. "But I don't want him to hurt you. I know what it's like for him to be inside your head, leading you down that stupid tunnel with no end in sight, burning his way through every good feeling you have. Please, take the necklace back."

Elice once again stopped Alice's hands from removing the charm. "I don't need it. Lenore taught me how to navigate the mind realm, and if that's where the dreams take me, then I know how to protect myself." *I just need to remember what she taught me.*

Tears slid down Alice's cheeks, and Elice wiped them away. She pulled her sister down on the bed and they held each other until they both fell asleep. This time, Elice didn't have a nightmare as she lay curled in her sister's arms.

They all sat around the sitting room, the fireplace roaring and keeping them warm.

Andre slowly sipped his spiked cider, making tiny sighs after every sip to fill the void their silence took up. After several beats, he couldn't take it anymore and finally spoke. "It's our last day."

Everyone nodded, and Elice got the distinct feeling no one wanted to say a word about yesterday, especially after last night. She didn't feel like talking after only getting a couple hours of sleep.

Andre eyed his glass. "This cider is really good."

James cleared his throat. "I'll be sure to tell Miss Lucinda you like it."

"She always made the best cider."

"Yup."

Then quiet overtook the room again as the men stopped talking. Elice shifted in her seat, hugging a fuzzy blanket to her chest. She didn't dare close her eyes, no matter how tired she felt.

Andre made a grunting noise, then set his glass on the short table in the middle of the room. "Are we really not going to talk about it?"

Alice met her eyes, a slight fear growing behind them. She turned her gaze on Andre. "Don't. Please, just don't."

"We can't avoid what's going on. What happened to Elice is what's been happening to you."

Alice covered her face with her hands, avoiding everyone's stare.

Andre leaned forward in his seat and gently removed Alice's hands. "I'm right, aren't I?"

Elice pulled the blanket further up her chest, wanting to hide like her sister did. Yet she knew they had to talk about her dream. Andre had been by Alice's side the entire time since Lenore's death, and James always showed he cared about their well-being in the aftermath. They deserved to know what Elice was now going through.

So, she took a deep breath and told them what she saw when she fell asleep. They watched her intently as she spoke—James's eyebrows furrowed, and Andre was breathing in hard as if he was getting angry.

When she finished, Elice took another shaky breath and closed her eyes as tears formed. She could almost hear the maniacal laughter in the back of her mind, so she threw her eyes open again.

James reached across the low center table and placed a gentle hand on her lap. "Thank you for telling us. I'm sorry you're going through this. Maybe we should go back to Madam Verna's shop to see if there's anything she can do."

"There's nothing a seer can do," Elice said, shaking her head.

"Then I'll find a healer. There's got to be someone who can make another protection charm like Lenore's."

Alice sat a little straighter. "That's a good idea. We could ask Madam Verna if she knows anyone."

"There's virtually no literature on this, though," Elice said. "I've spent weeks looking into these dreams. Even Madam Verna's suggestion was to enter the mind realm. That's what I have to do. I'll just have to get better at protecting myself while there."

Alice, James, and Andre looked at each other, the same question in their eyes. Elice ignored them, though, in favor of cuddling with the blanket.

She knew what she had to do, and that involved putting some trust in the one person she knew couldn't be trusted.

She had to trust Lenore. At the very least, she had to trust Lenore's teachings.

Thirteen

After lunch, the sun's rays peeked through the thick clouds in the sky. Elice leaned against the open doorway as a gentle breeze beckoned her outside. What she would give to be able to curl up on the soft grass, soaking up what little sunlight there was, enjoying the cool air as it blew across her body. She couldn't, though, because she knew as soon as her head hit the ground, she would be fast asleep.

And sleeping meant dreaming.

She blew out a sharp breath. Is this how life was going to be for her now? Unable to sleep, or even rest?

The sound of footsteps behind her made her turn to look over her shoulder. James hesitantly approached, his steps slow and deliberate. His smile didn't quite reach his eyes as he waved.

Elice had kept him, and everyone else, at a distance all morning. After last night, she was afraid to get too close for fear of melting down. She hadn't the slightest clue how to combat what she was going through, and she worried they'd *know* she didn't know once she started crying.

"I'm not going to ask if you're all right, because I know the answer," James said, his voice soft and full of emotion. "So, instead, I'll ask if you'd like to take a walk with me. There's a little bit of sun, and I can finally show you the grounds. If you're up for it."

She was grateful he always knew what to say. After a nod, she pushed off the door frame and turned toward the garden. The chairs still circled around the fire pit, but the staff had picked up the food and trash.

James stood beside her and motioned forward. They walked at a steady pace, enjoying nature and the fresh air.

Elice allowed her eyes to close for just a second as she sucked in the freshness. She could feel James's gaze on the side of her face for a moment, but he remained quiet.

As they walked past the fire pit, he pointed to the left, and they turned toward a path that led through the middle of the grove.

The trees were full of yellowing leaves, though she knew they would soon change into shades of orange and red, then fall to the ground in hues of brown. Only a few apples hung from the branches as they wandered down the path, most having been picked by the estate's staff for the festival or to be used in recipes for the household.

Elice stopped by a particularly large tree that had a few apples on some of its lower branches. They were bright red and perfectly ripe, so she reached for the lowest one and plucked it. She used the sleeves of her long orange dress to wipe across its surface before biting into it. The sweet juice flowed into her mouth, and she savored the fruity yet tart taste.

After the long night she had, this apple certainly reminded her of the beauty all around her. Her eyelids fluttered, so tired of staying open. Another bite and burst of flavor gave her mind something else to dwell on besides her exhaustion.

She turned to see where James had wandered off to, but he had stayed right behind her, watching her eat the apple. His expression was soft, and his hands were casually stuffed in his pockets like he had all the time in the world.

Knowing he got caught staring, he tried to hide his smile by turning to look at the tree behind him, pulling a slightly yellow leaf into his hands.

To break the awkwardness between them, Elice swallowed her bite of apple and spoke. "These are almost better straight off the tree instead of in a pie."

James turned, shocked that she said anything since she was so quiet all day. "Don't tell Miss Lucinda that. She won't want to make her pies for you anymore."

A hint of a smile broke free from her face. She missed this carefree side of their relationship and how they could have easy conversations with each other. She forced down the weird, nagging feeling that had hung around her since last night and walked closer to him. "I suppose I'd miss her cider, too."

James chuckled, then walked closer to meet her in the middle of the path. A strong wind blew, blowing her hair in different directions. He raised a hand, and it hovered in the air tentatively before it continued toward her face. Slowly, he tucked a few strands of her curls behind her ear, and as the wind died down, he brushed the tip of his thumb down her jawline.

Elice trembled, partly from the cold breeze, but also from the look in his eyes. She could see so many thoughts swarming around in them. He hesitated again, opening his mouth before then closing it right away.

After the third time, he shook his head and stepped away, pushing his hands back inside his pockets.

"Shall we continue?" he asked, then motioned ahead.

Elice nodded, but her insides churned in a confusing way. She wanted to know what he had to say, what he was thinking, but she didn't have the energy to push.

Instead, they walked in relative silence, taking in the rest of the orchard and the small pond in the middle of the grove. The winding path led them back to the central garden just as the wind picked up. The clouds completely blocked out the sun, and Elice could sense a storm coming.

"Just in time," James said as he eyed the sky.

"I can feel the rain." Elice wished they could stay outside to enjoy it. She closed her eyes a fraction and spun in a circle, her arms outstretched. When she stopped spinning, she noticed James staring at her with the same expression in his eyes that he'd had earlier when they were in the field. He wanted to tell her something, she knew it, but what?

"Do you..." He trailed off just as a drop of water fell on his cheek. He looked up, then back at her. "Is this you?"

Elice shook her head. "Not this time, I promise." She sighed as more drops fell all around them.

James shifted closer, his eyes roaming over her face. "Do you want to stay out here a little longer?"

Her heart soared, thumping a loud "yes" in response. She didn't get to speak her answer aloud as a streak of lightning spread across the sky above their heads. James's eyes widened, and he latched their hands as they hightailed it toward the back door. More rain fell, and the crack of thunder rang out behind them somewhere near the orchard.

They were now drenched as the rain led to a downpour. Just a few more feet and they would be in the safety of the house.

James stepped through and pulled her inside as another ominous brightness lit up the sky. Elice huddled close, shivering from the cold wetness that made her soaking dress cling to her body.

He pulled her close, rubbing his hands across the long sleeves of her gown, trying to give her some warmth. "I'm glad we weren't in the middle of the orchard."

She nodded. Getting struck by lightning would have only made her mood worse.

James tucked more of her hair behind her head, but she knew it wouldn't make a difference. A few pieces of wet hair stuck to her face, and he tried to pry them away, to no avail.

She laughed and placed her hands on top of his to halt his motions. His hands stayed there, cupping her cheeks as he looked down at her with wet eyelashes.

Now Elice noticed how close they were. It reminded her of the time he walked her back to the east wing after her birthday party. She could feel his breath near the top of her head, smell the mixture of fresh air and rain combining with his natural earthy scent.

He leaned forward, and her eyes closed. She couldn't keep them open any longer, and she couldn't watch his next movements. A light, hopeful flutter bumped around in her chest.

As his lips pressed against hers, the gentlest ghost of a whisper on her lips, her fears and apprehensions melted away. It felt like a fire had been lit, burning the doubt that had been plaguing her thoughts since yesterday.

And just like that, he was gone. She opened her eyes and noticed he had taken a few steps away. He shook his head and water flew in different directions. His eyes didn't meet hers, and she wondered what had gone wrong. Did he not feel the same warmth? Something twisted in her stomach at the thought of him not feeling the same thing she felt from that kiss.

"I'm sorry," he whispered, still looking at the floor. "I shouldn't have done that."

Before she could respond, the door in the next room opened. Miss Wanda walked through, carrying a pile of letters. She stopped upon seeing them, and her eyes narrowed.

"I'll get the mop," she muttered, then sighed and turned back the way she came.

Elice turned as well, wanting to run to her room and hide under the blankets. James called out to her, but she refused to let him see the burning tears in her eyes. When she made it to the safety of her room, she buried herself in the bed in her wet dress, and as sleep slowly pulled her under, so too did the nightmares.

⁓

The carriage was loaded, and everyone hung by the front steps to say goodbye to the staff. The sun wasn't up yet, and Elice's eyes hung low, threatening to close on her. After another night of little sleep, she wanted nothing more than to go back in time to when she used to sleep comfortably. Even sleeping on her flimsy cot in Lenore's old cottage was preferable to this.

Lauren came up to her with her hands behind her back. The way her eyes crinkled let Elice know she was worried about her. "I hope you have a safe trip back home, Your Highness."

Elice smiled, her lips only making a thin line. "Thank you, Lauren. I'm so happy to have spent time with you this weekend."

Lauren's eyes lit up. "Me too, my lady. I hope we see each other again soon."

Elice pulled the girl in for a hug, and her body sagged in Lauren's arms. Lauren laughed and patted her back before Elice pulled away.

Miss Wanda had a few last-minute words with James, imploring him to continue keeping a good watch on the royal family and letting him know she would continue to handle everything at the estate. "But don't forget to write to your mother," she said, lifting a finger and pointing it at him. "If she stops by unannounced again, I'm going to ask for a raise."

James ducked his head, hiding his laugh. "I might have to give you a raise anyway, Miss Wanda."

"You're darn right." She placed her hands on her hips, then sighed and wrapped them around James. She caught Andre's snicker and waved him over. "Don't think you're leaving without getting your hug. Bring it in."

Andre kicked a pebble before shuffling over, and Miss Wanda let go of James so she could hug Andre. Alice squealed and ran over for a hug too, and soon Elice was being pulled in by Miss Wanda's warm arms for a hug of her own.

"Don't think any of you are strangers around here. We want letters and visits way more often than what we've been used to the last few years. And that goes double for you, Lord Talin."

"I'll be better, I promise," James replied, a hand over his heart to emphasize his vow.

After more goodbyes from the rest of the staff, the four of them slid into the carriage. Michael closed the door for them, and as they settled in their seats, the carriage began rolling away. Elice sat up straight in her seat, refusing to get too comfortable, which didn't go unnoticed by anyone, as they each gave her a sideways glance.

As soon as they crossed the bridge over the River of Might, Alice and Andre dozed off. James continued to look out the window, but as soon as Andre began snoring, he turned toward her. "Why don't you get some rest? I'll wake you if I see you're having a nightmare."

Elice shook her head, but pushed herself back a little more. "I'll be fine."

He stared at the side of her face, but Elice didn't want to turn toward him to meet his gaze. What would she see if she looked at him right now? Regret about the kiss? Disgust?

"Elice," he called, his tone low.

When she didn't turn, he placed a hand on hers in her lap. "Did you get any sleep last night?"

She blew out sharply. "How am I supposed to sleep when all I see is that same tunnel?"

He swallowed before reaching over with his other hand, placing it on her chin to turn her head toward him. "I'm sorry."

Elice pulled away from him and finally met his gaze. She couldn't quite name the look he gave her, but sorrow and guilt were present. His eyebrows hung low and his eyes glistened. She looked away, not wanting to have this conversation with him.

But she knew, in that moment, whatever they had budding was not growing anymore.

Fourteen

Elice stood before the new floor-length mirror in her room. When she arrived from her trip, Serena had barely held back the smile on her face. She escorted Elice to her room and showed her the new gift, courtesy of Tabitha. Now, Serena gushed nonstop about the mirror—how big it was, how Elice could now see her entire outfit from head to toe, and how this would make Serena's job much easier.

"It even reflects more light, which will come in handy when the days are as cloudy as today," Serena continued, running a comb through Elice's freshly washed curls.

Elice barely heard her. She didn't mean to ignore the girl. Her mind just wasn't as focused as it used to be.

Over the last week, her sleep had been full of those same nightmares. She barely slept, which meant her body was feeling the effects. Her eyes were constantly heavy, her shoulders were slumped, and her emotions were wrecked. To make matters worse, James had barely spoken more than a few words to her, which made dinners even more awkward than before.

Alice, on the other hand, had been a ball of sunshine during this otherwise stormy fall season. She waltzed through the halls with more energy than Elice ever had, and she had been in and out of town more often than not. Elice suspected her sister had been visiting Donovan, a local artist and her true love, and was shocked to find out Alice went with only her guard—without Andre by her side.

Serena went to Elice's jewelry box and selected a necklace with a striking blue gem in the center. "This one matches your dress perfectly," Serena announced. She hung the necklace around Elice's neck and secured the clasp in the back. "Though I do miss your old one. It's nice of you to have gifted it to your sister. I can imagine how much it meant to you."

Elice absentmindedly ran her finger along the chain of her new necklace. "I think I'll head down early."

Serena nodded and bowed, but Elice didn't miss the way Serena frowned at her. Elice couldn't worry about that now. Her moods were always so up and down recently, and she didn't have the energy to spend rectifying her relationships with those around her.

Lifting the flowing hem of her dress, Elice walked out of her room and down the staircase toward the sitting room. Lately, she had been the first one there, followed by her parents. James and Andre, surprisingly, had been arriving together, though they pretended it was merely a coincidence each time. Alice usually sauntered in last, right when everyone couldn't take the wait any longer.

Now she knew how everyone else had felt when they had to wait on her in the past.

The room was empty, so she took a seat near the window and drew her gaze outside. It was another stormy day, and the temperature hovered just above freezing. Elice wondered if there would be an early winter this year.

Movement by the door caught her attention, and she turned to find James sticking his head in. He saw her and faltered, looking as if he were contemplating backing out of the room.

Elice looked away, not wanting to see what his decision was. On their first day back, she met at their usual spot for training, only to receive a message from a young soldier that he wouldn't be able to make it. She hadn't returned to the field since, and he never brought it up, so she assumed he was avoiding her.

The couch dipped next to her, and she glanced sideways to see him plopping into the empty seat next to her. She shifted as much as she could on the tiny two-seater couch to give him enough space.

The silence pounded in her ears. She thought it could have been her heartbeat, but that would have expended too much energy she didn't have. With shaky hands, she wiped at the bags under her eyes, forcing her eyelids to stay open long enough to make it through dinner.

"You don't look well," James whispered, even though it was just the two of them in the room.

Elice gulped, not wanting to have to explain anything to him—or anyone, for that matter. "I'm fine."

"You don't have to lie to me, my princess." He leaned in closer, and she tried to block out the way it made her feel to have him this close again.

"I'm not the one lying." She angled her body so she could fully face him. It had been on her mind a lot recently that he was too nice, almost too perfect. No one acted that kind, and it grated on her frayed nerves. The only thing that made sense about it was that he was either not normal or he was faking it.

He snapped backward as if she had slapped him. "What are you trying to say?"

She threw her hair over her shoulders. "Nothing."

"No, you're accusing me of lying about something."

"*Are* you lying about something?" She held his gaze, watching every emotion that shifted through his eyes.

He blinked several times before he faced forward. "I don't know what you're talking about."

"You've been avoiding me. Why?"

Looking down at his hands, he clasped his fingers together and moved his thumbs in circles. "I feel guilty, I suppose."

Ha! She laughed in her head. She knew it. It was too good to be true. She wanted to stand up and face him, but her legs were too weak with all the emotions flooding through her—not to mention she might just pass out from exhaustion if she stood too quickly.

He turned toward her again, his eyes narrowing in on hers as he reached for her hands. "I didn't mean to push you, or to push you away. I figured you'd be mad at me, and I couldn't face it. But this past week has been torture without seeing or talking to you. I promise I won't do anything like that again. I hope you can forgive me so we can go back to being friends again."

Elice blinked. Her brain tried to process what she'd heard, but she couldn't understand what he meant.

James sighed and moved to the edge of his seat, completely facing her. "I'll be honest with you. After meeting you, I knew how special you were—*are*. Being around you makes me happy, and I've never felt this way about anyone before. I don't think I'll ever feel this way about anyone else. I really like you, Elice. But I know what you're going through right now, and the last thing you need from me is to push the boundaries you set up for us. I meant what I said about wanting to be your friend, and if that's all we'll ever be—if that's the only way you'll ever see me—then I'll be happy knowing at least I have your friendship. That ... that will be good enough for me."

She swallowed down the emotions that popped up. Her heart wanted to beat right out of her chest at his words. Did she really hear him right? Was he really falling for her? The warmth she had felt when they kissed returned, and her cheeks turned hot.

But he said he wouldn't push her boundaries, the ones she had set up when she realized her parents intended on marrying her off. Her eyebrows furrowed as she glared at him. Was he really so dense he couldn't see how she felt about him?

All her worries about his trustworthiness vanished, replaced by a softness, and then, finally, by frustration. Did he not even intend to ask her if she felt the same way, or was he content to assume her feelings remained unchanged after all they had been through together?

Her mother's voice came from the other side of the door, and James recoiled. He turned from her glare, his shoulders sagging and weighing him down to the couch cushion as the king and queen entered the room. Andre and Alice were right behind them.

"Excellent. We're all here," Edgar exclaimed, and he walked to the dining room, arm in arm with Julice.

James flew out of his chair to follow, and Elice shook her head. She wished she had some of her fire back so she could have a long conversation with James, but it would have to wait until she felt better.

If she ever felt better.

They all took their usual spots, and their bowls were topped with a deliciously warm soup. Every now and then, Elice would look at James, but he never met her stare. He didn't seem like the same man she knew, and it must have meant it hurt him to think Elice didn't return his feelings.

But she now had just the plan to get him to understand, and, thankfully, it wouldn't cost her too much energy and time. All she had to do was say the right words, and he would understand.

Elice cleared her throat, but no one looked her way. If she wanted to make her announcement, she would need to raise her voice. She coughed again, and this time Alice banged her glass of water with the side of her fork.

"Thank you, Alice," she said, readying herself. She didn't want to stand, but she thought people usually stood when they did this, so maybe she should, too.

Alice nodded at her, then stood from her chair. Elice titled her head, her eyebrows coming closer together as she stared at her sister. Was she making an announcement as well?

"I have something I'd like to say," Alice exclaimed, a grin gracing her beautiful face. Elice had never seen her sister look so radiant, even after she first put the charm necklace on. "As you know, everything seems to have fallen into place in my life recently. My mind is clear, my body is healthy, and I finally feel as if things are going my way. I owe it all to my wonderful sister."

Elice placed a hand on her heart as her sister tipped her glass toward her before continuing. "Without you, Elice, I don't know where I'd be. You've inspired me to be strong, to be brave, to go after what I want in life."

Edgar raised his glass and shouted, "To Elice!" Everyone shouted her name, raising their glasses in a toast to her. A blush crept up her face. She wasn't used to this kind of attention.

"You're the reason I've made the best decision of my life," Alice said after everyone toasted. "I've decided to abdicate my place in succession to the throne as Queen of Norraine."

The air in Elice's lungs froze. Beside her, Edgar's glass fell to the floor, shattering into a hundred pieces. Julice gasped and covered her mouth with her hand, her napkin quieting the noise.

"What?" was all Elice could squeak out.

Alice looked around the table, taking in everyone's expressions. Even Andre and James had their mouths hanging open. She addressed Edgar, taking a few careful steps until she stood before him. "You know I've never been cut out for this role. You trained me all my life, had me work with the best governesses and leaders our kingdom had to offer, yet my heart wants something else. My heart wants *someone* else."

A sharp inhale came out of Elice's mouth. What was her sister planning, and how come she never discussed it with her?

Alice now looked at both of her parents, her head turning to one end of the table and then the other. "So, if I want to be with the man I love, I am more than willing to give up my title, the crown, everything."

Julice's napkin slipped from her hands, and Elice watched it flutter to the floor.

Edgar worked his jaw, clearly at a loss for how to best handle the situation before him. "Alice, I need to make sure you've thought this through."

"Are you in love with a commoner, Alice?" Julice asked.

Alice nodded. "He's anything but common, but yes, he's not of the nobility or a soldier who could rank up. He owns a shop in town."

"A shop owner?" the king bellowed, his hands balled up on his armrests.

"And this is why I'm giving up my title!" Alice shouted. The king's eyes widened at her raised voice, which was so unlike the old Alice. "This is why I want nothing to do with this life. I want to live in a small house somewhere in a field, near the mountains, where I can paint every sunrise and sunset. I don't want to worry about picking the right outfit or saying the right thing to the right lord or lady. And I don't think I'm the right person for the job, anyway."

The king's face took on a reddish hue as his anger grew. "Then who do you think will rule this land when I'm dead and gone? Will you have Norraine fall because you want to live a simple life?"

Alice didn't falter. If anything, her smile only grew as Edgar's anger rose. "Well, who do you think, Father? You know you didn't have only one child. And she truly is the best person for the job."

All eyes turned to Elice, and a new kind of shiver rolled down Elice's spine.

Despair.

Fifteen

Elice could feel the pressure, the heavy weight as massive as the Emori mountains.

What in the Fates' name was Alice thinking?

Alice gave her attention to Elice, drilling her with a sharp stare. "You're the only person for the job, Elice. I feel as if I've been pretending, forcing myself to live the expectations set up for me by the Fates. But you taught me that I have a choice. I'm not good with politics, and I don't know how to make people come together. With the new Fire Lord threat, you're the only one who can make us all band together—mages and non-mages—to stop them. To stop him."

"But I don't know the first thing about being queen," Elice cried, her voice pleading with Alice to reconsider.

Her sister only chuckled. "Well, it's not as if you're going to be queen tomorrow. You'll have time to prepare. And I'll be here to help you."

As if the matter were closed, Alice returned to her chair with a plop and picked up her fork, continuing her meal.

King Edgar leaned back in his seat and scrubbed a hand down his face. "Well, if you're sure—"

"Absolutely sure." Alice cut him off over a mouthful of food. "And I'll have to talk with Miss Tabitha about canceling my wedding. Oh! Andre, I almost forgot."

Everyone now turned to Andre, who looked shocked for once to have the attention on him.

Alice squeezed his arm. "Now we don't have to marry each other. You're free to be with whomever you want." Then Alice went into a long discussion about her plans to have a small wedding with Donovan next year.

But all Elice noticed was the way Andre's intense stare turned to her. She avoided it for a long time because she knew what he was thinking. He had already confessed his feelings to her, much the same as James had just a few minutes earlier.

When she finally looked his way, she felt the looming question in his eyes. Now that he was no longer engaged, would she choose him?

Her eyes strayed to James, and he was looking back and forth between Elice and Andre, the furrow in his eyebrows and the slant in his eyes asking the same question.

She knew she had to make a choice, and deep down, her heart had already chosen. Yet she didn't want to hurt Andre. He just lost his place as the would-be husband to the crown princess of Norraine, the second most important person in the kingdom once

Alice was crowned. Now, he wouldn't need to come to these nightly dinners, attend important balls or meetings, or otherwise show up to accompany Alice anywhere. Alice would now have another man on her arm.

Though they never were in love with each other, it would surely come as a blow to lose such an important standing in life. He wasn't even a high-ranking soldier in the King's Army, so he would have to rely on his title as Lord of Copita.

But was protecting Andre's heart more important to her than being with James? She knew what she wanted, so the question was how to let Andre down gently so she didn't lose a friend.

With her heart made up, but her brain completely exhausted, she resigned to make her choice known when she had more rest. Even if she knew rest was unlikely to come easily or soon.

"That settles it," Edgar said, clapping his hands together in one loud motion. "I will confer with the council about Alice's new title and how to handle her trust now that she's given up her claim on the throne. I also want to meet this *Donovan* person, so you must invite him to dinner. And we will need to make a few announcements to the public about these changes. Once I get confirmation from the council, we will proceed. Until then, Elice, you will need to start studying. I'll write to Miss Tabitha to get started on your training, since she is knowledgeable about the process and she can handle ... well, *you*."

"So, that's it, then?" Elice asked, looking at her mother and father.

Julice nodded, her face downcast at this turn of events. "Yes, darling. You are now the crown princess of Norraine."

"Well, after we make the official announcement," Edgar cut in. Then he downed his wine in one go before pushing his chair away. "If you'll excuse me, I have a few letters to write."

And just like that, Elice's new fate was sealed.

Andre and James excused themselves from the dinner table right after Edgar, leaving the women to talk. Elice didn't add much to the conversation as Alice told their mother everything she could about Donovan.

After dinner, Elice paced the library floor. The book she was reading now lay forgotten on the table. It was useless, anyway, since it didn't give her much information about how to access the mind realm. She didn't think any of the books in their vast library could help her, but she had to try.

Giving up for the night, she began to worry about how to tell Andre she would not choose to be with him. She owed him so much, and he was her first friend. He was fun to be around, when he wasn't being a jerk. But she couldn't see herself being with him the way she saw herself with James. The feeling of a rumbling river only happened when James touched her hand or kissed it the way he always did. Not to mention that brief, mind-numbing touch of their lips. Her face warmed just thinking about it.

With her jaw set, she determined to tell Andre her decision. She wouldn't put it off.

～

Three days. It had been three days since she had made her choice, yet she still hadn't sought Andre out. It had also taken three days

136

for the council to make their decision about the new situation they faced.

Elice had sat in on each meeting, which lasted most of the day. She listened to the council members argue back and forth as to whether Alice could keep her trust and title, if she would have to forfeit both, or if she could keep one or the other. Elice was surprised to find she had more sway with some of them, and they allowed her to speak her mind on several occasions.

Of course, she argued her sister was still a princess, even if she gave up her claim to the throne and chose to marry a commoner, and deserved to keep both her title and trust. Out of the ten council members, three of them completely agreed with her. Two were of the opinion that Alice could keep the trust with no title, and two thought the opposite. Another two thought she should lose everything.

The final member, James, was nowhere to be found. In fact, Elice hadn't seen him at all since he left the dinner table the night Alice dropped her announcement. She had seen the way his eyes scrunched up and his shoulders slouched, so she guessed he was still avoiding her. Especially if he thought she wouldn't choose him. When she found out he had returned to Talin, a pang of something hollow hit her stomach. She wished he were there so she could tell him just how she felt.

This also meant the council was at a standstill without the full council being present. Without his deciding voice as one of the army's officers, the council couldn't make the necessary decisions.

That night at dinner, the family got to meet Donovan officially. They all sat around the table, Donovan taking Andre's old spot.

"So," Edgar said between bites, looking hard at Donovan from his seat. "You ... paint?"

Donovan gave a nervous nod, just a quick up and down movement of his head.

Alice waved at her father. "He owns his own shop, Father. He's a businessman. And yes, he paints. He even sells paint supplies and his artwork."

Edgar rubbed his beard, his lips pursed as he took in the man who had claimed his daughter's heart and threw them all for a loop. "Does that actually give you an income?"

Donovan sputtered his wine, then hastily accepted the cloth napkin Alice passed him. "Yes, Your Majesty. I just bought a second home out in the country."

"Where in the country?" Julice asked, her tone light but probing.

"Just east of Copita, My Queen."

"So, in the middle of nowhere, then," Edgar said. He huffed and took a large gulp of his wine.

"Yes," Alice said, her smile full of pride as she looked at Donovan. "It's the perfect spot. Close to the Jani Forest, but close to Copita and the local markets."

Edgar narrowed his eyes. "You want to live in the forest?"

Elice shrugged, hoping to save her sister some of the heat she'd been getting from their father. "It's not so bad once you get used to it."

Edgar turned his glare on her.

"Oh, Father, don't worry," Alice said. "We'll have it all figured out by next summer."

"What's next summer?" he asked, lifting his fork full of roasted turkey to his mouth.

"The wedding," Julice answered, as though he should have known.

"That soon?" Edgar raised his voice. "But you just met!"

Elice could almost laugh at the irony of his words.

Alice was unfazed by his outburst. "Mother and Miss Tabitha are helping me plan it all."

Edgar mumbled something under his breath, but no one pressed him on it.

Julice cleared her throat before she turned her attention to Elice. "How are your lessons going?"

"Miss Tabitha hasn't threatened me yet," Elice responded. "So I imagine they're fine."

"And how are … other things?" Julice coughed again.

Elice avoided her stare. Her eyes blinked closed for a little too long and she almost fell asleep at the table. That wouldn't have been a good thing. So far, she had successfully avoided telling her parents about her nightmares.

"Elice?" Julice called, bringing Elice back to attention.

Elice opened her eyes with a start. "Right, yes. Other things are great. Just fine."

"I mean…" Julice shifted uncomfortably. "How is James?"

Elice looked at Edgar, who was pushing his food around the plate in front of him, his eyes glaring at the vegetables. "I don't know," she answered. "I haven't seen him."

"You know, once we announce your succession change, some things will need to be addressed."

Elice looked down at her plate. "Like my marriage?"

Edgar perked up at this, sitting straighter in his seat. "James is a fine young man. A perfect match."

Elice didn't miss the way her father stared down Donovan as he said that, or the way Donovan cowered in his chair.

"Well," Julice continued, "there are other matches, you know."

Elice also didn't miss the way her mother stared knowingly at her.

~

That night, she only slept a wink, making it hard for her to roll out of bed the next morning. Serena threw open the curtains, letting in what little light the fall sky gave them, and wished her a good morning. Elice pretended to wake up, faking a yawn and stretching her arms wide.

After dressing and having a quick breakfast, she escaped the house before Alice could catch her. She didn't need any distractions, and her sister seemed to be the biggest distraction these days with her nonstop talk of wedding plans and love. The only other possible distraction was Michael; however, he rarely spoke to her when he followed close behind wherever she went.

The barracks were alive and busy, as always. Soldiers scampered to the training grounds or to carry out other duties, leaving her to wander undisturbed through the main courtyard.

That's where she saw him. Andre leaned against the side of the building, smiling and laughing with a group of soldiers. As if he sensed her, he turned his head and froze, his smile only falling a fraction.

Andre excused himself and made his way over. His shoulders and hips swayed a little, making Elice even more nervous. He seemed happy—almost *too* happy—to receive the words she was about to give him.

"Good morning, Crown Princess," he murmured, only loud enough for her to hear. He looked over her shoulder at Michael, who stepped back a few paces to give them room to talk.

"Can we talk somewhere?" she asked, knowing she couldn't have this conversation with him out in the open.

He smiled and waved behind her, where two buildings met to create a secluded corner. It wasn't exactly private, but it was out of the way enough that she hoped people wouldn't be able to hear. Turning, she nodded at Michael, who copied her movement. He would stay where he was, close enough to keep an eye on her, but far enough to give them privacy.

She readied herself by taking a deep breath as she walked. When she made it to the corner, she spun around and almost ran right into Andre's chest. He was too close, so she backed up a few steps more so she could maintain eye contact.

"Dre," she began.

"Elice," he said, smirking.

She rolled her eyes. He was not going to make this easy. "I wanted to talk to you about what happened the other night at dinner."

He leaned an arm against the wall, his body angled and showing off the muscles in his arms. "I had no idea Alice had that planned. I kind of wish she would have told me, but I'm happy for her."

Elice gulped and nodded. "I am too. I hated that she wasn't

happy. Now she can be with the person she loves."

Andre smiled, leaning in a little closer. "Exactly. And I'm glad you're here now, so we can talk."

"About that." She cut him off, not wanting him to continue. "I have to let you know what I want. It's only fair, considering what you've done for me."

She paused, breathed deeply, then let it out, ignoring the way anticipation rolled off his body in waves. "You're one of my best friends. I only want the best for you. And I know you're smart enough, talented enough, strong enough to get what you want in life."

He took another step forward, and she backed up until she was against the wall. Putting a hand on his shoulder to stop his progress, she rushed her words out. "But that's not going to be with me."

Andre stopped. His eyebrows wrinkled before he shook his head. "What?"

She cringed, the confused tone in his voice making this harder. She knew she had to get straight to the point. "I want to be with James."

As if she had thrown rocks in his face, he stepped away from her, his eyebrows contorted even more than before. "You want James? But I thought, after everything we've been through, after everything that's happened, we could finally be together."

"I know this is hard to hear, but I have to tell you the truth. What James and I have... Well, that's what I want."

He turned away from her, not wanting to hear her.

She placed a hand on his shoulder, coaxing him to turn around.

"I know you'll find someone one day. Someone you'll be able to love who will love you back."

His shoulders tensed. He understood her meaning. She didn't love him, not the way he might have loved her.

Without another word, he stormed off, turning the corner and bounding out of sight.

Elice caught Michael's eyes and those of a few other people wandering close by, and she knew, once again, her conversation was not as private as she had hoped. With another roll of her eyes, she left the corner and went straight to her favorite place. The library.

Sixteen

Wildfire. That's how quickly gossip spread across the castle grounds. Secrets lit up like flames, and it was only a matter of time before every ear caught fire with the recent story about Andre and Elice.

As soon as Elice made it down to the dining room table for breakfast the next morning, she had heard several people around her whispering about her dumping Andre.

She ripped a piece of her breakfast bun and shoved it in her mouth, chewing angrily as she thought about it. She wasn't even with Andre, so how could she dump him?

Grabbing her glass of fresh apple cider, she took a sip, then almost threw the glass to the floor. This was not how it was supposed to go. She was supposed to still be on friendly terms with Andre, run straight into James's arms, and maybe, *finally*, get a decent night's sleep.

Instead, she had lost a friend, still hadn't seen James, and her mind was still weary from the little sleep she had gotten the past few days.

With the back of her hand, she rubbed at her tired eyes, then opened them wide as she made a silly face. She had resorted to stretching out her facial muscles every few minutes lest they continue to sag until she fell asleep. But she couldn't keep this up forever, and she definitely couldn't sleep well with the nightmares hounding her.

The door to the dining room flew open, and Serena stood in the doorway, panting and hanging on to the frame for dear life.

"He's here," Serena said between gasps.

Elice jumped out of her seat. She had asked Serena to keep the maids on the lookout for when James arrived from Talin. She knew they would be the first to know, seeing as how they always knew everything.

She rushed to the door, but Serena stopped her before she could leave. The maid adjusted Elice's hair, pulling loose a few strands so they curled around her face. Then she pinched Elice's cheeks and pulled at the hem of her dress so it wasn't crooked.

Elice pulled her in for a hug when she was done. "Wish me luck."

"You don't need it, but I'll wish you good luck, anyway."

Elice set off at a quick jog, Michael hot on her heels, pushing past the various servants and the odd lords and ladies who visited the castle. Everyone she passed gave her weird looks, but she didn't care.

She had to find James before the gossip did. She wanted to be the one to tell him her good news. *Their* good news, if he still felt the same way about her.

Once in the barracks, she wove her way down the inner corridors and straight to James's office. With a few loud bangs, she knocked on the door. A voice yelled for her to enter, and she had to remind herself to breathe before she opened it.

She pushed the door and came face-to-face with the man she'd been wanting to see for the past four days. He stood before his desk, a sheet of paper in his hands. When he saw her, he froze, nearly dropping the paper.

"Elice," he said, his voice croaking. Once he cleared it, he tried again. "Excuse me, my princess. What are you doing here?"

Michael leaned against the wall a few paces down. She stepped fully into the room and closed the door behind her. This time, she wasn't taking any chances at having people eavesdrop on her private conversation. Finally, she had learned her lesson.

The office was bigger than she originally thought. By the door was a small sitting area with a sofa and a chair. In the back was James's desk, made completely of metal that matched the walls of the building. The desk was as organized as everything else in his life, with everything in a clear, distinguished spot. Off to the side was a door that Elice presumed to be his bedroom, and she now realized she probably should have kept the door open. Was this space too private for her to be in?

James shifted, then placed the paper in his hands behind him on the desk. "I just got back from Talin, so I have a lot of work to catch up on."

"I know. I had the maids looking out for you."

He raised an eyebrow. "You were waiting for me?"

She sighed. For such a smart man, he was acting very foolish. "Of course. I've been wanting to talk to you ever since that dinner."

James turned toward the desk and shuffled some papers around, his back toward her. "Whatever you have to say, I already know."

"Oh, do you?" Her hands went to her hips.

Slowly, hesitantly, he faced her again, a hint of sadness in his eyes. "You don't have to tell me, my princess. I just want you to know that I'll always be here for you. I'll always be your friend."

Something tugged at her heart and her mouth went dry. This amazing, handsome, perfect man thought she wouldn't choose him. Yet he still offered her the one thing she needed above all else. A friend. Someone to trust.

Tears pricked at her eyes as she closed the space between them. They were so close she could feel the warmth from his body, his chest rising as he took measured breaths.

"James," she began, "are you serious right now?"

He drew in a sharp breath. "I mean, I think so?"

She chuckled and shook her head. "Why did you leave High-more so quickly?"

His eyes shifted to the side. "I couldn't stay and watch as you told Andre you wanted to be with him."

There it was—what she figured he thought would happen. She laughed again, this time a loud and uncontrollable sound.

James swallowed as he stared at her, his eyebrows knitted together. "You did choose him, right?"

"No," she exclaimed in between her laughter. She took a step back to gather herself again. "I'm sorry. I don't mean to laugh. It's just..."

He crossed his arms. "Wait, you didn't tell Andre you want to be with him?"

"Of course not," she said, finally composing herself. She had seriously lost her mind and clearly needed more sleep. "Why would I tell him that when I want to be with you?"

Slowly, his arms lowered to his sides. He opened his mouth to say something, but she cut him off. "That's what I wanted to tell you in the sitting room before dinner. I just couldn't find the right words. Then everything happened so quickly afterward, and you took off."

"What exactly did you want to tell me before dinner?" His eyes opened just a fraction more, hope beaming out from them at her words.

"I probably should have said something sooner, but I'm not good with this stuff. It seems you're not either."

He blew out a breath of a laugh, still unsure what to do or say. "I thought I messed everything up when I kissed you without your permission."

"That kiss was…" She paused. "That's why you were worried and avoiding me, wasn't it? You thought I didn't like it?"

He took a step forward, bringing them closer to each other. "*Did* you like it?"

She nodded, feeling the heat of his stare as he tried to read what was on her mind through her eyes. "I've never felt this way about anyone before."

James held her hands, bringing one to his lips. "Not even about him?"

Andre. James was jealous of him. All the glares and sarcastic words toward the other man must have meant he was jealous of a possible connection between her and Andre.

Elice held his gaze as she shook her head. "I already told him how I feel. He's currently not speaking to me."

"His loss." He kissed her hand again, causing a shiver to roll up her arm at his touch.

"I have a plan," she said, pulling her hand from his lips to lace her fingers through his. "But I want to see what you think."

"Anything you want."

"The council is still deciding what to do about my sister. In the meantime, there's a ceremony taking place tomorrow to announce my change in status. You would know that if you had been around." She gave him a pointed stare.

He looked down at his feet before meeting her eyes again. "I'm sorry I left without talking to you. I'm ashamed to admit I'm not as strong as I thought."

She playfully batted at his arm with her free hand before resting it on his biceps. "I would like you to be there with me. And, if you'll accept, I'd like to announce our official courtship. Not engagement—I'm sure I'll have to fight my dad on that point. But, if you'll accept, I would like to make things official. Finally."

His smile grew, making the blush on his cheeks shine as he looked into her eyes. "Yes, I accept. Although, I thought it was supposed to be me asking you."

"Times are changing," she said with a shrug and a wave of her hand. Then she wrapped her arms around his neck for a hug.

He squeezed her in return, burying his face in her hair. Finally, for the first time in over a week, she felt a semblance of peace wash over her. Things with James had worked out, and her life felt right again. Maybe she could finally get some proper sleep.

～

James showed up for dinner, and so did Donovan, much to everyone's surprise. Elice assumed Donovan would have been too afraid of the king's glare to show up again, but there he was, enjoying his meal, while her father simply stared at him from his side of the table. Elice was relieved Edgar had yet to say anything too terrible to Donovan. She knew how headstrong her father was, and how hard it was for him to keep a calm head. Maybe it was James's presence that lighten his mood or the good news they agreed to at the council meeting earlier that day.

King Edgar stood from his seat and all eyes turned to him. "Alice, with the help of your sister, and with James's influence on the presiding council members, they have concluded that you will continue to be known as Alice, Princess of Norraine. You will also get the money that was promised to you from birth."

With James's sway and wise counsel, he managed to get several other members to agree with Elice's stance—that Alice should keep both her title and trust. With the council split eight to two, the majority deciding in favor of Elice's vote, Alice would still be a princess after she married Donovan next summer, and she would get a hefty trust that would fund them comfortably for many years to come.

Julice squealed her delight, clapping her hands and congratulating her daughter.

Alice frowned and looked at her father. "But I don't want any of that. I refuse to keep anything."

Edgar groaned and sat down. "Is there really no pleasing you? With the title and the funds, you and your future husband will be set for the rest of your lives. When you have children, you won't have to worry about feeding them. Isn't that what you want?"

"I already told you what I want. Donovan and I will be able to handle everything on our own."

Edgar looked at Julice with mad eyes, unable to hold his emotions together any longer.

Julice leaned on the table, also exasperated. "Why don't you take the money, at the very least? If you want to lose the title, that's fine, but think about the security the trust will provide."

Alice and Donovan held a silent conversation with their eyes before Donovan sat up in his seat. "I will provide everything Alice needs and more. If she doesn't want to keep her title or take the family's money, then I support her decision completely."

Elice looked at Donovan with new eyes. He was willing to lose out on everything the title and money would give them, simply because he loved Alice that much. Her own heart swelled when Donovan smiled at Alice, the two of them having another conversation that only they would understand.

She looked at James to find his soft gaze on her. Beneath the table, she reached over and squeezed his hand for support, soaking up the encouraging smile he gave her.

Standing from her own chair nearly caused her to trip. She caught herself in time, but the motion caused her head to go dizzy. After steadying herself, she realized she successfully captured everyone's attention.

"I have my own announcement," she said, then she remembered to clink her fork against her cup. She lifted her glass, then tapped it with the closest eating utensil. James blew out a breathy laugh, and she turned a quick glare on him before she addressed her family. "As you all know, Mother and Father tricked me into becoming engaged to James."

Edgar sighed, thinking it was Elice's turn to give him a hard time. "Here we go," he muttered.

"But," she said, dragging the word and staring pointedly at her father, "the Fates seem to have a mind, and plan, of their own. Obviously. Well, anyway, things couldn't have worked out any better. I'm happy to say that James and I are ready to make things official between us."

Both Julice and Edgar shifted, practically jumping out of their chairs.

"Are you saying you're ready to be married?" Edgar raised his voice.

"Not yet," James answered.

Elice took that as her cue to sit down, thankful to be off her feet. "We're officially courting now."

Julice patted James's arm. "That's good news."

"I can use this information in tomorrow's proclamation," Edgar mused. He seemed to be deep in thought as he slowly sipped from his glass.

Across the table, Alice beamed. "This is not just good news. This is great news! I'm so happy for the two of you."

Elice met her smile, and, although she was bone tired, her mind told her this was right. This was the beginning of many good things to come.

If only she could shake the chilling laughter in the back of her mind every time she closed her eyes.

Seventeen

Her nerves bundled tight in her belly, like a knot of vines unwilling to separate. She stood behind the castle's grand front doors, both sides closed for now. James held her hand to stop her from wringing them, so she squeezed his instead.

"Hey," he called to her in a low tone, catching her attention with his deep voice. He grabbed the bottom of her chin with two fingers and turned her head to face him. "Just breathe. It'll be all right. We're just talking to the people. You've done that before."

She looked into his eyes. "Yes, but not like this. This is an official proclamation ceremony. There are going to be hundreds of people outside, waiting for me to mess up. They're going to scrutinize everything I say, the clothes I'm wearing, the way I look at them, and they'll probably wonder about the bags under my eyes. They'll think I'm crazy."

He laughed, moving his hand from her face to her shoulder.

"Well, you are crazy."

She gave him a light shove, but she laughed along with him. "Not helping."

"What I mean is," he paused, pulling her close, "you're crazy strong, crazy powerful, and crazy beautiful. They're going to see all those things in time. And they'll know just how lucky they are to have you as their crown princess."

Her shoulders relaxed at his words. Maybe she could do this. All she had to do was stand beside her father, hold James's hand, and read a few words from her script.

James frowned, looking across her face. "Wait, are you not sleeping well?"

Her eyes widened. After the hectic week and not seeing James for several days, she hadn't had the chance to talk to him much. Therefore, he hadn't really noticed how dead on her feet she was.

He pulled away to look at her fully. "Are you still having those nightmares?"

Before she could speak, her father came down the hall, flanked by several of the guards. Michael was among them, and he greeted her and James with a respectful hand-over-heart gesture. Her personal guard had given her even more space whenever James was around, and she wondered if it had anything to do with their new status changes and the fact that James was a highly skilled soldier capable of protecting her if she needed it.

"We're just waiting on your mother and sister," Edgar said. "And Donovan," he added with a grimace.

Elice held back her eye roll. This was not the time to get on her father's bad side.

James leaned closer and whispered in her ear. "We should talk more later."

She nodded. She didn't want to attract her father's unwanted attention by talking with James about her dreams, because he still didn't know about them.

Julice arrived, with Alice and Donovan just behind her. After Crystal, their speech writer, briefed everyone on how the ceremony would go and Elice was handed a sheet with her speech, they all lined up behind the double doors leading to the promenade. Edgar led the way with Julice on his arm, and Elice followed, James standing next to her. She latched onto his arm for support as the doors opened and the shouts from the audience reached her ears. Alice and Donovan exited behind her, followed by several guards.

Edgar walked to the podium while her mother came to a stop right beside him. There were no thrones since they stood on the front steps overlooking their citizenry. They all lined up next to the king as he spoke to the crowd. He couldn't be heard over the continued shouts and applause, so he raised a hand above his head.

Almost immediately, the crowd hushed. Elice shivered at the sight. Her father had such a command over the people. To them, he was their savior. He single-handedly ended a decades-old war that saw many lives lost and even more families ripped apart. The people respected him, they loved him, and they would listen to every word he had to say.

She didn't know if she could ever hold such power over the people.

"Thank you," Edgar said, loud enough for everyone to hear him. "Thank you for coming out today to join me on this special occasion. As you know, we recently welcomed my daughter, Princess Elice, to the castle after her many years away. We held a special ball in celebration of her first birthday with us, and many of you were in attendance."

Elice looked out into the crowd. She recognized a few members of the nobility, but she was shocked to see many people from the town mixed in with the crowd. The mismatched flow of people in heavy gowns and suits, together with the plain outfits of the common citizens, created a new and amazing sight. There were also a lot of unfamiliar faces. She didn't know who had come to witness this ceremony, or from where they came, but it warmed her heart to see people from different classes all here for her.

"But this ceremony is different. Today, we will pass on a special title to Princess Elice, and we want to share this momentous occasion with everyone, regardless of where you come from or how long it took you to get here." Edgar scanned the crowd and pointed to a man near the center. "I see you, Harold Thrum. We welcome you and our other guests from the Fishing Villages."

A man raised a hand and laughed. He wore a cap on his head and a simple tan shirt. Elice didn't know someone from the fishing ports would be there, but sure enough, several others near him all raised their hands and waved to the crowd that gave them light applause.

"Now," Edgar continued, "before we carry on with the ceremony, my daughter has a few words to say."

Elice took shaky steps to the podium as the crowd clapped again. Once they quieted down, she set her sheet of notes on top of the stand and looked out at the sea of people. "Hello," she muttered, knowing it wasn't loud enough for the people near the back to hear. She eyed those standing near the castle gates, watching as they leaned forward to hear her better. She cleared her throat and raised her voice. "I'd also like to thank everyone for coming. Since I've never given a speech before, I hope you all can bear with me while I fumble my way through this."

She had gone a little off script, but the laughter she earned from the audience bolstered her. It fed a bit of life back into her and fueled her sleep-deprived brain. Turning the paper over so she couldn't see the words, she decided to speak from her heart.

"You know, I had this whole speech prepared about how I would be a great crown princess and, ultimately, a great leader once the time comes for me to be your queen. But you all don't know me. You've only just learned about my existence, and for all you know, I'm untrustworthy."

Someone to her side coughed, and Elice knew it was her father's voice that whispered, "Stick to the script."

She continued anyway, letting her words flow. "So, instead of reading you words I didn't write, I'm going to speak from my heart in the hope that you will see me for who I really am. Because, at the end of day, it matters not the words I say, but the actions I take. It matters not how well I read a script, but how well I treat my people. And, when you need me most, it doesn't matter if I can stand at a podium reciting a memorized speech. What matters is that I stand with you, beside you, fighting for you. That's the kind of person I am, and that's the kind of crown princess I will be. And, when the Fates call our great King Edgar, the Defender, home to the spirit realm, I will continue to be there for you as queen.

Though these words may ring hollow now, I vow to always keep them in my heart. One day, I'll prove to you just as my father did, and the great kings and queens before me, how much I will protect this kingdom and its people."

She closed her mouth, and silence followed. No one moved, no one spoke. She looked out at the crowd as they blinked at her. Slowly, she raised her hand and placed it over her heart, showing her respect to the people.

One by one, hands raised to cover chests. Elice saw as the sea of people before her matched her, giving her the same sign she gave them. Then, as if a spell had broken, they erupted in a loud cheer. People hollered and whooped, using their fingers to whistle or their hands to clap. The sound was deafening to her ears, so she turned around and ran straight into James's waiting arms.

He caught her and held her tight, lowering his mouth to her ear. "That was amazing."

She pulled back enough to smile before she disentangled herself from his grasp.

Edgar walked up and held his hands out again. This time, it took the crowd a few moments longer to quiet down. "Well, now you know the force I've been dealing with." He paused as the crowd laughed along with him. "Now, on to the good part. General Thiery, if you will."

The general walked away from the line of guards at the bottom of the steps to pass the king a scroll. Edgar unrolled it and turned sideways so he half-faced the crowd.

Elice took this as her cue to step forward. She faced her father, ready to take on the new role bestowed upon her. After her speech, the people seemed to be on her side. They encouraged her, shouted for her, laughed with her, and she felt as if she could really do this. With a little bit of training, of course.

Her father began reading from the scroll, which was the official proclamation of her title of Crown Princess of Norraine. "With the unanimous approval of the Council of Ten, and the official seal of His Majesty, Edgar, the Defender, of house Moore, King of Norraine, I hereby proclaim you Crown Princess Elice of house Moore, future Queen of Norraine."

Her heart stopped beating. It happened all at once. As soon as her father finished the proclamation, the crowd erupted in a series of shouts and screams. At first, it sounded like the same joyous shouts from earlier. It took a few seconds for her to realize they were not the same.

A horrified scream wrenched the air, followed by several others. The crowd parted in the center, forming a circle in the middle that seemed like it didn't belong.

Edgar turned to see what the ruckus was about right when Elice saw it.

A fireball.

It flew from the middle of the circle and came hurtling straight for her. With her mind so slow and exhausted, she barely had time to register anything as she was tackled to the ground.

James fell on top of her just as the flames went over the same spot where her body had just stood. Her breath came out in pants as she stared up at him.

"Thank you," she muttered. Someone screamed again, and they both looked out toward the crowd to see more flames flying around.

"Stay down," James shouted over the sound of the fray. "Then, as soon as you can, get inside the castle and go to the safe room."

"What? No," she sputtered, trying to push him off. He wouldn't budge, so she grabbed his biceps. "I'm not going to the safe room. I don't even know where it is."

He groaned. "I'll have Michael escort you."

She pushed him again, but he stayed still, his heavy body protecting hers. "After my rousing speech, you think I'm going to hide while there's an attack? I'm staying."

Someone fell to the ground beside where they lay on the porch. Elice saw the charred remains of a face and her eyes went wide. He was a soldier; his uniform shirt was scorched, but she could see the king's emblem on the right breast pocket. She looked around the front steps and didn't see anyone else. Her family likely had gone with the other soldiers straight to the safe room. As long as they were safe...

"I'm staying," she said again, locking eyes with his.

He gave a short nod then pushed himself onto his knees. He pulled on her arms until she was sitting in front of him. "We'll need swords. Stay here until I can find some. Hide behind the podium until I get back."

Elice nodded as he got to his feet, his back bent low as he scanned the crowd. She was on her way to the podium when she remembered a very crucial bit of information.

She was a mage. The people attacking the castle were fire mages. If she used her water magic, and maybe a little of her earth, she would be able to neutralize their threat enough until the soldiers could take out the attackers.

With her head peering over the wooden podium, she took in the scene. More than half the crowd had dispersed, but a lot of people were prevented from escaping past the castle's gates, stuck behind a wall of red cloaks.

Fire Lords.

They had come out of hiding to attack here, on her special day. Had they meant to kill her?

Shaking her head, she continued to scan, taking in the fallen soldiers and a few of the citizens on the ground. Smoke billowed from bodies that lay crumpled, disregarded. Screams pierced the air as those who weren't dead, yet suffered from severe burns, crawled along the ground. The Fire Lords blocked the only exit through the front gates, hurtling more fire balls out from their hands and into the crowd to prevent them from escaping.

In the last few weeks, Elice had learned a lot about fire magic. Since it was the only element she couldn't control, she had to rely on stories from the townspeople and the few books that had information. She learned how the fire mages could draw on their power much in the same way she could draw on the other elements, and the way other mages, like healers and seers, could channel their own powers.

Rather than pulling from the air, earth, or water around them, fire magic was more of an internal power. Their body heat was their fuel, pooling in their bellies and pouring out from their hands. Once the heat reached their fingertips and met with air, it stoked into a flame.

A few flames flew into the air as a couple of fire mages hollered.

The smug looks on their faces enraged her now that she could see them.

Stepping out from behind the stand, she took the steps down to the stone walkway and made her way through the crowd. They shuffled out of her way, fear shrouding their faces as they looked at her.

"Princess," an older woman whispered, holding Elice's hand.

"Where are you going? You should be inside." Someone else tried to grab her shoulder, but she kept going.

She kept walking until she stood several feet in front of her people, facing the four Fire Lords and their smirks.

Eighteen

Smoke filled her nostrils. The scent choked her, making her gag. Her eyes stung, and she forced her sagging eyes to close for only a few seconds. Fatigue set in during those precious few seconds of rest her eyes so desperately needed, and she wondered for a brief moment if she had the strength to do this.

She didn't know if she was strong enough to protect her people. She cast a wary look over her shoulder at the small group of non-mages huddled behind her. A soldier peered out from the crowd, his eyes wide, looking on as if she were crazy.

And she was crazy.

Crazy strong, crazy powerful, crazy beautiful.

The words gave her a bolster. James's trust in her breathed new life into her lungs, and she sucked it in like fresh air.

Facing forward, the four mages looked at her, flames licking up and down each of their arms.

The one on her left strode forward, his red hood hanging off his head to showcase his face for all to see. Her eyes narrowed at his boldness. He didn't care if he was recognized.

The other three attackers walked sideways until they had her boxed in. She had the presence of mind to understand the looks on their faces, the gravity of her precarious situation.

They thought they had her. They thought they had already won.

Heat rose inside her, and for a moment, she could have sworn she could create fire. Lifting a hand, she tried to summon the heat, but no flames came out.

Upon seeing her move, the first mage stopped walking toward her. He stood a few feet away, close enough to cause serious burns on her body.

He sneered. "What do you think you're doing, little one? Surely you don't think you can take on four fire mages by yourself?"

The others laughed, readying their hands as well. Elice noticed all sound around them stopped, as if everyone in the promenade watched the scene unfold. She vaguely wondered if James stood behind her, two swords in his hands, looking at her with a horror-filled expression.

Elice met the Fire Lord's eyes. "You need to leave. Now. Before it's too late."

The man raised a single brow, then, after a beat, bent over with laughter. He sucked in several breaths as his fellow attackers joined in. "You think..." he said, then wheezed. "You think that, just because you beat that old hag, you could beat me?"

The four of them laughed again. Elice turned in a slow circle, staring at each of them as they laughed at her words. Two of the mages were women, both with their hair cut short to their chins. The fourth was a male, his eyes sunken and almost hollow.

Let them underestimate me, she thought as she completed her circle and stared down the first mage. "Fine. Don't say I didn't warn you."

She called on her surroundings, separating the water from the air, holding each element in a different hand. She aimed one hand backwards, shooting a gust of wind so hard she went flying toward the mage in front of her. With her other hand, she sprayed as much water as she could in the man's face, effectively soaking him.

He sputtered for only a moment before he grabbed her hand and swung her around. The movement made her dizzy, and with her already waning focus, she couldn't tell the difference between the ground and the sky.

The man let go of her, letting her fall on her bottom to the ground. As soon as she was out of his hands, he called on his flames and shot them toward her in a long stream.

She felt the scalding hot lick of fire on her body and screamed. The heat caused a sharp, stinging pain to light up the front of her face. She threw her hands in front of her, using water like a wall to block the flames.

His smile grew as he stared through the wall of water. When his fire died out, Elice let the water go, then took in shuddering breaths to calm herself. The burns on her face weren't as bad as they would have been if she hadn't blocked it, but the heat remained on her nose and cheeks.

He strode forward, and the three behind him followed, inching closer to her. Elice scooted away on her bottom, backing up until she ran into a foot. Looking behind, she saw the dead body of someone she didn't recognize. A normal citizen who came to see her. And now they were gone. She wondered if they had a family, a parent or sibling who would mourn for them.

She turned when the mage approached, grabbing her leg and pulling her across the dirt until he stood over her.

With a snicker, he lifted a flaming hand. "Say hello to Madam Lenore for me."

Only a second. That's how long she knew she had before he lit up her body like the one behind her. Just one second to plan.

Elice placed her hands in front of her. A force field of dirt covered her body just as the fireball slammed down. The attack bounced off and returned on its trajectory, and the fire mage had to shift his shoulder to avoid it.

Keeping the shield in place, she sat up, then she pushed it forward. It barreled the man into the other mages, almost knocking them off their feet and covering their faces with bits of dirt.

Using this distraction to her advantage, she sucked up as much dirt as she could. A cloud of dirt surrounded the four Fire Lords. She heard them cough and yell at each other to continue the attack.

But she couldn't let them get to her again. Her body grew weaker, her focus dwindled. Even her eyesight worsened, and it wasn't from all the dirt in the air.

If she didn't end this soon, she wouldn't be able to keep fighting.

In her peripheral, she saw James. He only had one sword, but he was running toward her from the crowd, right behind the attackers.

"Stop," she yelled. Her hands were shaking as she held them up, trying to maintain the dirt cloud. She didn't pay attention to James long enough to find out if he had stopped moving closer.

She released one hand from the first spell and used it to gather the air. Then she spun it in a circle, making the air move around the giant dirt cloud. The air encased the dirt, creating a sphere. The dirt inside spun with the force she created. Every so often she could see a hand or a leg fly around inside her spherical prison, and she knew the Fire Lords were trapped inside her dirt storm.

Wanting to add water inside, she closed her eyes, drawing as much of her power as she could. A tiny hole opened near the top, and she poured in as much water as she could. The sphere filled up with a muddy mixture that she kept churning.

"My princess," James called from her side, proving he hadn't stopped.

"I don't know what to do now," she admitted. Her eyes began to water, and her legs threatened to give out.

James placed a hand on her shoulder, the one holding her earth spell, while her other hand continued to move in a circle with the air. "You can stop now. We've got it from here."

We? Slowly, she turned her eyes to the side and saw several soldiers beside James, all with their swords drawn and aimed at her spinning ball.

All at once, her arms and legs collapsed. She fell to the floor, the magic stopping with her.

The last thing she saw as her vision failed was the wet splat of her prison as it dropped the attackers in front of the soldiers.

A soft whisper met her ears, and her groggy eyes opened.

Elice had to blink a few times before she could see clearly. Then she shot up into a sitting position, her hands gripping the blanket around her waist. The laughter, the tunnel, the water—it all faded from her mind as she became fully awake.

She shivered at the memory. She didn't want to fall asleep, but she didn't even remember going to bed. In fact, the last thing she remembered...

Looking around, she wasn't in her room. The soft cot she was lying on was encircled by a thin cotton sheet, blocking her view of the surrounding space. Shadows danced on the other side, and she heard more whispers. And wails.

She swung her legs over the edge of the cot and slid out of the bed, but her legs faltered as she tried to stand. Her body protested as she pushed the curtain away.

There were several cots scattered all around the room. No, it wasn't a room, but a makeshift metal building. Was she in the barracks?

On the cots were the bodies of injured people, either moaning or crying out in pain. Some had others around them, likely family or friends. Others were by themselves.

Elice covered her mouth with her hands as tears slid down her cheeks. The woman closest to her sat quietly on her bed, her eyes staring straight ahead as a female doctor spoke to her.

"There was nothing we could do to save the arm," the doctor explained. When the woman didn't react, the doctor touched her shoulder above a white bandage that covered the nub of her amputated arm. Still, the woman stared off into the empty space.

"I'll send the nurse over soon with more medicine to make you comfortable."

The doctor turned around and jumped when she saw Elice. "Your Highness, my name is Doctor Palm. You should be in bed."

"I'm fine," Elice said, the lie becoming normal now. She continued to look around the room, taking in the scene. "How many people were injured?"

The doctor sighed, then gently guided Elice to the side, away from the patient. "I'm treating almost a dozen. There's only one nurse at the moment to help me out, so the patients have suffered greatly. We've sent word to the neighboring towns for assistance. We're hopeful more doctors and nurses will arrive soon. But..." The woman's eyes flittered to the side as she hesitated.

"What is it, Doctor?"

"Our normal medicines aren't enough. These wounds... We don't know how to treat anything like this. Normal burns require healing salves, sometimes pain-relieving ointments and teas. But the burns these people received aren't responding to our routine procedures."

"Because it's magic." Elice's eyes surveyed the wounded people around her. Pain was written all over their faces, in the way their tears streamed down their soot-stained faces and the way their lips quivered endlessly. Even their loved ones looked on with furrowed eyebrows, dealing with their own variation of pain as they watched their family member suffer. When she returned her gaze, the doctor wore a frown. "That's why it's not working," Elice continued. "You won't be able to treat injuries caused by magic with simple salves."

"Then what do we do?" The doctor turned her worried look to the woman who had lost her arm. The end was wrapped in cloth just above the elbow. Tears now streamed down the patient's face, but she still hadn't moved an inch.

Elice got the doctor's attention by gripping her shoulder. "We need to treat them with magic."

The woman's eyes went wide. "I'm not a mage. I don't have magic."

"Then we get a healer," Elice said with a nod of her head. "And I happen to know one who can come immediately."

The doctor blew out a breath and nodded. "Thank you, Your Highness. I'm so glad you know what to do." She turned to leave, but then spun around again. "Please, stay in your cot until either the nurse or I can check on you again. I have a few more to see before you."

Elice assured the doctor she wouldn't leave her bed again, then returned to her little alcove in the corner of the building. A notepad and pen sat on the table next to her cot, so she began writing her note.

She just prayed to the Fates Madam Olivia would come.

Nineteen

The ache on her face helped her stay awake. She could feel the burn marks, and a headache was present near the front of her head, but she knew she was the lucky one in this building. As the cries continued throughout the day, her anger grew. The last thing she wanted to do right now was sit on the bed and wait. She wanted to go inside the castle, find out where they had locked up the attackers, and finish what she had started.

An hour after she woke, she still sat on her bed, the letter to Madam Olivia in her hands. The nurse had already checked in on her and promised to find someone who could deliver the letter.

As Elice understood it, they were left to their own devices in this building, which she learned was the medical station for the soldiers. Once she got back to the castle, she was going to have a few words with her father. If this was how they treated their wounded...

"Thank the Fates." James's voice came from the end of the building. He jogged past the array of cots and sat on the edge of Elice's bed. Elice let him squeeze her hands and place kisses on each one. "I'm so glad you're all right. One minute you were holding a ball of mud two stories tall, and the next you were on the ground. I was so worried when you wouldn't wake up. You don't know how many times I came in here to find you still knocked out."

Something warm settled in her chest. "I didn't know you came to check on me."

He held her face in his hands, looking into her eyes. "Of course I did. Your father is beside himself." Then he dropped his hands, and his breath hitched. "My Fates, you don't know." He stood from the bed and began pacing, which she was sure he learned from her.

When he said nothing further, she pressed him. "Please tell me they didn't get away."

James tensed, then stopped moving. He stood facing away from her and pulled the curtain so no one could see in. Then he crouched beside her bed and held her hands again, his expression tight and his lips in a thin line. "We have the four you caught locked in the dungeon. But there were others. They made it into the castle during the initial frenzy."

She held her breath when he paused, sensing something was wrong. "James, what happened?"

He lowered his voice. "Some got into the dungeon and freed the soldier who was with Madam Lenore."

"The one you captured at the cottage?" She squinted, trying to remember his name.

"Freddy. Freddy Owens. He was still waiting for his trial."

"Well, I'm sure we'll catch him again."

James shook his head, then leaned in closer, raising her bunched hands to his chin. He held them there, but his gaze was on the wall in front of him. "There's something else. And I don't know how to tell you this."

She pulled on his hands until he stood before her. "Just tell me. I haven't heard a thing from anyone, and the doctor doesn't want me walking around until they know I won't pass out again."

He sat on the edge again and angled his body toward her after a deep breath. "They took your sister."

It felt as if a rock became lodged in her throat. She didn't move, and James had to shake her a bit to make sure she heard him. "They took Princess Alice," he continued. "Michael tried to take her to the safe room, but there were too many of them for him to fight. He... He didn't make it."

She shook her head. This wasn't real. She must be stuck in a different nightmare.

Letting go of his hands, she pinched her cheeks, making her burns light up in pain across her face. James pulled her hands away, but she yanked them from his hands and jumped out of bed.

"Where is she? Where did they take her?" She paced, her legs threatening to fail, but she couldn't stay still anymore.

James stood with his arms crossed. "We don't know."

"Is there a search party? What about my mother? Is she safe?"

"Your father called for an emergency council meeting. We're on a break right now, which is why I came here. And your mother is safe. Distraught, but safe in her room."

"I need to go." Elice stopped pacing and turned to the curtain.

"I have to find her."

James caught her arm before she strode out of the enclosure. "We're organizing a search party. The council is readying all of our resources. We'll find her, Elice."

She snapped her eyes up to his. "You just called me—"

"I'm sorry. My princess," he blurted.

"No, it's okay." She raised a hand to his cheek, cupping it. "I like it when you call me by my name."

He leaned into her hand, and Elice could see the bags under his eyes. The nurse had told her it was the middle of the night, so they must have been in the meeting the entire time since the ceremony and subsequent attack. Which meant her sister had been missing for several hours.

She ran her thumb across his cheek and enjoyed the way his eyes fluttered closed. "But I'm the crown princess now, right? I have to be there when decisions are made."

He pressed his lips together. "Yes, you're right, but you need to rest."

"Then I'll sit in a chair."

His chuckle was short. "You aren't going to listen to me, anyway."

She rubbed his cheek softly. "Let's stop by the mail room on our way."

Walking in the cool night air helped refresh her mind, especially since she was running off more than a couple hours of sleep for the first time in days.

When she and James entered the council room, the meeting had already resumed. Her father looked up from the paper in front of him, and soon after, all heads turned her way.

"By the Fates, you're all right," Edgar said, his voice sounding hoarse and breaking on each word.

She met each member's eyes before settling on her father's, and she walked to her seat. Right now, she had to be the crown princess, so she wouldn't cry. But as soon as the room was empty of council members, she would collapse in her father's arms.

"It wasn't a terrible burn," she said. James pulled her chair out, and she sat down, only now noticing her dress was a mess. The only two members in the medical ward, understandably, weren't able to ask for new clothes yet, let alone change her if she had a clean outfit.

Lord Torenti leaned forward, his arms leaning on the table. "It's a blessing by the Fates. We're all glad you're safe."

She nodded at him, then looked around the table. "Where are we with the plan to find my sister?"

Edgar cleared his throat, bringing the attention to him. "Now that you're here, we can finalize everything. General Thiery will lead a group of soldiers into the Jani Forest, where the attackers were seen disappearing into. They'll scour the entire forest until they find her. If there's no evidence of them there, they will continue to the Emori mountains and follow Explorer's Pass through the entire range until they make it all the way around to Fort Emori.

"I've already requested aid from the other forts to send parties out into their surrounding villages. The villages of Highmore and

Copita will supply our soldiers with the necessary food for the trek, and the village of Torenti will supply extra weapons and other armaments before the general's group leaves in two days."

"Two days," Elice exclaimed, cutting off whatever her father had to add. "We've already lost half a day. Alice can't wait that long."

Lord Cove spoke with the same grumble in his voice he always had. "What would you have us do, then, Princess? Send our troops in without food and water? No swords or shields?"

Elice gripped the armrest. "Don't we have plenty in our storehouse?"

"It takes time to gather the proper resources," Captain Yusef answered calmly. "And if we go in without a proper plan, we'll be ill prepared to fight these rebels."

Edgar leaned in closer to her. "Any tools and weapons in the storeroom are to be saved for the soldiers stationed here. Special missions require specialized equipment, depending on the mission. These soldiers will mostly be on foot, with a few scouts on horseback riding ahead to scope the area. They will need lighter materials and clothing that will keep them warm and dry during fall storms."

Elice nodded, resigned to accept the facts. "Okay, so in two days' time, we will leave. And what about the prisoner who escaped?"

General Thiery opened his mouth to answer, but James interrupted with a raised hand. "What do you mean 'we'?"

Edgar seemed to catch on. He balled a hand and rested it on the table. "Not this again. Hear my words, Princess. You are not going on this mission, and that's final. Your sister is already missing. If something should happen to you—"

Elice interrupted, meeting each and every eye on her. "You're not seriously thinking of fighting fire mages with swords and shields, are you?"

Her father sat up in his chair and pushed his shoulders back. "I defeated them last time."

"They just went into hiding after Orser's aged body weakened enough for you to strike him down. And, if what Lenore said is to be believed—"

Now Elice was interrupted by Lord Cove's sharp voice. "Ha! Like we are to believe anything that mad woman said."

Elice ignored his outburst. "Then the Fire Lords are trying to bring Orser back. They must have found a way, and it might have something to do with Alice."

"Why would they need Alice?" Lord Torenti asked.

Elice eyed her father, waiting for him to decide to tell the council or not. After he studied their faces, he gave a gruff nod. "Alice has been suffering from dreams—nightmares, if you will. That's what some of us thought they were. Elice seems to believe they're actually visions."

"They are visions," Elice said.

"Well, she seems to have stopped having them, whatever they are."

She looked at James for help, then realized she couldn't have this conversation without telling them the reason Alice was cured from her dream sight. That would lead to her having to explain why she wasn't sleeping, and they needed to stay focused on finding Alice.

"The point is," Elice said instead, "you won't be able to fight the Fire Lords without my help."

"You're still recovering from the attack," James reminded her, his voice gentle but firm.

Edgar shook his head. "You are not going. I can't risk losing you."

To change the subject, General Thiery raised his voice. "Who will spearhead the logistics of the supplies?"

"Captain Yusef will continue to lead that department," Edgar answered.

After writing it down on a large notepad, the general looked at the king again. "With both myself and Captain Yusef leading the two groups out in the field, who will run the camp here?"

Edgar nodded toward James. "Captain Taylor will manage the soldiers in your stead."

James's chest rose and his shoulders straightened. His gaze was fierce as he felt the importance of his position being solidified in front of the entire council.

Elice sat straighter in her chair as well, the beginnings of a plan brewing in her mind.

Twenty

James set his jaw. "Absolutely not."

Elice narrowed her eyes at him. "Wow. You didn't even let me finish."

He sighed, his shoulders slumping and his arms hanging limply by his sides. "You're right. I'm sorry." He scrubbed a hand down his face, the mental and physical exhaustion weighing visibly on his body. He reached for her, and she gave him her hands. "Please forgive my outburst. I think I need some sleep."

It was early the next morning, and the council had just adjourned. Elice and James were in the sitting room just outside the dining room after having a quick bite of food to finally sate their hunger. Since the council usually met at noon every day, they only had a few hours to eat and rest before they would reconvene. Which meant Elice only had a few hours to convince James of her plan.

But one look into his eyes told Elice now was not the time to push it.

"All right," she said, putting off her plan for another time. "You get some rest. I'm going to check in on the wounded."

James gave her hands a squeeze. "First, we should talk about you. And *your* rest."

She looked at a spot above his shoulder, not wanting to meet his eyes. "I'm fine. I got some sleep yesterday."

"That doesn't count. You were passed out." James lifted a hand to her chin and moved her head so she had to look at him. "Why aren't you sleeping well?"

"Who says I'm not?" Her eyes shifted to the side, but he rubbed a thumb across her cheek to get her attention.

"It's the nightmares—the dream sight? Are you afraid to sleep?"

She closed her eyes and heard the briefest whisper of a laugh. The same laugh that haunted her sleep. "It's not like that."

He groaned, stepping away and running his hands through his hair. It had grown since their time in Talin, and all Elice wanted to do was run her fingers through his tight coils. She shook the thought from her head as he looked at her with a slight grimace. "Why won't you talk to me about it? I want to help you, Elice. If you're serious about us—about our relationship—then you'll need to let me help you."

She squirmed, her shoulders turning to the side to get away from his harsh words and glare. Never before had she ever had someone try so hard for her or be so mad that she wouldn't let them in. James wanted a relationship with her, and she did, too. But she didn't know the first thing about making one work.

When she turned back to him, he stood against the wall, his hands in his pockets and his head cocked to the side as he watched her. "Sometimes I forget," he said, "you're not used to this."

"I have no idea how to behave around you now," she confessed. "Not like I had an idea before, but now that we're officially courting, I don't know how that changes things."

After a breath, he pushed off the wall. "It shouldn't change anything." He strode toward her, one slow step at a time, as he spoke. "The way I feel about you hasn't changed. I still find myself drawn to you in a way I can't explain. And I'm still your friend. *That* will never change."

She closed her eyes, his words relaxing a part of her mind she didn't realize had tensed. Nothing needed to change between them—at least, not in a bad way. "Then I need your help, James. I need to find my sister, and I can't do that stuck here in the castle. You know that. You know what I can do. I should be out there looking."

He stopped his approach, his eyes roaming over her face. "I can't go against the king. Besides, I can't risk you getting hurt—and you're changing the subject."

The smile on his face made her laugh. He knew her so well, and she wouldn't be able to keep this secret from him for much longer. "I haven't been sleeping," she confessed.

"You mean at all?" His eyebrows rose.

"I only get a couple hours a night, at most."

He blew out a breath. "How long has this been going on? Since Madam Verna's?" Elice nodded, and James closed his eyes at the information before continuing. "Why didn't you tell me?"

"What was I supposed to say? That I'm too afraid to close my eyes because I can hear his voice? That I can't sleep because I'm instantly transported back to that same tunnel? That my mind and body are so weak I can barely keep myself standing?"

He pulled her in for a hug as her body shook. When her face met his chest, she realized she had been crying. Her tears soaked his shirt, reminding her of that day in Talin with the thunderstorm. He held her for several minutes, one hand cradling the back of her neck and his other pressing against the middle of her back. Once her tears stopped flowing, she wiped her face clean with her dirty sleeve and looked up at him.

"You need sleep," he told her before she could say anything else. "But first, you should talk to your mother. Maybe she could stay with you while you get some shuteye. It might make you feel more comfortable while you rest."

It made sense—the first night she had the nightmare, Alice held her, and she didn't have the dream. Maybe if her mother was there, she'd be able to sleep without seeing the tunnel.

"I'll talk to her," Elice said, pulling back from his embrace.

"You can get a few hours before the next meeting if you do it now."

She shook her head. There was something she needed to do first. "I'm going to spend a few minutes with the victims first, and then I promise to find my mother."

James pursed his lips, debating whether he should try to talk her out of it. "I'll walk with you to the barracks, since I'm going that way, anyway."

She smiled as she hooked her arm through his. He knew he

couldn't change her mind, but at least he decided to show his support in some other way.

They walked arm-in-arm to the medical ward, and the first thing she heard were the cries. James's jaw hardened as he too heard the sounds of pain. He pulled the door open for them, and they walked through. Her nose caught the scent of blood and burned flesh, and she brought her hands up to cover her nose and mouth. She didn't know how she missed that scent the first moment she woke up, but returning to the building caused the smell to hit her with full force.

The same cots took up the majority of the space, each with a person either writhing from their pain or lying motionless on their bed. Her heart broke again as she took in the sight.

James leaned close to her ear. "Are you sure you want to be here right now?"

With her eyes on the people in the room, she forced her hands down and stood tall. "I have to."

He squeezed her elbow, and she looked at him. "I'll be in my room if you need me."

She gave a nod and a wave as he left. Once he was out the door, she set out in search of the doctor or nurse, but she saw them right away on opposite sides of the room. She took a step toward the doctor when the sight of a familiar face stopped her.

"Madam Olivia!" Elice yelled in her excitement, forgetting where she was.

The healer looked up from the patient she was working with, then looked back down, her eyebrows knitted together in concentration. Elice took careful steps toward her side, observing the patient as Madam Olivia held her hands to the person's chest. His shirt was torn to shreds, barely held together near the bottom by a few inches of fabric. The majority of his chest was scarred from a severe burn, and Elice fought the urge to cover her eyes.

Even though he had this horrific injury, his face was calm, almost as if he were taking an enjoyable nap. As Elice watched, the outer edge of the wound changed. New flesh appeared where the burned skin was, the same color brown as the surrounding skin. The wound continued to close as Madam Olivia kept her hands directly in the middle of his injured chest.

Once his flesh looked completely healed and free of the burn, the man opened his eyes and sucked in a huge breath. His eyes met the healer's, then he looked at Elice and finally down at his chest, where Madam Olivia's hands still pressed upon him.

"Drink plenty of water, eat, and continue to rest," Madam Olivia instructed. She removed her hands, now covered in dark soot, and wiped them on the brown apron she wore.

The man had wide eyes as he mumbled a stuttered, "Thanks."

With a nod, she turned and walked a few steps away. Elice followed closely by her side as the woman's eyes roamed the room. "When I got your letter this morning, I came right away."

Elice gripped the woman's upper arm. "Thank you so much for coming."

Madam Olivia's dark eyes caught Elice's. "Don't mention it. But we might need more healers. I've already worked on a couple patients, and my energy is drained. At this rate, it would take longer to heal these people than the amount of time they have. Some are just on death's door, tempting the Fates to take them."

A shudder gripped Elice as tears formed in her eyes. "I don't know who else to ask."

Madam Olivia pursed her lips. "I know of one. If you tell him I sent you, he might come help."

Elice nodded, willing to do what she could to help these people. In the meeting, she was informed a total of ten people lost their lives, and she didn't want to lose any more to that atrocious attack. "Where can I find him?"

Madam Olivia pulled a folded piece of paper from her pocket and ripped a piece off. After finding a pen from the same pocket, she wrote something down and passed it to Elice. "This is his location. He might not answer his door, though."

"I'll try, anyway."

The doctor made her way over, eyeing Elice with slightly narrowed eyes. "You disappeared last night, Your Highness. Please have a seat so I can look you over."

"I'll do it," Madam Olivia tugged on Elice's arm, pulling her to a nearby chair. The doctor hovered as the healer placed her hands along Elice's arms, torso, and legs. Wherever she touched, Elice felt a warm, tingling sensation that breathed healing magic into her body.

Madam Olivia reached for Elice's head, but she snapped her arms away as if it hurt to touch her. She searched Elice's face, settling on her forehead. With one finger, she poked the center of her head quickly, then closed her eyes. "What's happened to you?" she asked with bated breath.

Doctor Palm looked on in concern, her eyes trying to see whatever Madam Olivia's magic could.

Elice pulled away, standing up and waving the paper. "I need to hurry if we want to save all these people. I'll be back as soon as I can." She turned to leave, but stopped after a couple of steps. "And thank you, both of you. I'll make sure you're properly compensated for your work here. Nurse Beth, too."

Before they could respond, she hurried out the door, bumping into someone on her way out. When she looked up, trying to find whomever she had run into so she could apologize, her eyes zoned in on the one person she didn't think she'd talk to for a long time.

Twenty-One

Andre leaned his back against the wall and slid, cursing on his way down. The smell of alcohol hit her nose, and his bloodshot eyes were unfocused as she stood in front of him.

"Are you drunk?" Elice asked, her hands flying to her hips.

He chuckled as his bottom hit the ground, making him laugh louder. "I don't know. Maybe?"

She narrowed her eyes at his slurred speech. "Alice is missing, and you're drunk. Unbelievable."

He didn't seem to hear her, because he pushed off the floor and staggered down the hall.

Elice followed him, wanting to take her anger out on him by yelling. "Where have you been this whole time? I didn't see you at the ceremony."

He stepped out of the barracks and walked toward the front gates. "I've been... I don't know. 'Round. The tavern."

"The tavern? Your best friend's been kidnapped, and you think your best chance of finding her is by visiting the tavern?"

He stopped short of the metal gates, then spun to the side and threw up. Elice stepped away before she got hit by the mess. Her anger grew as he wiped his mouth with his sleeve. "What'd you say?" he asked, his words still running together incoherently.

Elice shook her head. "Your best friend's been kidnapped, and you—"

Andre cut her off, grabbing her by the shoulders. "Alice has been kidnapped?"

Her eyes widened as it dawned on her. "You didn't know?"

He groaned, then ran a hand down his face hard enough to leave nail marks across his cheeks. "I've been at the tavern—"

"You didn't even know because you were getting drunk!" she yelled, pushing against his chest. When he didn't respond, she let out a high-pitched scream. "If you had been there—if you had been a *good friend*—you would have been there. You could have gotten her to the safe room. You could have protected her, like you swore an oath to do. Michael..." She couldn't get the words out, still not wanting to think about her guard not being there anymore to annoy her with his hovering.

"She doesn't need me," he mumbled, then turned and headed out the gate, waving at the guards manning it.

Elice's frustrated groan escaped her mouth before she stomped after him. The guards looked at each other, silently asking if she was allowed to leave the grounds after the attack, but she didn't pause long enough for them to stop her.

Jogging, she caught up with Andre and grabbed his arm. He

shrugged her off, but she wouldn't let him go that easily. A root shot up into the air from the yellowing grass at their side. She pushed it toward him, willing it to wrap around his wrist so he wouldn't walk away.

His eyes screamed at her with fury at being stopped. He yanked and pulled, but she wouldn't let go. "This seems vaguely familiar," he said, looking down at the bondage.

"You were supposed to be there for her," Elice said, her voice cracking with emotion. "And now she's gone. You made an oath to always protect the royal family, but you weren't there."

"She doesn't need me anymore, Elice," he repeated. With his free hand, he ripped pieces of the root off his arm, throwing them to the side until his hand was free.

Elice simply called another one and trapped both hands in front of his body. She took a few steps forward until he had no choice but to look into her eyes. "Then what about me? You weren't there for me."

His eyes searched hers, his breath coming out shallow. He examined her face, taking in the burns on her cheeks and forehead. "You said you don't need me either."

She shook her head, then stepped away, not wanting to smell the remnants of alcohol on him. "You're wrong. I never said that. What I need is my friend back."

He scoffed, then in one swift motion, yanked the root from the ground and stalked away, dragging the plant behind him.

She stood, looking at the spot he just stood at, when a glimpse of red passed by her peripheral. Her gaze shot in that direction, and she took off. "Wait! Stop," she yelled as she ran after what she thought was a red cloak.

Standing in the middle of the square, she looked around, hoping to catch another sight of it, when footsteps came pounding down the walkway after her.

"What is it?" Andre asked, panting as he caught up to her and throwing the last of the root to the ground. "What did you see?"

"What does it matter to you?" Elice asked in response, her voice clipped. Another flash of red dashed down a side street, so she ran after it again, this time with Andre right behind her.

She hurried down the cobbled path and turned down the alley she saw the red coat in, determined not to let it out of her sight.

As soon as she entered the alley, a fully cloaked figure stood before her. Elice froze, causing Andre to bump into her, almost knocking her over.

There were several doorways in this alley, all leading to small homes and lofts. Several windows looked down on them from the outside of the two-story buildings that encased the space, and at the end was a stone wall, the perimeter of the town's outer wall. Elice relished the fact that the Fire Lord before her was cornered in with nowhere to go.

The person stood with their arms at their side, palms facing her and Andre. The hood of their red cloak completely covered their head, creating a shadow that hid their face. Their feet stood shoulder-width apart, slightly bent at the knee.

Elice's eyes narrowed as she took in their fighting stance. She brought her arms up, readying herself.

The figure took a single step forward, and flames licked their arms.

Elice immediately called forth water to create a ball in her hands. "In case you missed yesterday's show," she called out, "I'll give you the same warning I gave your friends. You know, the ones currently locked in the castle's dungeon. But before you surrender, you'll tell me where my sister is."

The hood of the cloak tilted to the side, and that was the only warning she had before two fireballs shot in her direction. She threw the water ball toward them, extinguishing the first ball on impact. Andre pulled her by the waist, and she narrowly avoided the second. She threw a look over her shoulder at him before she pushed him to the ground.

He landed on his rear with an "oof," and she motioned for him to stay there. The last thing she needed was to be distracted by having to protect him.

The Fire Lord threw another flame her way, this time as a long stream of fire. She had a moment to react, pouring her own water stream to douse the fire attack. It didn't seem like she had enough water as the flame continued to approach, minimizing her water attack. It came closer and closer, creating a hot steam that misted over her face.

She took a few stuttering steps backwards. Her water stream faltered as she tripped over a pebble. That was exactly what the other mage needed to up his attack, and he stepped forward with another onslaught of fireballs.

Falling to the ground, Elice put up a shield of strewn rocks and pebbles, absorbing the attack and the heat of the flames as several balls bounced off it. She turned to the side, catching Andre's eyes. He looked shocked, his raised eyebrows causing creases across his forehead. With her eyes, she signaled for him to leave. She couldn't be responsible for him. Whoever this fire mage was, he was clearly stronger than the others she faced on the castle's promenade. The force of his fire was stronger, more powerful, and she had a hard time defending against the sheer firepower.

Andre's gaze hardened as he shook his head and pushed off the ground. He reached for his belt and grasped at air. His mouth formed a comical circle when he realized he didn't have his sword, and Elice shook her head. Of course he didn't have his sword, but it wouldn't have made much difference against such a powerful mage.

With no other choice, Elice threw her rock shield toward her attacker. Rocks flew directly at him, and the mage had to drop his fireballs to raise his arms, protecting his face from getting hit.

Using this distraction to stand, she called on as much wind as she could. It came running, gathering into a gust that blew her hair in all directions. Dust from the ground gathered with the wind, and her footing slipped as the air threatened to sweep her up as well.

The Fire Lord kept his hands in front of his face, but his hood flew back, and his cape billowed behind him. Squinting, she tried to see through the dust cloud, but the strength of her air prevented her from glimpsing his face.

As the stormy wind gusts continued to push, she had to plant her feet in the ground to avoid flying away into it. She looked on with a smile as the other mage threw himself to the ground on his belly, desperately holding onto the stone pieces cemented to the path.

It wasn't enough, though. She couldn't hold this wind for much longer, and her head and aching muscles begged her to stop, to rest. Her hands shook with fatigue, and a seam cleared in the middle of the forceful wind.

The fire mage looked up, saw the pocket of clear air, and pushed off the ground. He landed in the middle of the gap in her spell, and Elice saw his face.

He was old, with wrinkles all along his brown skin. A thin scar marred his jaw, running from his left ear all the way to his chin. His smile chilled her deep to her bones, and goosebumps spread down her arms. She dropped her spell, so enthralled with the face of her attacker that she barely registered she wasn't calling on her powers any longer.

"Elice!" came Andre's voice from behind her, warning her, and she lost focus on the man. She turned toward Andre's voice, and she didn't realize this mistake until a searing pain hit her side.

It crawled up her back and down her left leg, burning her flesh and making her scream in pain. The shock of it sent her falling, her head hitting the ground as she cried out. Her body continued to burn as shouts reached her ears. Squeezing her eyes shut to block out the pain, she tried to zone in on what was happening around her, but she couldn't hear anything besides her own screams.

Her knees scraped the cold, hard ground as she crawled toward the sound of Andre's voice. She didn't know what was going on, but she couldn't leave him to fight the fire mage alone. Forcing her eyes open, she lifted her head and saw three soldiers waving their shields at fireballs, deflecting them all around with reckless abandon. Andre stood behind them, and once their eyes met, he rushed to her side.

"It's okay," he whispered. He grabbed her shoulders and looked deep into her eyes. "I'm going to get you out of here."

She opened her mouth to speak, but no sound came out. Her throat was raw from all the screaming, and she couldn't form any words.

He pushed her shoulders down as a fireball flew over their heads. After a quick glance in the direction of the fire mage, he lifted her in his arms, avoiding her burned back. He slung her over his shoulder and swayed, clearly not sober enough.

She wanted to tell him to let her walk, but when she looked over his shoulder, she saw the fire mage. Sweat poured down his face, and he took deep, measured breaths. He stared directly at her, then his eyes flitted back to the three guards. Elice saw the two choices he had running through his mind: go after her and Andre before they escaped or continue attacking the soldiers.

One corner of his mouth rose as he threw a giant flame with both of his hands at the guards, creating an explosion so loud and bright, Andre went flying out of the alley with her still in his arms. She landed on her back, and Andre rolled a few feet away. Her head hit the stone floor so hard she thought she would black out.

When she lifted her head, her ears rang and her vision blurred. Everything was foggy, and her brain couldn't make sense of what she saw. She brought a hand to rub her eyes, hoping to clear the smoke from them.

A groan at her side let her know Andre was all right. "Elice," he croaked, "are you okay?"

She couldn't speak, couldn't see. She tried to reach for where she thought he was, and her hand clasped around his.

"I've got to get you out of here," he mumbled, more to himself, and she heard shuffling. His arms were around her again, picking her up and over his shoulder. He wobbled down the main courtyard, and once they were away from the smoke curling out of the alley, her sight improved. Dozens of people poured out of their homes, still dressed in their sleeping clothes. They looked on with fear, some with their mouths hanging open or covered by their hands, many shaking their heads as they saw the state their crown princess was in.

Andre carried her through the growing crowd, and as Elice looked through the people around her, hoping to give them some semblance of strength, she noticed a red coat standing near the back.

She pointed, opening her mouth to warn Andre. After a blink, he was gone, and she had to wonder if she'd imagined it.

No one could have survived that blast.

Twenty-Two

Elice sat on the cot while Doctor Palm cleaned the burns on her back. With her eyes clenched tight and her fingers gripping the sheet, she focused on staying awake. Not that it was a difficult thing to do, since her entire body ached and her side and back continued to throb from the pain.

Doctor Palm clicked her tongue. "I cleaned the wound as much as I could, but as we know, only Madam Olivia can heal you. She's currently resting in one of our spare rooms. As soon as she's back, I'll make sure you're seen first."

Elice shook her head. "There were still half a dozen patients that needed to be seen before me. I'll wait."

"With all due respect, Your Highness," Doctor Palm said, "you're our priority. While we wait for the healer, I'll apply some salves and wrap up your wounds. Considering the damage, I'll have to apply it to your entire back, midsection, and left arm and leg."

With a grim face, Elice nodded and allowed the doctor to work. As soon as she was done, Andre peered through the gap in the curtain. He had a cloth bandage around his head to stave off the bleeding, but there was a red bloodstain on the back of it from when he had collided with the ground after the explosion.

Andre pushed the curtain open and pulled a chair to the side of her bed. "How are you feeling?"

She shrugged, and the doctor patted her uninjured shoulder before she left them alone.

Andre reclined, wincing as his back hit the metal chair. "I didn't know that many people got hurt."

"Well, considering you didn't even know there was an attack…" Elice let her words hang, sighing as she leaned against a pillow with her good shoulder, pulling the sheet over her legs as they hung over the edge. Her dress had caught fire, and the doctor removed the frayed remnants to wrap a thick, breathable cloth around her torso and entire left arm. She wore a thin gown, and the chilly air managed to find its way into the building through the cracks between the metal panels.

He groaned, throwing his hands in the air. "Look, I know I messed up—"

"Messed up?" Elice raised her voice, not caring who heard her. Half the patients were too distracted by their own pain to listen in, anyway. "You didn't just mess up, Dre. You weren't even there. You gave up on her, and you gave up on me."

"What did you expect me to do, Elice? Wait around and watch as my best friend married the love of her life, while you and James run around, pretending you don't have feelings for each other?"

Elice pursed her lips. "We're not pretending anymore."

"Even worse." He closed his eyes and rested his arms behind his neck. "Don't be mad at me for not wanting to be left behind."

"Alice and I never planned on leaving you behind. You would have known that if you would have just listened to what I had to say instead of storming off."

He scoffed but said nothing else, further aggravating Elice's nerves.

"Fine," she grumbled, then readjusted the pillow to rest behind her shoulder. "You can go back to your own cot, since you want to be alone."

"I'm keeping an eye on you so you don't chase after any more Fire Lords." One of his eyes cracked open, then he closed them again as he breathed deeply.

"I don't need a babysitter."

Another scoff, and then his breathing evened out as if he had fallen asleep.

As soon as it became quiet, Elice's eyes drifted closed. Shaking her head, she fought off the sleep that called to her. The outer door slammed opened, the sound of metal banging against metal jarring her fully awake.

She and Andre angled their heads to look out beyond the curtain.

"Fates," Andre breathed as Edgar and James stomped toward them, their faces contorted in rage.

"What happened?" King Edgar asked, his voice booming and frightening several of the patients.

James immediately fell to his knees beside her, his eyes roaming over the bandages and cuts littering her body.

Elice cut her eyes to Andre for a moment before she looked at her father. "I was in town—"

"What in the Fates' name were you doing out of the castle?" Edgar's voice bored down on her, his imposing frame standing tall while his hands went to his hips.

"I was going to look for another healer." The last thing she wanted was to say she was chasing after a drunk Andre.

Edgar made a noise of annoyance in the back of his throat before he began pacing.

James traced a finger down her unbandaged arm, carefully avoiding the scrapes and cuts. "Why did you go by yourself?"

When she looked at Andre, he cleared his throat, and James turned a glare on him.

"I can explain, I think," Andre said, though his voice came out quieter than normal.

James clenched his hands into fists. "Why didn't you protect her?"

"Oh, was I supposed to start shooting fireballs out of my hands?"

"Wait," Edgar interrupted, coming to a halt in front of Elice's bed. "Did you say 'another healer'? And fireballs? Tell me you didn't run into a fire mage."

Where do I start? she wondered, gathering her thoughts through her muddled mind. "Okay, well, I wrote to a healer named Madam Olivia asking for her help with the patients. She's been able to heal a few of them, but we need at least one more to help since it's draining on her powers. She gave me a contact, so I was on my way to find them when I saw a red cloak."

Edgar's eyes bulged. "And you decided to fight this person on your own?"

"I thought I could handle him, but he was too powerful." Regret filled her, dragging her down until her eyes watered. If she were feeling completely healthy, she knew she would have been able to defeat him. She had him cornered, unable to counter her wind attack, but she couldn't go on.

James shifted on the floor. "Did you see his face?"

When she nodded, the man's face came back into her mind. "He was old, maybe in his seventies. His eyes were dark. And he had a scar on his jaw." She ran her hand along her jaw, indicating where the man's scar ran along his face.

Edgar froze, and his breathing stopped for a moment before he caught it again. "Red Cloud."

James sucked in a breath, looking at the king with wide eyes. "You mean General Samson?"

Her father made a growling sound. "He's no longer a general, Captain. He lost that title when he betrayed my grandfather. The day my father gave him that scar."

Andre looked uncomfortable in his seat. "I can't believe that was him. It's a wonder we escaped with our lives."

Elice didn't recognize the man's name. "If he was there during your grandfather's reign, how is he still alive?"

Edgar sat on the edge of her tiny cot. "Oh, he came around towards the end, climbed his way up the ranks quickly. Back then, there were a few other mages in the army. When Orser attacked the castle, my father and a few of his men protected the throne room my grandfather was in. Samson had already been compromised at this point, and he turned his sword on my father. He used his fire magic and felled the other guards. My father was the only one standing in between the king and Samson. Then Samson used his special attack."

"The explosion," Elice cut in, drawing a nod from her father.

"His fire can grow so hot, forcing a reaction so great it creates a cloud of fire. It's almost like an explosion of heat, of flames. That's what earned him the nickname. So, he attacked my father with his red cloud, but not before my father sliced at him with his sword, cutting up his jaw and leaving that permanent scar. My father survived, thank the Fates, otherwise you and I would not be here. But my grandfather, your great-grandfather, lost his life when there was no one left to guard the throne room."

Elice shuddered, unsure of what to say. Andre was right—she didn't know how they survived, considering the other three soldiers who came to help had been burned to death. Maybe with his old age, Red Cloud wasn't as powerful as he used to be. Maybe they had been far enough away to avoid the direct impact. Like her grandfather, perhaps the Fates were on her side.

Her mind went back to the flash of red she saw in the back of the crowd, limping away from the scene of the explosion. Had he survived his own destruction?

The sun was high in the sky now, and Elice didn't get to attend the council meeting since it was well after noon. Madam Olivia returned and set about healing Elice's and Andre's injuries. The healer frowned and warned them not to get injured again before she had a chance to see the other patients.

"I didn't get to see your friend," Elice told her once she had changed into a new dress. She stretched her arms, thankful she had no more pain.

Madam Olivia washed her hands in the fresh bowl of water by the side table. "Oh, Master William is not a friend. At least, not anymore."

"What happened?"

"That's grown folks' business. You'll understand when you're older."

Elice rolled her eyes. "Well, I'll go and see him now. Thank you again, Madam Olivia."

"Hold on, little one," the healer said, and Elice stopped moving toward the curtain. "Should you be leaving the castle again? What if there are more fire mages out there?"

"I have to find another healer to help you before you work yourself too hard."

"I can handle the work if I get proper rest in between healing sessions. It's the people I'm worried about. Some are on death's door."

"Another reason for me to go," Elice said. She squeezed Madam Olivia's hand before taking off.

This time, when she approached the gate, the guards held their heads high as soon as they saw her, and she knew they would give her a hard time.

"Open the gate," she tried, using a deeper voice than usual.

One of the two guards eyed her before looking straight ahead. "I apologize, Your Highness, but I'm under strict orders not to let you pass. King Edgar specifically told us not to let you through, no matter what you say or do."

She placed her hands on her hips. "Even if it's official palace business? To help the injured citizens under our care?"

The guards looked at each other, eyes wide. One of them opened his mouth slightly but shook his head.

"I don't know," he muttered to his companion. "The king told us not to listen to what she says."

The first one faced forward again, this time holding her gaze. "How do we know you're leaving for palace business?"

"I'm the princess, aren't I? The crown princess." She was grasping at straws, but she had to talk to Master William before it was too late. The patients needed her.

"Well, yeah, but..." He fumbled his words, not fully knowing how to respond.

"Listen," she said, lowering her voice. "If I don't leave, all those people sitting in the medical ward are that much closer to death. I can't just sit around and let more people die. If you let me through, I will be able to find a healer who can help. As soon as I find him, I'll come right back. But please, don't let those innocent people suffer any longer."

The second guard lowered his shoulders, sagging under the weight of her words. "I was there that day. I saw what you did."

"Yeah," the first one said, moving to the side. "I've never seen such bravery."

"I'm sorry about what happened to Princess Alice," the other one said, also moving to give her space to leave.

Elice nodded. "Thank you, so much."

They unlatched the gate and pushed it for her, and she walked past it to enter the bustling street.

Looking down, she pulled the sheet of paper with the healer's location on it. It had scorch marks on the edges, and even a few drops of blood, but it had survived the attack. "Ten-eight B, second floor."

She wandered down the main path, nodding at a man walking down the street lighting the town's lanterns. The sun would be setting soon, so she wanted to hurry before it got too dark.

The first alley she passed was numbered twenty-three, the shiny black letters painted on the side of the alley, and she remembered from previous trips into town that the numbers went down the closer she got to the outer gate. "Only thirteen more to go," she muttered to herself.

As she passed buildings and storefronts, a few people noticed her and gaped. In hindsight, she should have worn a hooded cloak to cover her face, but she had no other choice now. She would have to walk faster before more people realized who she was.

At a quick pace, she continued down the main street until she finally arrived at row ten. She entered the alley, then sought door number eight. She turned the knob and entered the tiny hallway, taking the stairs up to the second floor. The first door she came across had the letter A, and the one beside it had the one she was looking for.

She knocked on the door to apartment B and waited for the door to open. After several seconds and no answer, she knocked again, this time harder.

When there was still no answer, she banged again, not stopping until the door swung open.

"What?" a man exclaimed, his voice rough with age.

"Oh, sorry," she said, then cleared her throat. "I'm looking for Master William."

"Busy," the man said. He went to close the door, but Elice pushed against it before he slammed it shut.

"Please, sir, this is important. There are lives at stake."

He eyed her through the crack. "Who's looking for William?"

Elice stood straight and pushed her hair away from her face. "Crown Princess Elice of house Moore, future Queen of Norraine."

The man scoffed, opening the door all the way and crossing his arms. "Is that all you are?"

She softened her gaze. "I'm also a mage."

He smirked, the wrinkles on his face scrunching up his cheeks. "That's more like it. From what I hear, you're a powerful mage. Three elements? Unheard of."

She loved the praise, but she didn't have time to stand and listen to it. "Please, are you Master William?"

The man walked away from the door, and Elice followed as he spoke over his shoulder. "I haven't been called that in a long time."

"So, you are him." Elice looked around the room as he bustled about. Only a two-seater sofa and a short table were in the room, and a hallway led to another space in the back. The couch looked almost as old as the man, and the table had stains along its surface.

The man lit a few candles on the wall, then turned around to face her. "That'd be me. You said there were lives at stake. I'm no warrior, as you can see, and I know the army is gearing up for some kind of battle, so I don't know what you need with me."

"I don't need any fighters, Master William. I need a healer."

He looked her over, and she fidgeted under his stare. She knew he could see the scars and bruises across her face. "I know about the attacks, and about the princess. I still don't know what you want me to do."

"There are a few people in our medical ward who are suffering from fire magic burns. They weren't responding to the doctor's treatments—"

"Of course not," he mumbled.

She nodded at his interruption. "So you see why we need you. We need a healer, and the one we have is not able to care for everyone on her own. Some will die from their injuries before she can even see them."

"Who is this healer?"

"Madam Olivia. She owns a shop—"

He turned sharply, grabbing his coat from the back of the sofa and throwing it on. "If Madam Olivia is there, I'm coming too."

Elice's heart leaped. Master William grabbed a key from the table and opened the door, waving for her to hurry.

She wanted to ask how he knew Madam Olivia, but she knew he'd give her the same response the other healer had. As curiosity bubbled inside her, a little bit of hope did, too. At least the people had a better chance of surviving the attack with two healers working together.

And, hopefully, others would see their kind act and be more

forgiving of mages in the future.

Twenty-Three

She walked with Master William to the medical ward while explaining what had happened in as much detail as possible. He wore a grave, dark expression as he listened to her talk about the attacks.

When they arrived, Madam Olivia greeted him with a hug. The warmth from the embrace gave Elice the impression the two hadn't seen or talked to each other in a long time. She thought this was strange, considering they both lived in the same small town, merely a few blocks away from each other. Making a mental note to find out more about their relationship at a later time, she wandered the ward.

It was late, a couple of hours past sunset now, but a few people were awake. She greeted each one, sitting with them and their families as she learned their names and those of their loved ones. Most people were from Highmore, but there were a couple from neighboring villages or towns who had come to see her ceremony.

The man with the burns on his chest that Madam Olivia had healed earlier was sitting up and speaking with a woman and a child who seemed no older than ten. The boy had tear marks along his cheeks, and he half-leaned onto his father's shoulder as he smiled up at the woman.

The man caught Elice looking and waved her over. "Your Highness," he greeted her as she came close. "It's a miracle. I can't thank you and the healer enough for all you did."

Elice shook her head, waving off the man's gratitude. "Doctor Palm and Nurse Beth have worked nonstop since the attack, too. They are doing all they can."

"But they couldn't save everyone," the woman said, reaching for her husband's hand. "Another patient died today. If it weren't for Madam Olivia, I wouldn't know what my boy and I would do."

She caught Doctor Palm's eye from across the room. It wasn't her fault she couldn't heal the injured people the same way Madam Olivia could. It's true that Madam Olivia was much needed, and so was Master William, but she couldn't discount all the doctor's and nurse's hard work.

Elice patted the woman's shoulder and gave the man a smile that didn't quite reach her eyes. "I'm so glad you're almost fully recovered. Please let any one of us know if you need anything."

They all nodded, and the little boy whispered a "thank you" under his breath as he continued to cuddle into his father.

As Elice walked away, she wondered how people had survived without healers for the past eighteen years. It was high time for things to change, and it all started with her father's proclamation that mages could use their magic. Now that she was the crown princess, she would need to ensure mages felt comfortable enough to practice their magic again without losing the non-mages' trust.

She found Madam Olivia in the back of the building, sitting in a chair as she sipped from a glass of water. Elice pulled a chair next to her. "How's everything going?"

Madam Olivia placed her drink on the side table and rolled her shoulders. "Once I finish this quick break, I can get back out there. Master William is old now, so he won't be able to stay on his feet for long. We'll alternate, with me taking the longer shifts. But I think by tomorrow night we should have all the patients healed. Doctor Palm and Nurse Beth have been relegated to ensuring the patients have everything they need to be comfortable while the Master and I work."

"I've never met a Master before." Elice tilted her head as she looked at the woman next to her. While Madam was the official term for high-level female mages, Master was a title given to their equivalent male counterparts. Full training and immense skill were required before a mage could receive either a Madam or Master title, though it had been almost eighteen years since the last mage was given that esteemed appellation.

Madam Olivia eyed Elice with pursed lips. "I might as well tell you now, otherwise you'll keep asking. He trained me, long before your father, King Edgar, banned magic. Once we couldn't use our magic anymore, we decided it would be best to avoid each other lest we be accused of using our powers. It was safer to just pretend we no longer knew each other. I hadn't seen him in years. It became that way for mages all across the kingdom."

"As soon as I said your name, he jumped out the door to come help."

Madam Olivia's eyes snapped to hers. "I thought he wouldn't even come."

Elice returned her eyes to the room, surveying the people around her. "How many other mages live in Highmore?"

"Oh, quite a few." She looked off into the distance, her eyes seeming to drift into another world.

"And have you seen any ... Fire Lords, by chance?"

Madam Olivia's eyes went wide as she looked around for listening ears. "You can't just ask that, little one."

"After the week—no, *month*—I've had, I deserve to talk about them."

The woman blew out a breath. "Then turn your voice down, lest you want others listening in on your conversations."

"Too late for that," Elice muttered, although she knew she should really follow that advice more often. "It's just, after the recent attack in the alley, I wonder if there are more of them around us than we know."

"Well, it's all just rumors," Madam Olivia began, then paused. "Mind you, now that the ban has been lifted, mages are slowly starting to relax. With that letting down of the guard comes those who mean to do harm. Like the attackers in red. I've heard they are also starting to come out of hiding, which is why they attacked. What I don't know is why they would take Princess Alice. What could they stand to gain?"

Elice turned in her chair so she faced the woman. "Princess Alice has—had something called dream sight."

Madam Olivia's eyes scanned the room. "What do you know of this cursed sight?"

"It's not really a cursed sight. She didn't start having bad visions until recently. And then, long story short, I was able to stop her visions. But maybe the Fire Lords don't know that she doesn't have them anymore."

"You took them, didn't you?" The healer looked at the center of Elice's forehead and slowly touched it. When she made contact, she jolted her hand away as if she had received an electric shock.

"I just don't know how I got them—how they transferred to me."

"It seems you might need to do some meditating and visit the mind realm to find out."

Elice nearly jumped out of her seat. "You know how to enter the mind realm? Can you teach me?"

Madam Olivia sighed. "You'll have to wait until I finish with the patients and recover. It takes a lot of energy for one to enter other realms. And with all my magic going towards healing, which I haven't done in years, it will take me a few days to fully recover."

Deflated and shoulders sagging, Elice accepted Madam Olivia's terms. It was all she could do since the woman was going out of her way to heal all these people.

⁓

The library was cold that night. Elice made sure all the windows were shut, but nothing was open that could let in the cool fall breeze. With a blanket huddled around her shoulders, she wandered the shelves, looking for anything about the mind realm or meditation.

A history book caught her attention, and she pulled it from the shelves to peruse as she continued stalking the aisles. She opened to a random page and started skimming the words, not really reading or understanding what it said.

Then she came across a word that made her stop walking.

Orser.

She backed up a few sentences to the top of the passage.

King Neo knew he must find and destroy the Blood Flower. By killing his parents, Orser was able to create a weapon so vile, so repulsive, it would grant unnatural immortality to those who consumed of it. The act of sacrificing a love spawned such a creation. However, it wasn't until King Edgar's reign that the abomination was found, and Orser was finally struck down in the place where it all began for him.

Elice reread the passage several times, and looked at the paragraphs above and below it, but it held no further information about Orser. She let out a frustrated screech. It was always the same: either there was too little information or nothing at all.

That same flower came back to taunt her. Looking back at the words again, she read them aloud. "The act of sacrificing a love ... struck down ... where it all began..."

Her heart pounded in her ears. Finding a nearby table, she leaned against it for support as she remembered Lenore's and Alice's words.

A human sacrifice.
The flower will bloom again.

He's coming back.

"No," she muttered as the book fell from her hands. Lenore had warned her. So did Alice. But how? And what did it all mean? She needed more information, but the Fates' forsaken books gave her nothing but a haunting whisper of knowledge. It wouldn't be enough—it would never be enough.

Not unless she spoke to someone who knew exactly what was going on.

With determination, Elice sat cross-legged on the floor. She closed her eyes and focused on her breathing, just like Lenore taught her.

Her mind wandered, and her breathing slowed. Any moment now, she could fall asleep. But that wasn't what she wanted to do.

She remembered the mind space she entered with Madam Verna in Talin, and she willed her mind to take her there.

The room around her slowed down until, suddenly, it all began to spin. The movement made her want to open her eyes, but she clamped them shut against the sensation.

When it finally felt like it stopped spinning, she cracked one eye open, then the other.

She saw the bright space before her and knew exactly where she was. In her mind, she stood and sprinted down the room until the light dimmed to a normal brightness.

At the other end of the space was the young Lenore she had met last time. Her braids hung over her shoulder, cascading down to her lap as she sat on a black metal chair.

Lenore sneered at her. "Are you ready this time?"

Elice stood in front of her, glowering. "Is he back? In my time."

The seer puckered her lips in thought. "Not yet."

"Then when? Please. They took Alice. I need to know how to find her."

"And you think asking about Orser will help you find your beloved sister?"

Elice held her harsh response, but her chest inflated with the air she wanted to blow out at the woman. Lenore was as infuriating as ever. "Then tell me what I need to do to find her. Please."

Young Lenore threw her braids over her shoulder and stood. "You need to find the place where it all began."

The words echoed in Elice's ears. "That's the same thing the book said. Do you know where it is? This place I'm supposed to find? Is that where they've taken Alice? Is it Orser's birthplace?"

Lenore held up a hand before Elice asked another question. "He wasn't born there. He's actually from a little spot in the Lowlands, but that's not important." She turned and walked away, beckoning for Elice to follow. "The place where it all began is important to us all. By that, I mean it's important to you, me, and Orser."

Elice hurried behind the seer. "So a place we all have in common. The castle? We've all spent time there."

Lenore shook her head. "The place you seek is saturated with darkness."

Elice groaned and grabbed the woman's shoulder to stop her from walking. "Why can't you just tell me?"

Lenore smirked. "Always so impatient. Needing answers right away."

"That's because my sister has been kidnapped," she exclaimed, losing her patience. "What if they hurt her?"

"They will not hurt her. They only mean to use her."

"For what? Some kind of crazy ritual?"

Lenore turned out of Elice's grasp and kept walking. "They plan to use her as bait."

A tightness tugged at her chest. "They really want me, don't they?"

"They know you will try to find her. I left them detailed instructions."

"Hold on." Elice grabbed the woman's shoulder again. "You told them to kidnap Alice?"

"Not explicitly. I merely told them what I saw happen."

Elice gripped her own head in frustration. "What am I even doing here? For all I know, you could be trying to lead me down the wrong path." She turned to go back the way she came.

"You know what you must do, girl. And you know where you must go—where it all began."

Lenore's voice faded as Elice walked toward the blinding light. When she couldn't take the brightness anymore, she sat in meditation and willed herself to return to her body. Her mind slowed until it started spinning. Once the spinning in her mind stopped, she opened her eyes to find herself back in the library.

Her head throbbed and her stomach rumbled. She hadn't eaten since this morning, but nothing else mattered until she found her sister.

Twenty-Four

When Elice emerged from the library, she was surprised to find two guards stationed outside waiting for her. A pang of loss hit her as she remembered her guard, Michael, had died trying to protect Alice. She had only ever given him a hard time, avoiding him and making him feel like a nuisance when he was only trying to do his job.

A tear rolled down her cheek. She needed to do better this time, if only to honor Michael's bravery and sacrifice.

The two guards nodded at her, their swords sheathed at their belts, and she recognized their faces but not their names. "Did my father assign you as my new guards?" she asked as she stood before them in the hall.

The shorter one nodded once. "Yes, Your Highness. I'm Ross, this is Brighton." His voice was gruff and taut—as if he meant business—which matched his stout frame.

Brighton adjusted his stance so his tall body stretched even higher above Elice. He had lanky arms and thin legs, but he had a layer of muscle under his brown skin. Both guards seemed to be in their mid-twenties, younger than Michael had been.

She gave them a nod and proceeded down the hall at a slow pace so they could keep up. "I'm going to stop by my mother's office before dinner."

"If I may, Princess," came a voice higher pitched than Ross's, and Elice understood this to be Brighton's. "Dinner has already been served, and the queen has already retired to her chambers."

Elice frowned, turning the other way down the hall to head toward the east wing where the rooms were. "I'll just have dinner sent to my room, then."

Now heading to her parents' room, she silently asked the Fates for help. She didn't know how to approach Julice, and she hadn't seen her since the day of the attack. Her mother must have been distraught. Elice knew she should have visited her right away, but there was so much going on she didn't stop to think about how her mother might have felt.

Two more guards flanked her parents' door, and she gave a sturdy knock, though the woman didn't answer right away. Elice knocked again, this time receiving a quiet answer to enter the room.

Ross and Brighton stood beside her mother's guards as she walked in and passed the sitting area to open the bedchamber door. Immediately, a heartbreaking sight met her eyes.

Her mother sat on the floor by the foot of the four-poster bed, her curly hair frizzy and sticking up all over. She wore a nightgown and a thick robe around it, but the robe hung off her slumped shoulders. Julice wiped at her eyes with a handkerchief, attempting to cover the traces of her tears, but Elice saw her red and puffy face, anyway.

"Oh, Mother," Elice said with a sigh as she entered. She kneeled before Julice, touching her mother's bent knee. "I'm so sorry I didn't come sooner."

Julice sniffled, then wiped at her nose. "I don't know what to do. Your father's been in the council room all this time, and you were in and out of the medical ward. But I was too scared to see you, because then I would be reminded of Alice." She lifted a hand to touch Elice's cheek. "You look so much alike."

Elice leaned into her mother's touch. "I'm here now, Mother. I'm here."

Julice closed her eyes and let out a trembling exhale. She grabbed a book that lay forgotten on the side. "I found this in your sister's room."

Elice took the book from her mother's hands, recognizing the soft brown leather cover. "Alice never let me look at it. Did you open it?"

With a nod, Julice pulled herself up from the floor and sat on the edge of her bed. "It's horrifying."

Sitting next to her, Elice snuggled into Julice's side as she slowly opened the front cover. Alice's name was scrawled on the inside, a single flower etched in pencil right below her name.

Turning the page, she found another pencil sketch. Her heart sank at the drawing of a shaded stone tunnel, the stones beautifully detailed along the walls. A shadow loomed in the corner, but Elice couldn't make out what it was.

As she turned page after page, the same tunnel system from her dreams was drawn in vivid detail. Sometimes the corner wasn't shaded in, but most times, Alice had furiously scribbled across it to create darkness. Towards the middle of the book, she saw a few doors hastily drawn inside the walls, and she remembered seeing those same doors in her dreams.

One door stood out to her. It was the only one that was partially open, and a shadow crept underneath as if it were crawling out of the room. She ran a finger along the page, touching the door and the ominous smoke. She hadn't seen that door in her visions.

Julice sighed beside her, and Elice closed the book. With a swallow, she looked at her mother, and the woman's knowing eyes stared back.

"I have something to tell you," Elice began, then segued into what happened in Talin and what had been happening to her since they came back.

Julice's eyes turned teary as she listened, and she gripped Elice's arm so hard it hurt. But Elice continued, knowing she had to get this off her chest. When she did, they sat quietly for a long time, Julice still with an iron grip on her daughter.

Then her mother stood with the book, wound her arm backward, and threw it across the room. It thudded against the door, and Elice wondered if their guards would burst in to see what was wrong. A knock on the door let her know she was right—the guards were worried.

"It's all right," her mother yelled back at them. "Just leave us."

Julice glared at the book where it lay, her hands on her hips as she panted. Fury raged all around her. Elice was too afraid to speak, let alone move.

Julice finally turned around. Elice panicked when her mother's glare met her, but then Julice's features softened. "It's all my fault," the woman whispered, then buried her face in her hands.

Elice stood, slowly making her way to where her mother stood. "You couldn't have known about this. We should have told you as soon as we returned. Alice should have told us what she had seen. I should have told you everything sooner."

Julice shook her head and uncovered her face. "I should have known one of you would have this curse. I should have warned you."

Something in her words reminded Elice of what Madam Verna had said. "You know about the cursed sight."

With her shoulders low, Julice walked to the other side of the room. "I know it very well." She opened her chest of drawers and pushed aside several folded clothes before she pulled away with something shiny in her hands. "I wore this necklace for many years when I was young. They're very common where I'm from. Every Newton born to my family wore it to protect us from the curse."

Julice walked forward and placed the necklace in Elice's hands. It looked similar to Lenore's necklace. However, this one had a gold chain with thick links and a larger clear gem at the end.

Elice knew exactly what it was as she placed it over her neck. "It's a protection stone."

"This one has been passed down for generations, to me from my mother, and hers before that. I only took it off when I moved to Norraine and married your father. By then, I knew I wasn't cursed.

I still kept it, though, even after the magic ban. Your father never knew it was imbued with magic."

"But," Elice began, her mind reeling, "what is the curse? And does our family in Newton have magic?" She wondered if there were others like her, perhaps cousins, aunts, or uncles.

"What you and your sister have is not the same curse, I'm afraid. That one is far less forgivable. You two seem to have a variation of it. Though, there are others outside of our family who possess dream sight. As you know, dream sight can come in different ways—from pleasant visions, like your sister had of you, or nightmares, like this tunnel. The cursed sight is only about death."

Elice shivered, hugging herself as she thought about having visions of death. Her mother was right—that would be worse. "So you don't have visions? What can you tell me about our people in Newton?"

Julice pulled Elice to the bed, and they sat together. "No, I wasn't blessed with magic. The cursed sight doesn't appear often, but it is something that only our line has. So, to protect ourselves against it, we all wore a necklace similar to this from birth. Then, as we get older, we find out whether or not we have it. It's been many generations since we last had someone in the family with cursed sight. And there are many mages in Newton. Magic is viewed differently where I'm from. There are whole communities full of mages, those who practice and teach others. Even the other kingdoms to the south have those strong with magical power."

"There are other kingdoms south of Newton?" Elice's eyes almost popped out of her head. She thought she knew the history of her people, but she only knew of Norraine's history.

Julice chuckled and stroked the top of Elice's head. "My dear, the world is much larger than our two kingdoms. Perhaps one day, when you are queen, you will be able to learn more about them, and you can teach that knowledge to the people of Norraine. We are so far removed from the rest of the world. Especially after your father's reign. No offense to him, but when he closed our land off against mages, it cost us dearly in terms of inter-kingdom relations."

Her mind reeled with the news. There were others just like her all throughout the world. Now it seemed Norraine was just a tiny speck of land. Inside, she was dying to visit these far-off lands. What would she learn? And who would she meet? Maybe there were other mages who could use three elements just like her—or those who could use all four. Maybe she wasn't as special as she once thought, and she was perfectly fine with that.

Her world just grew, and her trivial day-to-day events paled in comparison.

Then she thought about Alice. She needed to find her so they could talk about what she had learned. But to do that, she needed some sleep, and perhaps some food.

She looked up at her mother when her stomach grumbled. "I haven't eaten since breakfast."

Julice gave her a look, then called out to her guards. When one poked his head through the door, she asked him to send for a maid to bring something from the kitchens.

After Elice finally filled her belly, she cuddled against the pillows with her mother, wrapped in the thick woolen blankets. With her mother stroking her hair, she drifted off to sleep, and this time she didn't fear it as it overtook her.

She immediately entered a dream, but with the protection from her mother's charm, it was a calm dream. A normal dream.

Elice dreamed of a field full of tall grass, surrounded by enormous trees that blocked out the sun. She walked through it, her hands sweeping low by her sides and running through the top of the overgrown grass. Lenore's cottage stood off to the right, and weeds overran her old garden.

Something caught her attention as it shimmered in the tiny rays of light that peeked through the treetops. She squinted her eyes, trying to capture the sight again, but all she could see was a slight cloud, almost like smoke.

The hazy image blinked in and out of existence, and as she approached, it seemed to move faster. She reached a hand out, and it touched nothing but air.

With a jolt, she sat up in her mother's bed, jarring Julice awake. In a daze, Julice reached out to her. "What's wrong?" she asked, her voice groggy with sleep.

"It's nothing," Elice answered. Her breath was ragged, and it took another minute for her to steady her breathing.

When she calmed down, she lay next to her mother again, who still looked at her with concern. Before Elice fell asleep, she had already made up her mind.

And she knew where she had to go.

Twenty-Five

The sun was just beginning its ascent into the sky when she entered the metal building. Only a few soldiers were awake, but soon, the entire barracks would be alive with movement and noise, so she would have to hurry.

With her new guards in tow, she walked up to James's office door and gave a resounding knock. He opened it almost immediately, his eyes finding hers and narrowing in confusion. Before he could speak, Elice pushed against his chest until he was fully in his office, and she followed, waving at her guards and closing the door on her way.

"Is something wrong?" he asked, stepping back to give her room to pace.

She didn't answer right away while she gathered her thoughts. She had crawled out of her mother's bed just before dawn, mumbling that she needed to bathe and change. After getting ready in her room with Serena's concerned gaze on her the entire time, she rushed to James's office, her mind buzzing with what she needed to do.

"I had a dream," she finally said, though her voice sounded thick and muffled to her own ears. She cleared her throat and tried again. "I had a different kind of dream last night."

James watched her pace the floor, his arms crossed on his chest. "Are you all right?"

She paused to nod and make eye contact with him. "I was with my mother all night, and she gave me this." She pulled the necklace from underneath her loose tunic and recounted what she learned about her mother's history.

"So there might be others like you," James said once she finished.

"Who knows what kinds of mages exist outside of our little kingdom? But that's not the only thing I wanted to talk to you about. It's about Alice."

James lowered his eyes, finally taking in her loose pants and hiking boots. "What are you planning?"

"Just hear me out first," she implored, reaching out to grab his forearms. "I know where Alice is. At least, I think I do."

"Whatever it is you're thinking, no. Your father already said he doesn't want you leaving the castle."

"And I've already told him I'm no prisoner. Not anymore." She placed her hands on her hips and lifted her jaw. "I came to you first because I trust you the most. But if you won't help me, I'll go by myself."

James's eyes softened, and his arms slumped to his sides. "Of course I'll help you. I just don't want you to get hurt. Your father doesn't want you to get hurt, either."

Elice shook her head. "I'm stronger than he gives me credit for."

"I'm sure he knows that. I think he's just afraid of losing you again."

She turned her head away, staring off at the wall above his couch. "I'm the only one who can find her. He's too afraid to see that, and because of his fear, he's unwilling to do what it takes to get her back."

"And I'm afraid I won't like this plan."

When she met his eyes, she could sense his apprehension. There was little she could do to make him feel better about this. "We need a mage to enter the mind realm. I think that's where they've taken her. The tunnel I keep dreaming about—I think the dreams kept trying to tell me where I need to go."

He stepped closer and held her hands. "How do you know that? What if it's a trap? Every time you've entered that space, you've had a bad experience."

"Not every time. I meditated last night. I was able to come and go with no issues. All I have to do is have a clear mind."

James bit his lower lip. "I don't like it."

"You don't have to like it. You just need to trust me. Lenore told me I have to find a place that is connected to me, her, and Orser."

"So we're actually trusting Lenore?" He closed his eyes and shook his head.

She ignored his interruption. "And last night I had a dream about the field where I grew up. That can't be a coincidence."

"It sounds more like a trap to me."

She turned around, facing the door and crossing her arms. "You don't get it, James. In my dream, there was something..." She trailed off, not knowing how to explain what she saw.

James came up behind her and wrapped his arms around her shoulders, squeezing her into a hug. "I'm sorry. You're right, I don't get it. So why don't you help me understand?"

"That's what I've been trying to do." She turned around in his embrace and stared straight into his eyes. "What happened to your open mind?"

He brought a hand to cup her cheek. "When I first saw you in the medical ward, the only thing I could think about was keeping you safe. I can't keep seeing you like that. It hurts knowing there's nothing I can do to keep you safe from those fire mages."

Elice leaned into his touch, splaying her hands on his chest. "Maybe I'm supposed to be the one to protect you. To protect everyone."

He chuckled and kissed the top of her head. "I'm starting to believe that more each day."

"So you'll help me?" She titled her head up to catch his eyes.

"Always," he whispered before leaning forward.

Her eyes closed involuntarily, and she leaned in closer. She felt the moment he connected their lips. The softness of his lips against hers made her sigh, and she melted against him. The warmth she felt the first time they kissed crept up her cheeks.

He pulled away with a smile, his hand still caressing her face. "What do you need me to do?"

She met his smile. "First, we need some supplies. And ... we also need to recruit some more help."

His smile faltered a bit. "Who else do we need?"

≈

Andre lifted his head from his pillow and looked at them as if they had grown two heads each.

James sighed and leaned against the door, his hands in his pockets. "I told you this was a bad idea."

Elice threw him a quick glare before returning her attention to Andre. "Come on, Dre. You owe me."

"I saved your life. My debt is paid." He yawned and went back to his bed, throwing the blanket above his head.

Elice stomped toward him and ripped the cover off. "Then what about Alice? Don't you want to help her, or does she really mean nothing to you?"

He groaned, trying to grab the blanket from her, but she threw it to the floor on the opposite side of the room. "Can you stop yelling? I have a hangover."

James blew out a breath of frustration. "Let's go, Elice. He's obviously not worth our time."

Andre sat up in his bed. "Excuse me?"

"Are you serious?" Elice yelled. "You'd rather fight James for telling the truth than find your best friend?"

He turned his glare on her. "So you think I'm worthless, too?"

Elice rolled her eyes. "Why are you being like this?"

Andre grumbled something under his breath before standing up and walking to his dresser. "I'm going to be late for training."

With pursed lips, Elice stared at him for a moment longer before she turned her head. "You know, I thought you were my friend, too. I guess I was wrong."

A tightness clamped her throat, and when she caught James's gaze, he nodded at her and opened the door. They walked out without saying another word. When they stepped out into the hallway, he pulled her into a hug. He didn't say anything, and she didn't really want him to. She knew the situation was awkward, but she didn't have many friends. Losing the first friend she had made hurt more than she could describe.

She pulled out of his hug and forced a smile. "We might need to expand our recruitment a bit."

"Who else do you have in mind?" James held her hand and together they walked back to his office.

Elice looked over her shoulder and motioned to her two guards. "They're supposed to follow me everywhere, anyway."

James followed her line of sight. "Ross and Brighton are loyal and trustworthy. We can talk to them. I can think of a couple more soldiers, if you think we need to add anyone else."

She nodded. We might need all the help we can get.

When they returned to his office, they invited Ross and Brighton inside to discuss their plan. At first, they stared wide-eyed at her as she explained what they needed to do. Ross's hands were balled into fists and he looked like he might walk out of the room, but when Brighton nodded along with what Elice said, Ross's expression lightened. Though he still wore a slight scowl, which Elice began to think was his resting face.

"So," she said at the end of her long explanation, "are you in? Can we trust you to help us?"

Ross cut Brighton a sideways glance, and when Brighton nodded once more, Ross turned to face Elice with a tilt of his head. "We're in, Your Highness. We'll make sure nothing happens to you when you're in the … mind space place, whatever you called it."

Brighton grinned at her. Then he sobered his face and straightened his back. Elice couldn't help the smile that found its way onto her face as she looked at her new guards.

After they finalized their plan, the guards posted themselves outside of James's office while the captain went in search of the two soldiers he thought would be a good fit for their mission. Elice continued to pace the room, running the mission over and over in her mind until James returned.

He walked through the door with two soldiers she had seen around the barracks. Her guards followed behind and closed the door. The first soldier was a heavily built man with a burly mustache and a completely shaved head. James introduced him as Trey, and the man bowed with his hands over his heart. The next soldier was a petite woman with strong legs and a firm layer of muscles in her arms.

"And this is Victoria," James said, waving a hand toward her.

She frowned, her jaw clenched as she gave a bow of respect. "But please, Your Highness, call me Vic. No one calls me Victoria."

"Not unless you want to get pummeled," Trey cut in, earning him a punch in the arm from Vic.

Elice looked around at the group gathered before her as her heart raced. The compound would now be busy as soldiers hurried around, and the castle would likewise be occupied. It would be difficult to walk out the front gates, especially after her last escape with Andre, so they needed to get that last piece of the plan sorted before they could leave.

As if reading her mind, Vic stepped forward. "Captain Taylor said we need a way out of the castle grounds. I may be of some help with that part of whatever plan this is."

Since it seemed as if James hadn't yet explained the mission to the newest additions, she and James took turns filling them in while Ross and Brighton listened in again.

"I can't believe we're part of this secret mission," Vic said, smiling and pounding one of her fists into her other hand.

"Don't get too excited there," Ross said, leveling the other soldiers with his stare. He was the oldest of the group and would help them all keep a level head. "The king could very well punish us once we return."

"Not if we return with the princess—both of them—safe and sound," Brighton said cheerfully, and Vic punched him on the arm. He winced but matched her grin.

"Exactly. We'll probably get promotions." Vic seemed to only see the bright side of everything.

Elice eyed them carefully. "Let's not think about what's going to happen afterward. We need to focus on the mission and our main objective. Brighton is right. Alice is our priority."

"You too, my princess," James said, touching the small of her back. "We need to keep you safe when you enter the mind realm."

"You can count on us," Trey's deep voice came, and the rest of the group nodded along with him.

A knock on James's office door drew everyone's attention, and they all froze, looking around at each other. James hastened to the door, opening it just a crack.

"Oh, you've got to be kidding me," James said, his voice a whisper, but Elice could hear the disbelief in it. She tried to look over his shoulder to see who was at the door. James opened it just enough to pull the person all the way inside, then slammed it shut.

Andre stood there in his uniform, his cap hanging sideways on his head like it always was. He gave the room a thin smile and a wave before he looked at Elice. She narrowed her eyes at him, the glare cutting across the room.

"So, what's the plan?" he said lamely.

Elice didn't want to answer him. She didn't even want to look at him. But, the truth was, she wanted him to be there. With his head on straight, he was a good friend, and he knew the Jani Forest better than Elice did.

A heavy sigh left her mouth. "What made you change your mind?"

Andre shuffled his feet. "You were right, I guess. James too. Alice has always been there for me, so I need to be there for her."

The others looked back and forth between Andre and Elice, no doubt aware of the rumors and the tension in the room. Her father never had the chance to announce her courtship to James, and people were still unaware of their relationship. But, in that moment, nothing else mattered, as long as she found her sister.

Elice nodded and told Andre the plan, the others adding in pieces she forgot to say. Once everyone finally knew what to do, had grabbed one of the packs filled with supplies for the hike through the forest, and were armed with a sword and shield, they set out to begin their mission.

Twenty-Six

Elice quickly realized Vic was not someone to mess with. They all marched as one to the eastern tower, the one Elice used to sneak out, and faced off against the newest guard. He was a much younger man than the previous guard who always fell asleep, and he was now in charge of the night shift. Since it was just after dawn, he would soon be relieved, so Vic warned them to hurry before he left and she couldn't use her leverage.

Standing by the station in front of the gate was the guard, and his eyes nearly popped out of his head when he saw them approach. He looked at Elice, then at all of her companions, before finally resting on Vic. He gave an involuntary shudder as Vic stepped out in front of the group, her hands on her hips and her legs spread wide to create an imposing stance.

"We need passage through this gate, Jeremy," Vic said, her voice firm and demanding.

Jeremy swallowed and folded his hands in front of his body, then fidgeted with his interlaced fingers. "There's actually a protocol—"

Vic took a few steps forward until he cowered away, bumping into the metal grates behind him. "I'm sorry. What were you saying?"

The poor guard gulped again and shook his head. "I mean, I guess as long as the Crown Princess says it's okay…"

Vic sneered at him. "Thought so. If you would be so kind…" She motioned toward the gate, and Jeremy fumbled with the metal latch.

The gate swung, and the group filed through. Elice patted Jeremy on his shoulder as she passed him, hoping he understood she meant him no harm. When Vic finally walked through, Elice caught her celebratory grin and couldn't help but smile back.

"Do I want to know why he's afraid of you?" Elice asked as Vic came to a stop beside her.

Vic merely shrugged, but Andre answered for her. "Everyone knows she's the strongest out of all of us. She looks small, but we don't underestimate her power. She's a fireball."

Vic nudged Elice's side. "Kind of like you, Your Highness."

Elice smiled at the woman beside her. If only people were as afraid of her as they were of Vic, maybe she wouldn't have to sneak out of the castle every few weeks to get things done.

"All right," James said, interrupting her thoughts. "Let's get going. We can be at the cottage in less than two hours if we plow straight through, and most of us are experienced hikers, so it shouldn't be hard. My princess, please let us know whenever you need a rest." James looked right at her.

Elice shook her head. "I'll be fine. Let's hurry."

They began their trek, and Elice was not surprised to find the soldiers made easy work of their brisk walk through the forest. After only thirty minutes of fast-walking to keep up, she was begging for a quick stop to drink some water and to eat from the rations they had brought with them. They all took a few sips from their canteens and ate a bit of food, since no one had any breakfast.

"So," Brighton said in between bites, "how long will you need to be in that mind space?"

Elice swallowed a mouthful of water. "I have no idea. Every time I enter the mind realm, time flows differently in the real world. Once, it felt like I spent hours there, but only a second had passed."

Vic tilted her head. "So, all we have to do is blink and you'll be back with Princess Alice?"

Elice shrugged her shoulders. "I'm not so sure it will be that easy. Honestly, I don't even know what we'll find once we get to the cottage. I just know I saw something in my dream vision, and I think the only way to find it is to enter the other plane."

"By the Fates," Ross muttered under his breath. "You're talking about other realms as if it's normal."

"For a mage, it is normal," James said, finishing the last of his food.

After cleaning up their mess and stowing their water containers in their packs, they resumed their walk. Elice felt more energized this time around now that she had food and water in her stomach, and she was able to push through with only one more break.

Though the sun was up, a frigid blast of air kept beating down their backs. Elice was grateful she wore a thick cloak, and she was sure the others were thankful for theirs as well.

Finally, after almost two hours, Andre pointed out the break in the path that led to her old cottage. They stepped through the thick brush, the sound of crunching leaves beneath their boots the only thing they could hear.

Entering the clearing, Elice took in the familiar sight of her cottage nestled in the middle of the tall trees. Her heart clenched as she instantly remembered all the times she ran through this field, hiding from Lenore so she could practice magic.

She steeled herself and continued walking, leading the way until she stood in the middle of the open field where she saw herself in the vision. Twirling, she tried to squint to find the same haze as in her dream, but she couldn't see anything different.

"What now?" Andre asked, watching her closely.

Elice stopped spinning to face the group. "Now, I meditate. You should all form a circle around me, but please don't touch me and don't try to wake me, no matter how long I'm in the mind realm."

James shook his head, his eyes burning into hers. "No way. If something happens or if you're in there too long, I'm going to bring you back."

"I'm not leaving there until I either find Alice or find out where they're keeping her."

Andre rolled his eyes. "You know there's no use arguing with her."

James ignored him and reached for her hands, holding them tight in his grip. "It feels like I'm always asking you to come back to me."

Elice smiled, remembering his words the last time she made a trip into this forest. It felt like such a long time ago, and she never thought she would ever set foot here again. Yet here she was, with a new, more urgent mission. She closed the distance between them, placing a quick, gentle kiss on his lips, knowing this time he would understand the intentions behind her actions. He leaned into her, but she pulled back and squeezed his hand before pulling away completely.

She sat on the floor, crossing her legs in front of her and trying not to shiver. She didn't know if she was cold or nervous, but her body seemed to shake on its own. Before she closed her eyes, she looked around as everyone got into place around her. James held her eye until she shut them.

Okay, deep breaths, she told herself, and intentionally slowed her breathing. It was a lot easier to calm her mind out in nature rather than in the library or in Madam Verna's shop. The wind slowed, making the tall grass stop swaying against her legs.

Then, when she sucked in a slow inhale, she felt the familiar spin in her mind. She entered the mind realm, in the same bright space as before. Running, she took off toward the dimmer light, and found the young Lenore in the same spot as before.

"Well, look at you," Lenore said, smiling. "I didn't think you'd figure it out, yet here you are."

Elice walked until she stood just a few feet away. "I'm here now, so what do I do next?"

Lenore clicked her tongue and brushed her thick braids back over her shoulder. "That's not how this works and you know it."

Groaning, Elice covered her forehead with her hand, trying not to lose her patience. "You're going to tell me some kind of riddle I need to figure out, aren't you?"

Lenore only smiled. "It's much more fun this way."

"For who?" Elice yelled, then sucked in a calming breath. "In case you forgot, because time works differently here, Alice is still missing."

"I'm well aware of the happenings in the mortal realm."

"Then you know I need to find her before it's too late. I had a dream—"

"You mean a vision," Lenore interrupted, raising a finger in the air.

Elice waved her off. "And I think this is the place where it all began. The place that connects me to you and Orser."

Lenore looked around as if she could see where Elice stood in the mortal realm. "You're right."

"But there's nothing here. In my dream—*vision*—I saw a haze or something, but there's nothing there."

"That's because, while you're in the right location in the mortal realm, you need to go to the spirit realm. Or, more precisely, the tomb of lost souls."

Elice nodded. Finally, she was getting straight answers from this woman. "All right, so how do I get to the spirit realm?"

"You need to access your inner spirit."

Elice held back the eye roll she so desperately wanted to give. "And ... how do I do that?"

Lenore pursed her lips. "You already know the answer to that, girl."

Throwing her hands up, Elice lost all patience. "No, I don't. Otherwise I wouldn't be here."

"You need to leave the mind realm before you can enter the spirit realm. It requires deep meditation. I've already taught you this." Lenore quirked an eyebrow at her.

"Obviously I forgot."

Young Lenore shook her head and took a few steps away, gazing off into the empty space. "You'll need to meditate on your spirit. Access that part of you that only exists to serve the Fates. They will call to you, and when they do, you'll feel it."

"But how long will that take?"

Lenore shrugged a shoulder. "Who knows? It might depend on the Fates, and whether you're in their favor or not."

Once again, none of what Lenore said made sense to Elice. She turned to leave, knowing she wouldn't get anything else out of the woman.

Hurrying toward the blinding light, she thought about what Lenore tried to teach her all throughout her childhood. When she sat down again, she remembered a prayer Lenore used to say.

Let the guiding light lead you home.

As the room around her spun, she repeated the mantra in her head. Over and over again, the words played in her mind, until she felt a strange pull inside her heart.

She almost opened her eyes, but the spinning would only make her dizzy if she were to look. Instead, she focused on that pull, letting it guide her.

Her body jerked forward and her arms splayed out in front of her. She felt as if she were flying through the air, her long hair billowing behind her. Then, just as suddenly, she stopped. Her hair stopped blowing and her arms relaxed at her sides.

Elice squinted one eye open, then the other, and she found herself back in the forest, sitting cross-legged on the ground and surrounded by the group of soldiers.

Disappointment made her shoulders sag, and she let out a sigh before standing up. "I guess it didn't work," she mumbled. She dusted off the dirt from the bottom of her pants, looking around at the group.

They hadn't made a move to acknowledge her, so she spoke up. "I'm sorry I wasted everyone's time. Let's get back to the castle before I get you all into trouble."

She took a step toward James, and when he made no movement or sound, she realized something was wrong.

Elice touched his shoulder, but instead of making contact, her hand went through his body. She shrieked, but the sound rang hollow. She looked at Ross, who stood beside James, and his face seemed frozen in time. All around her, the soldiers were completely still.

Stepping out of the circle and careful not to touch anyone, she stood in front of James and took in his face. He was frozen mid blink, his beautiful dark eyes almost fully closed. As she leaned in closer, she noticed his arm was stuck in an awkward position, almost like it was on its way down, close to his side but hovering above his hip.

"Weird," she whispered, and once again, her voice sounded hollow. She turned to take in her surroundings when her breath caught in her throat.

Several feet away, in the middle of the field, stood a curved wooden door. It hovered there, with no building or walls on either side that it could attach to.

A strange haze surrounded it, and a light smoky shadow emitted from beneath the frame.

With shaking legs, she stepped up to the door and gave a knock on its hard surface.

Twenty-Seven

The echo of the knock reverberated in the empty field, and Elice sucked in a deep breath.

This must be the spirit realm, she thought. And this must be the entrance to that tomb I need to visit.

There was a reason her visions led her here, and she must have high favor from the Fates, because she didn't need to meditate long at all. So, either she was being set up in some sort of trap, or the Fates were guiding her on the right path.

Or it could be a little of both, she mused, then wiped the smile from her face.

After another breath, Elice realized no one was going to answer the door. Testing her luck, she gripped one of the metal rings hanging in the middle of the door and gave a slight push, but the wood didn't budge. Next, she tried to pull, and this time, one side of the door moved.

Gasping, she almost lost her balance as the bottom of the door bumped into her boot. She stepped to the side and continued to pull on the handle. The door groaned as it opened, and the gray smoke rolled out of the opening, covering the tops of her shoes.

It was dark inside the doorway, but the bit of light coming from her side of the door helped her see the first step. She placed one boot on the step, sinking down into the staircase.

In the back of her mind, she feared what she'd find at the bottom of the stairs. Pushing through her fear, she took another step down, then another, until she was fully immersed in darkness.

The air was suffocating, and she had to take measured breaths to make sure she was getting enough air into her lungs. It felt thick going in, a cold dampness that stuck to the insides of her nose and throat.

After a few minutes of walking, she realized she should have counted how many steps she had taken, but she was too far down now to return to the top.

Another minute passed, and she wondered whether this staircase would even end. She took another step, but her foot landed much sooner than she anticipated. Extending her foot forward, she slid it across the ground. Finally, she made it to the bottom.

A single torch stood affixed to the wall in front of her, but it was so dim she could hardly see anything else around her. One hesitant step and then another, she inched her way toward the torch. It illuminated the wall directly behind it. The wet stone glistened with water that slid down its surface ever so slowly.

Her heart sank in her belly, and she was drawn to look at her feet. Just as she suspected, she stood in a puddle of water. The thumping of her heart was loud in her ears.

She knew this place. She'd seen it so many times over the last couple of weeks. Looking down the tunnel, she envisioned herself running endlessly toward a light she would never reach.

Her throat tightened as she realized she was now inside her dream, living out the nightmare that had haunted her and her sister.

Closing her eyes, she waited for the maniacal laughter that always stuck to the back of her mind, but it never came.

Elice swallowed against the thick, heavy feeling in her throat and took the first step forward. Unlike her visions, she wouldn't run down the tunnel, crying her eyes out and begging to be saved.

No. She would walk calmly, even though her body continued to shake, and find the end of this Fates' forsaken place.

When she reached the first door, she pulled on the metal ring, but it wouldn't move, nor would it push open. At the next door, she found it was also closed, or perhaps locked. Door after door, she tried and failed to open it. After nearly half an hour of walking, she found a door that would open.

She was shocked that it creaked, giving way under her light push. Opening it all the way, she splashed her way inside, hoping she would find something of use here—at least a lantern she could carry with her.

Her eyes had mostly adjusted to the darkness, but she couldn't see more than a foot in front of her. With the tip of her boot, she accidentally kicked something solid, and she pulled back, ready to run the other way.

Whatever it was she ran into didn't move, but the way the dark hair floated in the inch of water made Elice pause. She stared at it, then the realization that it was a person hit her in the face. She bent down and turned the body from its side to its back, finding her sister's face staring back at her.

"Alice," she shrieked, the sound bouncing off the wet stone walls. "Oh my Fates, it's you!"

Her sister didn't move, and her eyes were closed. Touching Alice's cold cheeks, she gave her a little shake to stir her awake, but the girl continued to lie on the floor, motionless.

"By the Fates," Elice whispered, then slowly held her fingers against the side of Alice's throat. Feeling a faint pulse, she let out the breath she had been holding. "All right. Okay. Alice, I'm going to carry you out of here. I'll try not to drop you. But if you could wake up and walk out on your own, that would be great."

Elice looked down at her sister's dead weight and wondered if she'd be able to walk all the way back down the tunnel and up that long staircase. She placed her arms under Alice's shoulders and tried to lift, but she could only get her sister's upper body off the floor.

After gently resting her back on the floor, she went around and attempted to cradle Alice in her arms. Breathing through the exertion on her body, she was unable to stand while lifting her this way. She returned Alice to her spot on the wet floor, panting and trying to think of another way to get her out of there.

"Maybe there's something I can find to carry you, or at least drag you on." Elice looked around for a rope or cloth, but remembered there was nothing in the room with her. "I'll be right back. I'm just going to check another door."

Elice stood and hurried out the door, coming up to the next one, but it was also locked. She tried two more before she leaned her head against the wall. Water streamed down her face, and she closed her eyes. Resigning herself to carry her sister over her shoulder, she pushed off the wall.

A wet splashing sound came from behind her, and she spun around. Another splash, this time coming from further down. She followed the sound and saw an open door just in front of her.

Yanking to a stop, she eyed the door, waiting for someone to exit. After a few breaths, no one came into view, so she walked up to it. Light streamed through the open doorway, and as she came to stand in front of it, she was met with a room full of red cloaks.

She froze, hoping they wouldn't see her, but the one on the opposite side of the room faced her, and the head of the cloak titled sideways. The rest of the hoods turned toward her from their place in the circle. Wanting to turn and run was the first thought she had, but she couldn't abandon her sister. She would have to face off against these mages, but she didn't know if her powers worked in the spirit realm.

The circle parted, and Elice saw a ghostly black figure floating midair in the middle of the circle. The smoky form looked almost human, but the sides spiraled away from the center of the body. She didn't know if this was a spirit, but she could feel the energy it gave off, almost like a heated glow.

And it seemed to look straight at her.

"Finally," a voice said, the noise sounding thick and muffled, "I have the pleasure of seeing you face to face."

Elice knew the voice came from the shadow in the middle of the room. She stared at it, but her eyes cut back and forth at the fire mages in their red cloaks, and she waited for them to attack. "I'd say the same, if I could see your face."

An indignant huff resounded in the air, almost like a laugh. "Ah, but you know who I am, don't you?"

She forced a smile, holding back the shiver that wanted to run down her spine. "Not a clue. But I think you should be using past tense, right? I mean, we are in the spirit realm, so whoever you are, you must be dead."

Another laugh, this time high pitched, and another shiver rolled down her back and arms. "My dear, I have your father to thank for my current predicament—as well as your guardian, for betraying me."

Her heart stopped beating for a moment. "No," she muttered. "It can't be."

The figure moved forward, gliding through the air. "Oh, but it is. You see, when Edgar stabbed me through the heart with his mortal sword, my body died. But my soul... It was full of life, of revenge. The Blood Flower not only fed my body, but my spirit, so I was sent here, to the place where lost souls roam, awaiting the time when my soul could be reunited with my body. And thanks to you, that time has now arrived."

She shook her head at his words. "I don't know what you're talking about. I didn't—*wouldn't*—do anything to help you."

"But you did, my dear. All because of your worthy sacrifice."

Familiar words echoed in her mind. A human sacrifice. The flower will bloom again.

"Lenore," Elice muttered. "I killed Lenore in the field. Is that where the Blood Flower blooms? Is that where it bloomed before?"

The shadow merely shifted, flowing with the nonexistent breeze.

Elice took a step forward. "Who are you, really? Tell me your name."

"Ah, yes, we haven't been properly introduced." A thin part of the spirit moved toward the center of the mass, and the top part bowed. "My name is Orser, and I will soon be the king of Norraine."

A fire grew in her chest, and she wished she could let it out like the mages across from her. "That's funny, because my name is Elice, and I will be the queen."

"My dear," the figure said, then moved forward, "how will you be queen if you're dead?"

The fire mages seemed to shift all at once, taking a step toward her. Elice lifted a hand and tested her magic, but nothing came to her. Cursing, she did the only thing she could do.

She pulled the door shut and ran toward Alice's door, the water kicking up around her feet as she moved. Kneeling beside her sister, Elice shook Alice's shoulders, but the girl still wouldn't wake. With a groan, she lifted Alice by the arms and adjusted Alice's upper body behind her back and over her shoulder.

Taking a steadying breath, Elice pushed herself up, dragging Alice up with her. She couldn't hear any splashes running toward her, so she tromped toward the door and down the hallway that led to the stairs. Her body threatened to collapse under the weight of her sister's body, but adrenaline pulsed through her veins and gave her the extra strength she needed.

Every few minutes, she strained her ears to listen for the sounds of approaching footsteps, but none came. She didn't want to think of how strange it was they didn't chase after her. Maybe all those mages were spirits as well, and they couldn't leave.

It felt as if she had been walking for almost an hour, and when she approached the torch by the foot of the staircase, she leaned against the wall to catch her breath. "It's all right, Alice," she said aloud. "We're almost out of here. I'll get you home safely."

Closing her eyes, Elice willed herself to push against the wall with her arm and continue walking. The first step hurt, and her leg almost gave out. She pressed her shoulder on the wall and slid her other foot up to the next step, sliding her body against the stone enclosure. For several minutes, she climbed the staircase in that manner, half hanging on the wall, begging her legs to move.

Finally, after almost fifteen minutes, she saw the light from the open doorway. That gave her the last drop of motivation, and she pushed past the discomfort in her body to make it to the top.

Elice fell through the doorway, almost dropping Alice as she landed hard on her knees. Her breath came out ragged, and she struggled to suck in air. She could see the group of soldiers in front of her now, still frozen in time. Crawling on her knees with her sister's legs dragging on the floor, she made it the rest of the way, not caring this time around if she went straight through someone else's body.

She lowered Alice to the ground before sitting next to her. "How do we get back?" she asked out loud. She brought her gaze up to James's back, remembering how much he wanted her to return to him.

Straightening her back, she crossed her legs again and tried to find her breath. With her sister's limp hand in hers, she focused on finding the light, hoping it would guide her back home.

Twenty-Eight

The bright light hurt even from behind her eyelids. Elice fought against the curiosity urging her to open her eyes, knowing the brightness would likely blind her.

"Let the guiding light lead you home," she said under her breath, repeating the phrase so many times she lost count.

Then she felt the spinning, and she knew she was on her way. She waited for the dizzying spin to stop, and when it did, sound finally returned—a few chirping birds, the wind howling in her ears, and even the shuffling of feet.

Opening her eyes, she saw her companions encircling her, their backs turned. She looked down and saw her sister there, still slumped on the floor. "Alice," she yelled, then reached over to check her pulse again.

The soldiers all closed in on her, kneeling beside her with their eyes wide.

"You found her," James said.

"How did she get here?" came Andre's voice.

"She wasn't there a second ago," said Ross's gruff voice.

Feeling a pulse, Elice patted Alice's cheek, and her twin scrunched her face. "Ow," Alice muttered, finally opening her eyes. "Why did you hit me?"

Elice laughed as tears ran down her cheeks. She pulled her sister into a hug, and when she pulled away, Alice looked at her with furrowed brows. "Why are you crying?" Looking around, Alice took in the group of soldiers and the surrounding field. "What's going on? Why are we in the forest?"

Elice wanted to explain everything to her, but before she could, the sound of crunching leaves made her look up.

Sliding out from the cover of the trees, a few red cloaks emerged onto the field. Elice counted six of them, all with their hoods up. As soon as her companions turned to look, the fire mages lowered their hoods.

A familiar scarred face stood in the middle of the pack, and Red Cloud stepped forward. On cue, the king's soldiers unsheathed their swords and lifted their shields, forming a barrier in front of the twins.

They were equal in number—six mages versus six soldiers—but her group couldn't hold up to the strength of Red Cloud and the other fire mages. Not without her fighting alongside them. She pushed herself up, but her legs gave out on her, and she fell to her hands and knees.

James came to block her, standing directly in front. "Stay down, my princess," he said, his tone low and quiet. "You're in no position to stand."

"I have to," Elice mumbled, attempting to stand again. This time, she stayed upright, but her body swayed from the exertion she had put on it while carrying her sister out of the tomb. "You can't fight them on your own."

Vic stepped to the side and guarded Alice, her sword swinging in the air. "Just watch us, Your Highness. We got this."

The Fire Lords stopped once they were in close range, forming a semicircle with Red Cloud and another man Elice didn't recognize taking point in the middle. They readied their hands, bringing them to the sides of their bodies with their palms facing forward. Flames engulfed their entire forearms, licking their skin without causing any harm.

An icy wind blew all around, and a dark shadow crept along the ground from the middle of the field, heading toward the cottage. Elice hadn't noticed the shadow before, but the way it slinked across the floor made her shiver with awareness. Without warning her companions, she took off after it just as the mages began their attack.

Fire flew all around, and she dodged the few stray balls of flame as she ran.

"Elice!" James yelled, but she didn't turn to look. She knew what that shadow was, and she had a hunch about what it was going after.

As she approached the cottage, the front door stood slightly ajar. It swung lightly with the breeze, making a creaking sound. She never closed it after she left the cottage and found Alice and Andre out in the field, tied and gagged by Lenore and her fire mage minion, Freddy. It remained open all these months later, ominously waving at her as if welcoming her back home.

She came to a stop near the spot where it happened—where Lenore's lifeless body had lain on the floor, the knife she had threatened Alice with sticking out of her chest.

In the same spot, a single flower grew. One stem sprouted from the ground, thorns dotting the green surface of the stem. On top, a blood-red bud lay waiting to bloom.

And the shadow was heading straight for it.

With as much strength as she could muster, Elice gathered air in her palms and threw it toward the shadow. It moved straight through the figure and past the grass, blowing with her wind, causing the flower to shake on its thick stem.

The shadow reached the Blood Flower, swirling around the stem. As soon as it touched it, the shadow began to solidify. It rose in the air, completely engulfing the flower. The figure grew taller, taking the same form it had in the tomb.

She watched in horror as Orser continued to materialize in front of her. But once the shadowy figure reached its full height, it stepped away from the flower, its wispy legs gliding above the ground.

"You need your body," she whispered, just loud enough for Orser to hear over the sounds of shouts and fighting behind her. "You can't fully come back unless you have your body."

"Clever girl," Orser's shadowy self responded, the head portion titling to the side. "I merely needed a ride out of the Tomb of Souls, and thanks to you and your sister, I made it safely. You have my gratitude."

She clenched her jaw, her hands fisted beside her. "You possessed my sister. And I just carried you out."

He laughed, three short chuckles making his form shake with the motion. "It wasn't really a possession, since she wasn't awake. I just accompanied her soul, and you were unaware of my presence in your race to escape."

Now she knew the reason the fire mages didn't chase after her. This was their plan all along. They lured her there by kidnapping Alice, knowing Elice would come to save her. "But you're still just a shadow, a ghost. You can't do anything without your body."

"Which is why my lords will dig it out of the grave and finally reunite my soul with it. All we need is the Blood Flower—which, again, I should thank you for. Without you, none of this would have happened."

He was messing with her on purpose, and she could see the hint of a curl, like a smile, on his ghostly face. It infuriated her, lighting a fire in her belly.

She crossed one foot over the other, stepping to the side like she had seen James do so many times in their training sessions. "You're wrong, Orser. I haven't done anything. At least, not yet."

His head titled again as he ghosted closer toward her, following her arch. "Whatever it is you're planning, it won't work. Your wind will go right through me. Your water won't even wet me. And your earth won't touch me. As I am, I might be close to invincible. But once I get my body back, my powers back, I will be unstoppable once more."

Elice continued her sideways progression until she stood closer to the flower, and Orser was well away from it. "Maybe I should be the one thanking you."

He huffed, the sound coming out like a breathy laugh. "And why would you do that?"

"You've told me exactly what I need to do in order to defeat you." She gave a bow, her hand placed gently over her heart. "So, thank you, Orser. Without you, I wouldn't be able to send you right back to where you came from."

Before he had a chance to rebut, she turned toward the flower. She stood directly in front of it now, and with the last dregs of energy in her body, she poured her powers out. Air, water, and earth mixed in her hands before it flew forward, knocking the entire bud from its stem, and the deep red began to fade.

But she didn't stop once it fell off. Tiny bits of rock flew straight into the petals, slicing it to pieces, and the air and water pummeled it into the muddy ground.

"No!" Orser screamed, and his spirit form flew past her, right through her to get to the last bits of the flower.

Only pieces remained, but once it was removed from the stem, it had lost all of its vibrancy. Bits of the flower petals sat lifeless in a pile of mud. Orser's thin arms reached down, but it couldn't grasp them in its ghostly hands.

Elice fell to her knees, looking up at the scene before her. Now that she faced the fighting, she could see the fire mages and her soldiers—and Alice hiding in the middle of her friends. Fireballs flew everywhere, and the soldiers were doing their best to deflect them with their shields. Cloaks were half burned off, and a few of the soldiers had scorch marks along their exposed brown skin.

She had to end this before anyone got seriously injured. If Red

Cloud decided to use his special exploding attack, it would be all over for them.

Behind her, Orser groaned, the sound reaching her chest. He flew past her toward the mages, screaming as he went. The fire mages stopped their attack as he met them, and they knew something had gone wrong. They turned their faces toward her—wide and confused gazes met her triumphant one.

Elice stood on one leg, then pushed herself all the way to stand as straight as she could. "It's over," she yelled, pointing a finger at the mess of the Blood Flower that lay beside her. "You lost. The flower's destroyed, and he is never coming back. If you know what's good for you, you'll either turn yourselves over to my soldiers, and you will stand trial for your crimes against the kingdom, or you will run away and never think about facing me again."

James smiled at her before he turned his sword on the mages, the other soldiers following his lead. "You heard her. Now bow before your crown princess or run like cowards. She'll only give you this one chance."

Red Cloud puffed out his chest, his eyes flaming and his head shaking. "I'll never bow to the likes of her, and I'm not a coward."

"Fight, you fools," came Orser's threatening voice, the sound gravelly and hoarse from his screams. "End them now, and we will find another way to bring me back."

Elice shook her head, not understanding how these mages could follow someone like Orser. She stretched her arms and rolled her shoulders, asking the Fates to give her enough energy for what she needed to do. Closing her eyes, she tried to slow her breathing, finding each breath rough and hollow. Even though she was exhausted and weak, she entered the mind realm quickly, the spinning coming to an abrupt stop almost as soon as it started.

The light poured through her lids, and she opened them, absorbing as much energy from it as she could. She stood in the light for several minutes, breathing deeply and focusing her mind. It was the only thing she could think of, and it might not even work. All she knew was she needed to replenish her energy somehow, because her body was spent. If she could let her mind rest in this realm, perhaps she could go back with enough magic to form one last attack.

"You really are clever." Young Lenore's voice met her ears, and when Elice opened her eyes, the woman stood in front of her.

"What are you, really?" Elice asked.

Lenore smiled and linked her fingers together in front of her body. "What do you think I am?"

Elice looked around, trying to see through the blinding light. "You're not real here. I mean, you're not the real you. This is the mind realm, a meditative space. But it's not the spirit realm. So, I think you're a figment of my imagination."

Lenore's lips made a thin line. "And here I thought you were clever."

Elice rolled her eyes. "Then tell me what you are. Please."

"This *is* the mind realm, and anyone who meditates can come and go as they please. People can often meet each other here for talks, to share or pass information across long distances. For example, if you wanted to talk to someone in Newton, all you have to do is make a connection with them and meet at a designated time and place. It could be every day at noon by the Mighty Lake."

Elice thought over her words. "But you're dead, right? In the mortal realm. And in here, you're young. I don't understand."

Lenore turned and walked a few paces away. "I left this piece of myself here for you."

"Why would you do that?"

Lenore picked at one of her fingernails, looking down at it. "Because I was working by Fates' design. I always am—*was*."

Elice's mind reeled and tears burned at her eyes. "You always say that, but I don't know what it means. You still stole me from my family. How am I supposed to believe that was Fate, and not just you being evil?"

Lenore turned to Elice and sighed. "You're not supposed to understand. Not yet."

"Why are you always so vague?" Elice sighed as well, wanting this conversation to end.

Lenore chuckled and walked down the hall where the light dimmed. "If you ever need me, you know where to find me. Oh, and you should have enough energy now. When you get back, make sure you aim for the middle."

Elice closed her eyes, holding back the angry words she wanted to yell at the woman. Instead, she let the room spin, bringing her back to the mortal realm.

Twenty-Nine

As soon as she opened her eyes, she saw Red Cloud's smirk. He was getting ready to attack, and she had to get to him first before he blew up the field.

Aim for the middle.

Red Cloud stood in the middle of the group. If Lenore was right—and she was a seer, after all—Elice had to take out Red Cloud. If she could bring him down, the rest of the Fire Lords would either give up or flee. But did she really want them to run? She had given them a warning, and they didn't listen. She had to try to take them all in and lock them in the dungeons. But Lenore said to aim for Red Cloud.

With only a second to decide, she relied on her most trusted spell. She called on the elements she knew well, welcoming them into her hands.

The swirling storm built into a fierce tornado almost immediately, just as the first flames came flying her way. She couldn't see anything beyond her tornado, but she heard James's warning for everyone to get down. Of course he would know what was coming. He'd seen her storm before.

Rocks, leaves, dirt, and water swept up into the tunneling storm, and as soon as it towered above her head, reaching as tall as the trees, she let it go. It kept building in strength, and she funneled more wind and energy into it.

Her sister and the soldiers rolled out of the path, and a few fire mages dodged as well, running to the side to avoid getting hit. The tornado had reached the height of the trees, maybe taller, and wide enough to block Red Cloud's body from her view.

Once it hit him, she kept it going, angling it toward the middle of the field. It continued to spin, gathering more water and air, with bits of earth mixed in. It grew taller and thinner, reaching for the sky as Red Cloud's screams rent the air.

Suddenly, he flew upwards, skyrocketing straight out of the funnel. His body landed with a sickening thud, his limbs hanging at awkward and unnatural angles.

Elice dropped the spell. Her body was now taxed beyond its limit. She landed on her knees, then her hands came to the ground.

James was there in an instant, kneeling beside her with his hand on her back. "The rest fled," he said. "Should I send someone after them?"

Elice shook her head, looking up to meet his eyes. "No. It's over."

He nodded, his lips turned down into a frown. "Are you all right?"

She sucked in a wheezing breath, her entire body sore and

protesting the movement. "I just need to rest." Elice looked around the field. "How's my sister?"

James looked over his shoulder, where Alice sat on the floor, leaning her head on Andre's shoulder. "She has no injuries, from what I can tell. Maybe the healers should look at both of you when we return."

Elice nodded and tried to stand, but she slumped to the floor, unable to move anymore.

James scooped her up, her head and legs resting in his arms. "We should have brought horses."

"Hindsight," she said, chuckling. She rested her cheek against his chest as he carried her toward the group.

"We should head for the castle to let the king know what happened," James said in his best captain's voice. "And send a cart for Red Cloud's body."

Trey stepped forward. "I'll carry him back." He headed to the dead fire mage's body, and his thick muscles bulged as he lifted it up.

Everyone else sheathed their swords and straightened out their clothes as well as they could. They were covered in burns and blood, but they were the ones looking at her with concerned expressions.

Not wanting to look weak in front of them, she pushed against James's chest, and he set her feet down on the ground but kept his arm around her waist.

"Thank you all for your bravery today," Elice said, meeting everyone's eyes.

Vic reached over and patted Elice's shoulder. "It was my first battle against a mage. I can't wait to do it again."

Elice laughed, shaking her head.

Alice took a step forward. "I can't believe what just happened. Someone needs to fill me in."

Elice took a hobbled step out of James's arms and brought her sister in for a hug, wincing at the contact. "I'll tell you on the way," she whispered into Alice's ear, and Alice wrapped an arm around Elice's waist as they all made their way into the forest.

~

The throne room was always a menacing place to stand in, especially when King Edgar sat on his throne, staring down at Elice with his stone-faced glare.

"I can't believe," he began, then sucked in a deep breath, "you disobeyed a direct order. Again."

Elice winced at his tone, and the movement made her gasp in pain. "To be fair, you told me I couldn't go on your mission. So, I made my own."

Andre made a noise from his place in line, and Elice knew he was probably shaking his head at her, holding back his laughter.

Edgar stood, towering higher above them all. Then he began pacing on the raised dais, walking in front of Julice, who had tears down her face as she looked at Alice. Alice sat on her throne next to their mother, looking at their father as he moved.

"This isn't right," Alice said, her voice strong. Elice still wasn't used to Alice's newfound confidence. "They saved my life. They should all receive medals of honor, not a lecture."

Edgar turned his glare on her, and she met it with the same intensity. "Great. Now we have another one who is set on defying me," he muttered.

Julice stood and held one of his hands. "Princess Alice is right, you know. Without them, we wouldn't have our daughter back."

Her father's jaw ticked. He turned toward Elice, then surveyed the soldiers beside her. When he returned his gaze, he looked at her with a fierce stare. "Did you rally these soldiers to follow you into the forest? To risk their lives for you and your sister, even though you didn't know for certain your plan would work? To trust you, without knowing whether any of you would make it out alive?"

Elice straightened her throbbing back as much as she could. "I did, Your Majesty."

James brushed his fingers against hers. "And we would do it again, my king, if it meant keeping her safe."

"One hundred times over," Ross said from her other side. The rest of the soldiers voiced their agreement, and Elice's chest swelled with pride.

Edgar's eyelids lowered, squinting at each of them. He stepped down from the platform, taking one slow step at a time, until he stood before Elice.

Then he nodded slowly, his eyes glistening over. "That's my girl," he whispered, then cleared his throat. "None of you will face punishment for what you have done. But rest assured, if you disobey me again, there will be consequences. You're dismissed." He turned and stalked back to his throne, flowing his cape out to rest over the armrest as he sat.

Exhales went around the room as the group let out a collective breath. Without waiting to be told twice, they hurried through the double doors at the end of the hall.

Vic started laughing as soon as the doors closed behind them, and Andre joined in her laughter. "That was so scary," she said, wheezing in between her fits of laughter.

"I thought we were going straight to the dungeons," Andre added, holding his stomach.

Elice rolled her eyes. "It isn't that funny."

Brighton had a smile on his face. "You think the king will give us medals?"

Ross and Trey shook their heads.

"He's more likely to demote us," James said, his voice quiet.

Elice squeezed his arm, giving him a comforting smile. "I'm sure he won't, Captain. I'll talk to him, and Alice will help me convince him of everyone's bravery."

He touched her hand where it held onto his biceps. "We'll let the Fates decide what's best. I'm just glad you and Alice are safe."

Vic cleared her throat, a smirk hiding behind her hand. "So, what's the deal with you two?" She pointed at Elice and James.

Elice's cheeks heated as she looked around, avoiding Andre's face. "We're courting. Not officially. Yet."

"But hopefully officially soon," James added, his eyes on Elice.

"I guess congratulations are in order," Trey said, bowing.

Elice smiled as they all bowed, and her eyes flitted to Andre. He had his hand over his heart as he lowered his head, but he didn't seem as upset as she thought he would. She hoped this meant he would be back to his old self soon, and they could go back to being friends.

The weariness in her legs reminded her she needed rest, so she excused herself, thanking everyone again for their help. James escorted her to the east wing, stopping at the bottom of the stairs.

She leaned into him, resting her head against his chest while he held her by the waist. "I hope I can actually sleep," she muttered against his torn shirt.

"You think you'll have nightmares?" he whispered above her head.

Elice tried to shrug her shoulder, but found she couldn't move. "I don't know. But at this point, I don't care as long as I get some sleep."

He sighed, the movement blowing the stray hairs on top of her head. "Just don't take off that necklace and you should be fine."

She had actually forgotten about it. Her hand went straight to her chest, grasping the crystal and holding it tight. "Thanks for reminding me."

James nodded, pulling away enough to look at her. He cupped her cheeks and placed a soft kiss on her forehead. She closed her eyes at the feel of his lips on her skin.

When he looked down at her, so many emotions swirled in her stomach. But right now, she couldn't focus on any of them. She stepped out of his embrace, missing the warmth immediately, and turned toward the stairs, hobbling as slowly as she could while the muscles in her legs throbbed.

When Elice made it to her room, she shut the door and went straight to her bed, not caring that her clothes and hair were filthy. She didn't even pull the blankets over her body, too tired and weak to reach for them.

With the heat from the fireplace warming her room, she drifted off to sleep, finally resting nightmare-free for the first time in
weeks.

Epilogue

Elice took a steadying breath, eyeing each member of the council as they looked at her with mixed expressions. James and Lord Torenti gave her an encouraging smile. Captain Yusef and General Thiery looked on with concern in their furrowed eyebrows, and Lord Cove openly glared. The other members wore unreadable expressions, their faces relaxed as they listened to her.

"Let me get this right," Lord Cove began, then added a quick, "Your Highness." Once he had everyone's attention, he continued. "You want to start your own battalion?"

Elice nodded, her eye contact directly on him and his angry scowl. "Not just my own battalion, my lord. A specialized unit, specially trained and run by me and a few select others I deem leadership worthy."

General Thiery placed his elbows on the long desk, his thumbs resting under his face and his pointer fingers against his lips. "A specialized unit. That's interesting."

"They would need their own section of the barracks," Captain Yusef cut in, his head tilted. "And a separate training facility."

"We'd prefer to work outdoors, I'm sure," Elice said, a flare of hope building inside her chest.

"I'm sure we could allocate the appropriate funds," Lord Torenti spoke up, his tone light.

Colonel Bryce, the highest-ranking female in the King's Army, shifted in her seat. "And how will you find your recruits? Surely they're too scared to come out of hiding."

Lord Cove huffed under his breath. "Good luck finding anyone dumb enough to join your group. They'll all think it's a setup."

Edgar leaned forward in his seat, and Elice saw his pointed stare at the grumpy lord. She spoke up before they began arguing. The last thing she wanted was a distraction before they could decide on the subject.

"Once I gather my leaders, I'll be able to come up with a solid plan of action. But that's why we need this unit. Without people like me, we're vulnerable to another attack, unable to defend ourselves properly."

"And getting more mages on our side is surely the smart way to go," James added, earning a few nods.

"It would make sense to have a few mages under our employ," Colonel Bryce conceded.

"Shall we put it to a vote?" Edgar asked, his eyes roaming the room. The council members all nodded. "All in favor of the new measure, raise your hand."

Elice looked at the hands in the air and counted. With James,

Lord Torenti, General Thiery, Captain Yusef, Colonel Bryce, and three other members, she had the majority of the votes.

With a smile, Edgar continued. "All those opposed…"

Only two hands shot into the air, Lord Cove's and another lord Elice never agreed with.

"With the majority in favor," Edgar said, looking at Elice, "it seems you have your unit."

Elice nodded and smiled, then gave her thanks to the room.

Now that she had the council's approval, she could begin her search for other mages to join her new battalion.

~

A strong wind blew, threatening a late fall storm. The first rain drop turned to ice on its way down from the dark clouds, landing on a blade of grass and instantly melting.

A wet boot landed in the mud, then another, as more icy rain fell from the sky.

With a shriveled hand, a person in a red cloak reached down and grabbed a handful of mud. Mixed in with the mud were several specks of red, causing a smile to form on the person's wrinkled face. Lowering his hood, he brought the pile to his nose and inhaled.

More boots came to a stop behind him. "We must hurry, Lord Victor, in case they have this place under watch," murmured a woman in a red cloak.

The elder raised a hand, the other still by his face as he continued to sniff the mud. "There's no one else here. We must gather as many pieces as we can find."

Another mage stepped forward, picking up as much mud as he could and throwing it into the metal can he had carried with him.

With another sniff, the old man smiled. The ghost of a figure slid up next to his shoulder, seeming to look down at his hand. "Make sure you gather it all," the shadow whispered, and the elder nodded.

"Yes, Master Orser," the old man said. "We will not fail you again."

The ghost glided closer to the ground, and the elder watched in amusement as Orser attempted in vain to pick up pieces of his beloved flower.

Soon, Lord Victor thought, his focus still on the bits of flower in his hand. *Soon I shall have everything I ever wanted.*

Note from the Author

Thank you for reading book two of Elice's adventure! To continue the journey, read Army of Mages, the final installment of the series.

If you enjoyed this book, please spread the love by leaving a review to help other readers find out about it!

WANT EXCLUSIVE BONUS CONTENT?

DIVE INSIDE JAMES'S POV TO UNDERSTAND EXACTLY WHAT HE'S THINKING AND FEELING DURING HIS FIRST KISS WITH ELICE.

DOWNLOAD IT FOR FREE AT WWW.JENNIFERROACHFORD .COM.

To be informed about future release dates or to sign up for my Advanced Reader Copy (ARC) list, sign up for my newsletter at www.jenniferroachford.com.

Are you ready to join my Army of Mages? Join my exclusive street team, where you'll get first access to my books, as well as swag and other fun giveaways. Visit Jennifer's Army of Mages Reader

Group on Facebook to be part of the club.

Also by Jennifer Roachford

ELICE, THE GREAT

The Secret Mage (Book One)
Tomb of Souls (Book Two)
Army of Mages (Book Three)

≈

LENORA, THE CURSED

The Cursed Sight (Book One)
A Curse Awakened (Book Two)
Coming Soon (Book Three)

Acknowledgements

I still can't believe I'm blessed enough to be able to share this story with the world. This book is for my amazing beta readers who helped me make sure book two was ready to go.

Also, I want to thank each and every reader who continues to support my author journey. Your help fuels my passion for writing. I want to thank my Army of Mages for continuing to read my work and for being my biggest supporters.

To Aamna Shahid, MC Damon, and the entire team at Etheric Designs. You are all seriously amazing, and your work is spectacular.

Thanks to Angela Knotts Morse for being so remarkable. You continue to provide me with great insight, and you've helped my words shine.

A huge shout-out goes to my family and friends for their overwhelming love as I follow my dream.

Finally, but definitely not least, is the special thanks I give to my husband and children. You are my guiding light, making me shine brighter than I ever thought possible.

About the Author

Jennifer Roachford is a wife, mom, and the author behind the **Elice, the Great** and **Lenora, the Cursed** trilogies—diverse fantasy worlds built for readers who have always wanted to see themselves in the pages of a book.

As an Afro-Latina, Jennifer believes representation isn't just important, it's essential. Her passion for storytelling was born from a lifelong love of books, and she channels that love into every character she creates and every world she builds.

When she isn't writing her next novel or editing someone else's manuscript, you can find her in the garden daydreaming about books or hunting down the perfect cup of coffee on snow days. She also bakes—because every great story deserves a good snack.

www.ingramcontent.com/pod-product-compliance
Lightning Source LLC
Chambersburg PA
CBHW060913190726
48286CB00002B/488